THE BOOK CLUB KILLER

A DI BARTON MYSTERY

ROSS GREENWOOD

First published in Great Britain in 2025 by Boldwood Books Ltd.

Copyright © Ross Greenwood, 2025

Cover Design by Head Design Ltd

Cover Images: iStock

The moral right of Ross Greenwood to be identified as the author of this work has been asserted in accordance with the Copyright, Designs and Patents Act 1988.

All rights reserved. No part of this book may be reproduced in any form or by any electronic or mechanical means, including information storage and retrieval systems, without written permission from the author, except for the use of brief quotations in a book review. This book is a work of fiction and, except in the case of historical fact, any resemblance to actual persons, living or dead, is purely coincidental.

Every effort has been made to obtain the necessary permissions with reference to copyright material, both illustrative and quoted. We apologise for any omissions in this respect and will be pleased to make the appropriate acknowledgements in any future edition.

A CIP catalogue record for this book is available from the British Library.

Paperback ISBN 978-1-83617-806-4

Large Print ISBN 978-1-83617-805-7

Hardback ISBN 978-1-83617-804-0

Trade Paperback ISBN 978-1-80656-049-3

Ebook ISBN 978-1-83617-807-1

Kindle ISBN 978-1-83617-808-8

Audio CD ISBN 978-1-83617-799-9

MP3 CD ISBN 978-1-83617-800-2

Digital audio download ISBN 978-1-83617-802-6

This book is printed on certified sustainable paper. Boldwood Books is dedicated to putting sustainability at the heart of our business. For more information please visit https://www.boldwoodbooks.com/about-us/sustainability/

Boldwood Books Ltd, 23 Bowerdean Street, London, SW6 3TN

www.boldwoodbooks.com

For Sandra Rosser
A wonderful mum

MAJOR CRIMES TEAM

Detective Chief Superintendent
Andrew Troughton

Detective Chief Inspector
Sarah Cox
John Barton (acting)

Detective Inspector
Shawn Zander

Detective Sergeant
Maria Zelensky
Kelly Strange (retired)

Detective Constable
Imran Malik
David Leicester
Kevin Hoffman
Caroline Minton

Only the Good Die Young

— BILLY JOEL

1
DCI BARTON

Friday 6 December

The silence in the car was thick with unspoken thoughts. Barton had slumped in the passenger seat, while Zander drummed the fingers of one hand on the steering wheel, his focus fixed on the road ahead.

'So,' Zander eventually said, breaking the hush. 'Cox is back next week, eh? I saw her pop in today.'

'Yep.'

'What are you planning to do with yourself now your covering year is up?'

Barton shrugged, his gaze drifting outside the vehicle. The early December night was dark and cold, the street lights casting long shadows on the empty paths.

'I've been running through my options,' he mumbled.

'Chippendale? *Strictly Come Dancing*? Rhinos on Ice? Rewiring the International Space Station?'

'Sadly, none of the aforementioned. All my choices seem to involve me sitting behind a desk.'

Zander chuckled.

'Worried you'll be climbing the walls within a week?'

'Yeah, exactly. There's no current need for another DI at Peterborough

Major Crimes, so the possibilities here are limited. I spotted a position in Lincolnshire but decided I'm too long in the tooth for commuting anywhere.'

Zander's eyes flicked towards Barton.

'You look knackered, John. More than usual.'

Barton sighed. That was how he felt. His wife had bought new scales, and they confirmed what he already knew. He was back over twenty stone, but it wasn't only his body weighing him down. For months, the team had hunted for a serial rapist in the city. They'd finally caught him on Monday, but only after he'd damaged the lives of four women forever.

'This last case got to me,' he replied. 'With all the girls a similar age to my daughter, I haven't slept well...' He trailed off, the image of the final victim's bruises fresh in his mind.

'Yeah,' Zander said quietly. 'It was a gruelling investigation.'

Barton didn't comment, lost in his own reflections, as the familiar streets of his home town raced by in a blur of houses.

As they turned onto Barton's road, Zander spoke again.

'Did you hear what Malik said about A & E this afternoon?'

'No.'

'His wife took an uncle down to the hospital a little after midday. It was sick only inside. Companions were told to wait outside. She only got in because he'd had a stroke and she was pushing the wheelchair. Reckoned it was so busy the atmosphere reminded her of a bitter football match between two local rivals.'

'The staff and the patients?'

'Something like that.'

'I'm not surprised. There was an email from Uniform before we left the office saying ambulances are currently stuck waiting with patients onboard, but so are response vehicles with sorting out all the aggro. People are getting desperate. There were eighteen ambulances queued up one night last week.'

'Grim scenes.'

'I suppose it's always chaos in the run-up to Christmas. Our custody cells were filling up this afternoon from a drunken brawl at a works event. The boss had only taken his team out for lunch with the trimmings.'

Zander frowned.

'Sometimes it seems like everything's falling apart.'

Barton huffed out a breath.

'I keep having the same thoughts. Maybe I'm better off out of it. I could leave the force, become a private investigator. Be my own man. Live on my wits. Taking cases nobody else wants. Stealthily tracking people with cunning and guile.'

Zander laughed loudly.

'John, the only location you'd blend into the background at is a wrestling match, and only then if you were leaning against the ropes in a Lycra singlet, waiting to be tagged.'

Barton chuckled. 'They could call me Badass Barton.'

'Your family call you that already.'

Barton flicked his eyes over at the driver.

'You're in top form.'

Zander bobbed his head. 'The twins are happy at playschool three days a week. They'll be in the infants next year. Kelly says at last she's feeling human again and can't wait to work. And we've booked a short break away in January. Just the two of us.'

'Nice, but aren't your parents too old to babysit the boys?'

'They are.'

'Who's having them, then?'

'You and Holly.'

Barton grinned. 'I see. Lovely to be in the loop. I'd better warn the neighbours their peace is going to be shattered.'

'They're much calmer now.'

'Really?'

'Sorry, no.' Zander indicated to pull onto the drive. 'I'll pop in for a minute, say hello to Holly. Thank her for offering. I've not seen her for a while.'

'Nothing to do with me telling you she was baking different types of cookies and cakes today, which she hopes to use the best of when the business is open?'

'Cake never hurt a man.'

'Amen.' Barton smiled faintly. 'She'll be pleased to see you. Not getting out of the house for work means she appreciates visitors.'

'Is the café thing progressing?'

'Very much so. The loan has been approved, a site is all that's needed. She was checking out a promising one today.'

Zander nodded.

'Kelly still feels bad about not going in as partners, but twin boys have become more demanding than we imagined. A part-time job is all she can handle.'

'Holly understands, so no worries. By the way, don't mention me appearing exhausted to her.'

'Why not?'

'It won't be an opinion as far as she's concerned. Merely ammunition.'

As they pulled up outside Barton's house, a figure emerged from the shadows. Barton got out of the car and forced a grin onto his face. It was one of the homeowners who lived at the bottom of their cul-de-sac, Ken, a retired teacher and a gossip who could talk for England.

'John!' he called out, despite being only a metre away, his shout echoing in the quiet night. 'Just the person I wanted.'

Barton couldn't help being intrigued. Their resident whisperer and rumour-mill stoker was usually like a calm newsreader with his mundane tales. Tonight, he seemed unduly agitated.

'What's up, Ken?' Barton asked, stopping next to him.

Under the bright white glare of the LED street light, his neighbour's face was etched with concern.

'I went outside to lob a bag of rubbish into my wheelie bin,' he said, lowering his voice. 'Heard some bellowing at number nineteen. Nasty stuff. Sounded like she was really losing it.'

Barton frowned as he pictured the properties at the end of the road. Nineteen was a long, narrow semi-detached house that had been empty for a year after the previous, elderly owner had died. It was Ken who had informed him six months ago that a young couple had moved in and were planning to modernise the place. Barton had nodded at the woman a few times in passing not long after they arrived, but she'd avoided eye contact.

'What sort of stuff?' asked Zander.

'Angry tones,' replied Ken, his eyes wide. 'Furious. But also... kind of crazed, if you know what I mean. Like someone who's not quite right in their mind.'

Barton felt a knot of apprehension forming in his stomach. He remembered the case they had just solved, the vacant expression of the final victim, the devastated boyfriend, the weeping father, and the raging mother with murder on her mind.

'Did you see anyone about?'

Ken shook his head. 'No, the curtains were drawn. I daren't knock.'

'I don't suppose you rang 999.'

'No, I knew you'd help.'

It had been a few years since a neighbour had come over to ask Barton for assistance. Visits for aid or advice had been common when he was in uniform. Naughty kids, excessive noise, missing cats. You name it. Still, he wasn't relishing the prospect of getting involved in a neighbour's arguments, one he suspected might be fuelled by alcohol.

'I'm not the right bloke for dealing with a domestic. That's usually a task for stab-vest-wearing, baton-wielding, Taser-pointing officers in uniform.'

Ken's expression turned grave. 'It might be dangerous, but you're a brave man.'

Barton smiled despite thinking of the Billy Joel song about the good dying young, then puffed out his cheeks. God knew why he was debating the issue. Barton was always going to check the moment the man had opened his mouth. Uniform would probably be hours, anyway. He looked at Zander, who nodded with a tight smile.

'Right,' said Barton, his reply firm. 'Let's go and have a chat with our neighbour.'

As they trudged towards number nineteen, the tapping of their shoes on the damp pavement the only sound, a sense of foreboding swept over him. He hoped he was wrong, but the Barton belly told him this wouldn't be a pleasant social call. His relaxing night had taken an ominous turn, and Barton suspected, with a heavy heart, his working week was far from over.

Ken had set off with them but needed to scamper with his much shorter legs to keep up.

'The couple's names are Lily and Fraser, but I doubt he's there.'

'Why is that?' asked Zander.

'Fraser moved out three months back after he met another woman at work. It wasn't an amicable split with Lily, and I don't believe he's returned since.'

Zander scowled at Ken.

'Are you saying Lily's arguing with herself?'

Ken stopped in front of them at the entrance to number nineteen's driveway.

'That's why I'm so worried. I think it's just her and the baby.'

2

DCI BARTON

A chill ran down Barton's spine. A young woman, alone with a baby, shouting and sounding crazed. A recipe for disaster. He decided Ken would be calmer if he was given something to do, preferably something that kept him out of the way.

'Okay, Ken. Stay at the roadside. Grab your mobile. If there's any drama, ring 999 and ask for the police and an ambulance.'

Ken nodded, eyes narrowing. Back hunched, he took his phone out as though he were drawing his pistol.

Zander strode to the front door and knocked loudly. The shouting, which Ken had heard, had stopped. No lights were on. Nobody answered.

Barton rapped his knuckles on it.

'Police! Come to the door, please.'

After thirty seconds of continued silence, a howl of angst came from inside.

Barton and Zander exchanged a wary glance. Zander put his hand on the door handle and pushed down. There was a squeak as it depressed. He gave it a shove, and it swung wide open. With Barton leading, they stepped through the doorway to be greeted by a wave of frigid air. The temperature was lower than the winter night outside. Barton paused at the stairs and looked up them. No movement. The silence inside was more unsettling than the cry they'd heard.

Barton remained still as his ears and eyes strained. A dull ache throbbed in his shoulders and neck, the weight of a long and stressful week settling into his bones. He longed for a hot meal and the comfort of his armchair, but remembering the woman's scream, the raw desperation in her voice, he spurred himself into action.

'Lily! It's Detective Chief Inspector John Barton. I live down the road. Is everything okay?'

Again, no reply.

Zander tutted.

'Didn't you know she had a baby?'

'She was walking a big male golden retriever the last time I saw her, but I don't remember a pram. I must admit, it was quite a while ago, and I was in a rush.'

The house was eerily quiet, the only sound a hum from what was probably a fridge somewhere in the depths. The narrow, dark hallway pressed in on him. As Zander moved forward, the street light at the pavement was strong enough to shine in and unveil a threadbare carpet and peeling wallpaper. A faint, mouldy scent hung in the air. Zander flicked a light switch, and a dim, uncovered bulb came on above him.

Barton tested a door knob that he guessed would be for the lounge. It turned with a soft click. He nudged the door open to reveal a sparsely furnished room. A woman stood by the fireplace, her back to them, dressed in a grey T-shirt and loose jogging bottoms. Her dishevelled shoulder-length brown hair gave her the air of a mad scientist. But it was the bare feet that caught Barton's eye.

'Lily?' he asked.

In slow motion, she turned around. Clutched in her hand was a large kitchen knife, its blade shimmering in the weak light. She pointed it at them.

'It's too much,' she murmured, her words little more than a whisper. 'I want it all to stop, but he's angry. No sleep. Not for anyone. Voices. Outside.'

Barton and Zander shared another look. The woman mumbled again, her phrases rambling, incoherent. She appeared to be in a state of shock, or perhaps something worse.

'Lily,' Barton began, his voice calm and steady. 'We're police officers. Could you please put down the knife?'

She bared her teeth, and the hair rose on Barton's neck. Lily's skin was pale and drawn. Her skin, nearly translucent from the lounge light's glow, stretched taut over the delicate bones of her face. The chill of the house seemed to cling to her, her breath misting with each shallow exhale. Eyes, sunken and bloodshot from lack of sleep, burned with a dull inner fire, while her hand trembled as she gripped the handle.

'He's upstairs,' she muttered, pointing the tip towards the ceiling. 'It's not fair...'

A soft cry, clearly audible, cut through the silence. The unmistakable sound of a baby.

Barton spoke louder, firmer.

'Lower the knife, Lily.'

She peered down at her hand and appeared to see the blade for the first time. She let it fall onto the hearth with a clatter.

With a rush of adrenaline, Barton marched forward, swept up the weapon, then dropped it behind the sofa.

'Stay with her, Zander.'

Barton ascended the stairs, his footsteps muffled by the carpet. The baby's cries grew louder as he approached three open doors and a closed one. Barton checked the open rooms, all empty. He paused outside the shut one. A low rumble, almost bearlike, emanated from behind it. Barton's heart pounded. That didn't sound like a golden retriever.

With a deep breath, Barton slowly opened the door. The room was narrow and cluttered, with a smallish blue cot in the far corner and a wardrobe facing it. Clothes, mostly blue, were scattered on the floor, along with nappy bags and wipes. A stocky, long-haired yellow dog was sitting by the cot, eyes focussed on the baby, nostrils flaring. The beast dipped his head, then let out another lengthy growl as it twisted to face the intruder.

Barton lowered himself down, knees straining.

'Hey, there. Who's a nice doggie?'

After a couple of seconds of slow blinking, the hound wagged its tail furiously. It seemed to accept Barton was now in charge and released a soft whimper of relief as it crawled towards what must have seemed a big man. Barton reached down and stroked the animal from head to tail.

'Good boy. Stay there.'

Barton approached the cot with trepidation. The cries had subsided. He gently lifted the blanket, which mostly covered what he assumed to be a boy's face.

The child's complexion was white and pasty, eyes closed. Barton felt for a pulse, his fingers trembling against the cold skin. He couldn't be sure if one was there or not. The baby appeared lifeless. Then its eyes flicked open.

Barton nearly screamed the place down.

It had been a long time since he'd held a baby. He carefully picked up the child, cradling it in his arms. The infant was surprisingly light, almost weightless, but chubby fingers pressed against his face. A surge of protectiveness came over Barton, making him fiercely determined to protect this little life.

As he carried the bundle out of the room, he cast a glance around at the retriever. The dog whined again; its eyes filled with a strange sadness. Barton suspected the animal had sensed Lily's volatile behaviour and protected the baby. He decided not to think about when and why the knife had materialised.

Back in the lounge, Zander appeared to be holding the woman upright.

'She wouldn't sit, just started weeping. She's freezing, and so thin, but we'll never get an ambulance for this situation ahead of heart attacks or strokes. We could drive her down.'

Barton recalled their conversation about turmoil at the hospital. Where would this mother and baby fit in down there?

He scrutinised Lily, who had pulled herself closer to Zander, her face buried in his chest. She was probably trying to suck out some warmth. Barton normally resembled an elephant seal, but even he shivered in the dense cold surrounding him. They had a lot of questions to ask her but, right now, the priority was ensuring the mother and baby were safe and warm.

'Pick her up if you have to. We'll take them to my place.'

'Is the kid okay?'

'Yeah, seems to be.'

'Is this a crime scene?'

Barton understood if it was reported as one, the chances of this woman keeping her child would be slim.

'We can talk about that at mine. Get them in the warmth first. I'll ring Shirley from Social Services. Ask for some advice.'

'You're sure you want them at yours?'

'Just a neighbour being helpful.'

Barton found a changing bag, which contained baby products, and headed outside. He considered for a moment how wise it was to take Lily and her child back but decided that he wouldn't worry.

Barton would do what felt right, whatever the consequences. It dawned on him as he left Lily's place that thoughts like those might mean he'd made up his mind about his future.

3

THE BOOK CLUB KILLER

The biting December wind rattles the twinkling Christmas lights strung across the entrance façade of The Bell in Stilton. I involuntarily shiver but still pause to admire the stone building. A faint smile plays on my lips. It has always been my favourite pub. Strange to think I've been walking through this door for decades, long before the book club launched. I suppose it's one of my longest relationships, but I don't come as often nowadays. I suspect none of us do.

I should make more of an effort to visit because its leaded windows are glowing with a welcoming amber light, promising refuge from the cold and dark. Few establishments draw customers in like The Bell. Centuries of tradition await inside. Sometimes I feel as if the ghosts of long-forgotten guests are surrounding me. Enjoying my company. Benign spirits urging me not to leave. Perhaps never to leave.

I miss the monthly meets, too, but doing only one book a year before Christmas does make it special. Makes sense, too, after everything that's happened.

Still, the lively discussions, the shared passion for literature, the laughs and drink, the bonding and taking of sides, have become an important part of life for many of the group. You can usually see excitement on people's faces as they arrive, sadness when they leave, but nothing stays the same.

The Bell is a former fifteenth-century coaching inn set on the Great North

Road about ten miles south of Peterborough. History oozes from its every pore. The modern A1 bypasses it these days and the wide street is often devoid of traffic, but the pub remains a busy and popular place, frequented by locals, tourists and businesspeople alike. The staff are friendly, the fires always lit and the atmosphere warm and convivial.

All of which makes what I'm about to do harder, but needs must. I doubt there'll be any harm done to the pub's top-notch reputation. Suspicious eyes will soon wander elsewhere. I suspect numerous employees and regulars might relish the drama, even though they may not admit to it.

I stride through the striking doorway, into the courtyard beyond and past the well. Shame I can't lob someone in, but there's a grate over it now. Health and safety ruining my fun. The manager told me that, due to the inn being Grade I listed, there was all manner of fuss when the grate was being installed. Like a comedy sketch, with a large cluster of people with clipboards, all watching while one person screwed in four bolts.

I push open the heavy door to the bar. Despite not quite being seven o'clock, it's already bustling. The twenty-two bedrooms provide a steady stream of hungry patrons, even midweek. A table will have been reserved for the book club.

A counter sells cheese. Stilton, naturally. I may buy some later, but it's addictive stuff and different from what's sold in most supermarkets. I find it hard not to eat it all in one go.

The Bell remains a place of laughter, shared stories and spilled secrets. Friendships are forged, surrounded by the scents of woodsmoke, ale and roasted meat. But tonight, it will become something else.

The club evenings used to be raucous affairs, stretching until closing, but everyone's much older now. Many will wear the ravages of time this evening. Most still drink alcohol, though, so I expect voices rising and falling in animated conversation. Five couples, linked by work, enjoying life.

In the past, other customers peered over with jealous eyes, some even asking how to join, but there had been an agreement to keep the group small and manageable. It was a select and exclusive gathering. We felt lucky, and ten was a good number.

Of course, only eight of us remain.

4

DCI BARTON

Ken was standing poised on Lily's driveway when Barton came into view, hand raised, thumb quivering above the dial button, with an expression set firm. As though ready to verify the launch codes. He lowered his phone, and a brief flash of disappointment passed over his face.

'Everything okay?'

Barton gave him a respectful nod.

'Stand down, Ken. Lily's boiler is broken. I think she was shouting at it. We'll take them to mine to warm up. Great work for telling me. Nobody should be in a cold home, especially with a baby.'

'Tommy all right?'

'He is.'

'No harm done, then.'

'None. Night, Ken. See you soon.'

Barton patted his shoulder as he passed him, then marched back up the street. His hands were full, so he gave his front door a kick.

Holly came and opened it. She examined Barton's face, then his package.

'I've told you about making unhealthy food choices, John. Go and return that baby.'

'Very funny. It's Lily's down the road.'

The boy started to cry.

'Oh my God, what have you done now?'

She stepped back to let him in. Barton gasped at the welcoming warmth. He quickly explained what had happened.

Holly's mouth dropped open.

'Poor girl. I only spoke to her a few days ago and was a bit worried about her state of mind. Where is she?'

Zander appeared at the door, carrying Lily. She struggled out of his arms and groaned as she seemed to feel the heat. Holly pulled her into a hug.

'In the lounge, Lily. Let's get you cosy.'

Barton and Zander followed the women. Gizmo, the greyhound, was lying in front of the fire. He lifted one eyelid, then swiftly shut it.

Holly plugged in the heated throw she kept in the living room for when she didn't want to put the central heating on, bought for her by Barton as a 'gift' after he'd seen a horrifying energy bill.

'Sit down here, Lily. I'll turn this on, and you'll be toasty in minutes.'

Holly took the bundle out of Barton's hands. The baby was quiet now, but his little fists were clenched. Holly unwrapped the blanket, gently rolled him onto his stomach on the sofa, and tapped the back of his Babygro. There was a packed sound.

Barton opened the bag he'd brought from Lily's house and removed a fresh set of wipes and a nappy. He passed them to Holly, who couldn't help smiling.

'As ever, it was thus. Changing mat?'

Barton shook his head. Holly stared at him for a moment.

'Go back and get it. One of you carry the baby's cot if it's light enough. See if there're some small jars of food. Tommy should be on solids by now.'

Barton suspected she wanted them gone from the room.

'I'll ring child services,' he said.

Holly's eyes conveyed a message he'd deciphered countless times.

'Not yet,' she replied. 'Let me chat with Lily. We'll talk when you return.'

Barton studied Lily, who was head down, cowering under the throw.

'Okay.'

Holly poked a finger in his direction.

'And don't forget Vince.'

'Who the hell is that?'

'The dog.'

5

THE WAITRESS

The Bell Inn is absolutely buzzing, that lively, festive kind of energy you only ever get in a busy pub a few weeks before Christmas. Despite being rushed off my feet, I can appreciate the noise and the ambience.

Management did a great job with the refurb. The low, beamed ceilings and exposed brick walls, which were getting so marked and dusty, now shine from the new lighting. People bask in the plush velvet armchairs by the crackling fireplaces. Laughter and chatter dance over the clinking of cutlery, and the sturdy oak tables, polished to a gleam, invite you to settle in for a proper cosy inn experience. In fact, every single corner whispers comfort.

Tonight, though, table service in the bar is out of the question. There are simply too many people, too much of a throng. Even with my usual instinct to fuss over folk, I can't possibly manage that. It's a night for everyone to jostle their way to and from the bar, pint and wine glasses lifted high, and enjoy the hustle and bustle of the season.

I spot a young couple, both tall, step through the entrance, and my heart sinks a little because I've seen them in here a few times. He's got those hopeful, raised eyes, looking for a table. I shake my head even before he asks. Most people this evening are repeat customers, and they understand you usually need to book. The Tax Titans, a local group of professionals, for instance, made their reservation when they left a year ago, just as they've done for decades. I should know. I was working that night.

* * *

I remember when the club first started. Sometimes it feels like yesterday and others a lifetime past. Most of the members were already regulars. All lived in the village. The main connection, though, was that at least one person from each of the five couples had to work at Jones and Singh Accountants. Everyone seemed so young and vibrant back then, at the top of their games. Ageing has been kinder to some, but nobody isn't at least a touch weathered. I suppose we were all beautiful once.

Tonight, they've placed their meal orders, starters eaten, and the mains are arriving soon. For a moment, the crowd parts and my gaze drifts over the group. There's Vijay Singh, same as ever. The predatory glint in his eyes remains unchanged since his wife died. The same woman, Morwen Jones, is the object of his slow glances and compliments, as it was even when Avani Singh was present.

When the Joneses arrived this evening, Morwen's husband, Rhys, held the door for her, so she came into the bar first. His jaw bunched, just a touch, when she made a beeline for Vijay and took a seat by his side. She's laughing now. Honestly, Vijay isn't that funny. Her hand rests too long on his arm, her hair tossed back, those too-white teeth flashing.

I used to think Rhys was completely oblivious to it all, but he's such a clever man, a nice one, too. Maybe experience taught him to pretend, and the years have crafted him into an expert, but his mask is slipping. Perhaps he forgets why he turns a blind eye.

The cupcakes, another tradition, sit covered in cling film in their usual spot in the opening in the wall, which once would have been used as a passthrough, but now enables us to see inside that part of the bar. The person responsible for the cakes originally made them from scratch, but they get them from the supermarket now and stick various little edible book titles on top. They never admit to it, of course, but I spotted them buying the cakes in Waitrose near Peterborough railway station last year. It was a fluke encounter when the trains were delayed, and I fancied a decent sandwich. I pretended not to have looked, but the desserts were sitting in their basket.

They'll have forgotten that now even if they were suspicious at the time. That's clear because when I was collecting glasses, I overheard them telling Mary Thwaite how they had a new recipe for tonight.

I like Mary and her husband, Eric, although they're somewhat dull. Mary's a librarian, but Eric has long been retired. He's fading from this world, if you ask me, but I always get the impression he doesn't miss much. Those sharp eyes of his, scanning the room, they've got a sense of humour behind them, though he keeps most of it for himself.

Bernie Goodman is next to him. Deadman is perhaps more apt. He makes eighty-nine-year-old Eric appear positively robust. Cancer is a cruel disease. Killing by consumption, but taking its time, seemingly enjoying its spread. His wife, Beryl, is laughing too loud. A starling, chirping for attention but outshone by the parakeet, Katarzyna, beside her.

Katarzyna, who hailed from Poland long ago, just shines, as she has done since her husband's premature death. A woman reborn. She's never brought anyone else with her, unlike Vijay, who has paraded the occasional trophy after Avani passed. He catches my eye and waves. Such a clothes horse, that man. I've no idea if his suit cost five-hundred quid or five thousand, but he looks priceless. Yet, he only has eyes for one. Or perhaps two.

That's the eight of them, soon to be fewer.

I give the group a last glance as another staff member calls for my attention. There's something extra in the air tonight. I'm not completely sure what, but I sense it. From the outside, the book club members all seem to get on, but not everyone is as pleasant as they appear, nor as honest. There will be undercurrents of friction, even resentment.

How do I know? Because I have secrets too.

6
DCI BARTON

Barton had planned to return to Lily's property anyway, because it wasn't secure. While Zander went upstairs and manoeuvred the cot down, Barton checked the fridge. He discovered a four-pint bottle of whole milk, an elderly cucumber and not much else. The cupboards were equally sparse, save for a few jars of baby food and a pack of rice cakes. He noticed paperwork on the kitchen table as he put the jars in his pocket.

The top letter had lots of red writing demanding the recipient to pay now.

Barton headed to the front door and held it open. As Zander manhandled the cot through, Barton threw the changing mat in as he passed by.

Zander frowned at him.

'Let's go, John. Lock up.'

'There are only two tubs of food.'

'You've probably forgotten. They'll eat most things at Tommy's age. Holly will know.'

'Okay,' replied Barton, clicking his fingers at the dog, who'd been following him around. 'Come on, pooch.'

The retriever, tail wagging, barked at the coat rack near the entrance, where a lead was hung up. As Barton was attaching the lead to the collar, he saw a name on it. Vince. He took the key from behind the door, went outside, locked up, then set off up the road with the dog ambling beside him.

Zander followed, struggling with the cumbersome wooden cot.

'Sure you can cope with that animal on your own, John?'

'I've also got the baby food. Do tell me if that thing gets too heavy.'

'It's lucky I'm in the prime of my life.'

'That's the spirit.'

By the time they'd reached Barton's lounge again, Zander had sworn loudly a few times and knocked a porcelain ornament over in the hall, which had broken. Barton had never liked it, so at least the evening hadn't all been negative.

Vince edged into the room, peering around cautiously, nostrils flaring. After a few seconds, he dragged Barton towards Gizmo, who remained by the fire. Gizmo opened both eyes, stared at Barton as if to say, you're kidding me. His canine visitor gave the greyhound a cursory sniff, then flopped down beside him, close to the heat from the flames.

Holly had the little boy sitting on her lap, drinking from a plastic cup. He waved a plump hand at Barton like royalty greeting his adoring public. A gentle snore came from the brown throw Lily was under.

'He's fine, John. Plenty of puppy fat. Big poop, but no nappy rash. Lily's been caring for him.'

'It didn't seem that way. What did she say?'

'Just that she was so tired. I said she seemed pale when I met her walking past our house with Vince and Tommy this week. You'll never guess what her bastard husband, Fraser, did to her?'

'Left her for another woman?'

'That's not the half of it. He cleared off, took all the money, hasn't been in touch. When I spoke to her, she told me she was worried her credit card would be declined, but her kitchen cupboards were empty.'

'Yeah, well, they're still barren, so perhaps it was.'

'I should have pushed harder to help. She rushed off, saying she was fine, but it sounds like everything was far from okay.'

Zander dropped into an armchair. 'Shirley can give us the best advice.'

Holly's gaze swept from Barton to Zander, who received a smile more chilling than anything Medusa could offer. Holly was the only person who used Zander's first name.

'Good to see you, Shawn. Kelly will be expecting you. Tell her I've found something, and I'll call tomorrow.'

Zander took the hint and rose from his seat.

'Will do. Catch you later.'

Zander gave Barton a look of grim understanding, like a soldier who had been dispatched to warn their reserves of a huge approaching enemy force, while knowing those left behind were doomed.

When Zander had gone, Holly settled the drowsy Tommy in his cot, rested a thick blanket on him, then placed a cuddly bear at his side, which Barton had last seen in Luke's room.

'John. We don't need to ring social services. Let *me* help Lily.'

'Lily's a stranger. She could have any number of problems.'

'She can stay here for a few days, regain her strength. We'll support her.'

'Great. I can't wait to wake up with her hands around my throat, or, worse, the contents of our knife block sticking out my stomach.'

Holly's stare narrowed.

'I never ask you about anything concerning your work.'

'I don't mention my cases.'

'Do you think I've never seen the news? Seen your dark eyes? Heard your complaints in your sleep?'

'That's wind.'

Holly wasn't in a joking mood.

'Trust me on this. I know women like Lily well enough. I've dealt with them for decades at school. They try, and they try, all on their own, with no money, no support, until one day it all gets too much. They aren't terrible parents, but, for a moment, they're overwhelmed. With a little assistance and encouragement, they can swiftly get back on track.'

'Yes, and there are council departments to assist them.'

'You only said this week that vital services in the county were swamped.'

Barton perched on the sofa. 'That's true.'

'Lily needs a friend. Give me some time with her. If you still want to call Shirley on Monday, then that's okay.'

Barton reached into the cot and stroked the now-sleeping boy's arm. Tommy's mother was quietly snoring, as were Gizmo and Vince.

'Fair enough. I told Ken her boiler had broken and that's why she was shouting, but her heating shouldn't have been off, so I'll check it in the morning.'

'Okay. Let's talk tomorrow.'

'Shall I sleep down here?'

Holly chuckled.

'No, I'll do it. If she groggily woke up and heard you breathing heavily in the same room, she'd panic she was having a nightmare about a grizzly's lair.'

'Not to mention it smelling like one.'

'Exactly. By the way, there are some important matters I need to chat to you about.'

Barton trudged off to make them a hot drink, muttering under his breath, suspecting life had just become much more complicated.

7

THE BOOK CLUB KILLER

I'm pretty spaced out now. A few strong drinks, loads of lovely food, and the warmth and relaxing smells and sounds that only an open fire can provide. Saying that, it's been a long night with some nervous tension. The bill has arrived. Seems a scary amount, but there are eight of us, and I'm not so old that I've forgotten prices always rise. In a way, it's a bargain, purely for the cover the meal has provided.

Rhys rises from his chair. He pings a dessert spoon against his glass of Talisker single malt. When all eyes are on him, he smiles his most reassuring smile. The one that no doubt made his business such a success, at least at the beginning.

'Well, the votes are in on which book we're choosing from the eight that were put forward. I can reveal the winner of the novel we need to read in the next two and a half weeks is, da-da-dar, *The Slay Before Christmas*, by Desmond Finch.'

We all join in with whistles or boos.

'Now, now. The majority have spoken. Some of you aren't overkeen on crime, but hopefully this won't be too gruesome. Should be nice and festive, too, and something for us to get our teeth into, leading to meaty discussions next time.'

Rhys seems unsteady on his feet. He takes a moment, then continues.

'As always, we have a reservation here for 7 p.m. on Christmas Eve, which gives you plenty of opportunity to order the paperback or buy it on Kindle and read it. I'll look forward to seeing you all then. Our resident baker asked me to remind you all to take a cupcake home with you. Improved recipe this year and bigger than usual.'

Rhys retakes his seat, face flushed red. I wonder if that's from the whisky or the stress he's been suffering from of late. He seems distracted, confused. Perhaps he's not a well man, either. It's probably an age thing. The body's complaints become difficult to ignore. Turning a blind eye is harder. I suppose Rhys suffers at times, even though he can be a kind, thoughtful fellow. To a point, of course.

Rhys's eyes widen. He climbs back to his feet. Strange to see him so drunk. Has something happened I don't know about?

'Apologies, apologies.' Rhys puts seven blank envelopes in the middle and mixes them up. He theatrically chooses one, then adds another blank envelope, which will contain his name, and stirs them again with a flourish. Two of them fly off the table. The person next to him picks both up with a shake of their head.

Rhys puffs out his cheeks as though the effort has exhausted him. 'Secret Santas.'

Each member takes a pick, but Rhys doesn't sit down.

'I have another announcement. A commercial statement more than personal. Actually, I guess it's both. Everyone here has played a part in making Jones and Singh Accountants a remarkable success, even if it's been supporting from behind the scenes. I thank you all sincerely. So my heart is somewhat heavy, but also relieved, to make you aware I have decided to retire in the new year.'

There is stunned silence. None of us expected that. Interesting. Tonight, the eight surviving members of The Tax Titans' lives are going to change in more ways than one. Rhys's dropped bombshell will complicate everything.

Let's not forget the wild cards either, of course. Will those people play their hands? It could make all the difference.

8
RHYS JONES

Rhys Jones stayed sitting in the car while his wife stomped towards the electric garage door. She stood in front of it, hands on hips, as though sheer willpower alone would force it to fulfil its role. He tutted. Such an emotional, highly strung, passionate woman. Actually, that was being kind. Angry seemed to be more her default emotion lately. He supposed her fiery nature had initially been a significant part of the attraction.

Rude would be another word to describe her. She'd called him a fat chuff shortly before they'd left for The Bell. Normally her slurs bounced off him, as though his layer of insulation, which admittedly had grown considerably these past few years, made him bulletproof. Insult-proof. A visible shield, if you like, especially with him not knowing what a chuff was.

Tonight, it had been the expression of disgust on her face when she'd said it that had pierced his armour. Contempt and a mocking tone, mixed with revulsion. Ungrateful cow. He bit down on the cupcake he was holding, taking a huge chunk as a small, pathetic act of retaliation. It was a self-inflicted blow, especially considering her taunt.

Morwen pounded the metal door with her fist, then stamped out of sight around to the rear entrance. She'd need to lift the door by hand. He understood that was usually a blue job, i.e. one of his, but he'd felt weaker of late. It was his firm. The long hours, the arguments, the general stress-filled nature of it all, all of which had gradually drained the strength from him. There wasn't much left in the tank. He needed to pause, rebuild, and he'd be unable to do that working sixty-hour weeks.

Perhaps he should have discussed his retirement with Vijay beforehand. That was assuming the guy could have pulled himself away from chatting up Morwen for a moment. Rhys took a further big mouthful and nodded approvingly. Magnificent cupcake, although a new recipe, his arse. Rhys enjoyed his desserts, and this was shop-bought.

He stuffed the final little piece of chocolate chip loveliness into his mouth. Folded the paper and hid it in his suit's inside pocket. With a grunt, he heaved himself out of the vehicle just as the garage door opened. Morwen appeared. Arms raised like a biblical strongman. He meandered past her to open the front door of their house. Another nip of whisky in his office would help him forget his woes.

Morwen scoffed.

'I'll put the car away, shall I?'

He shouted back.

'I'm over the limit.'

'I believe the phrase is past your best.'

He ignored the barb and made his way to the drinks cabinet behind his desk. Two fingers of Glenfiddich went into a crystal glass. He liked that American saying, especially with having thick digits.

He dropped into his luxurious executive chair and finally relaxed. Felt brilliant, in fact. So chilled. So pleasant to be home. The book club had been nerve-racking earlier. Why had he felt so nervous? He'd done talks at accountants' AGMs with hundreds of high-powered people present. Surely this immense sense of relief indicated that he had made the right decision about taking time out.

So, retirement wasn't a choice. It was a solution. What lay ahead of him, though? Maybe he should dig out his tennis racquet. Although that would still leave plenty of time. Most of which Morwen would want to spend apart from him. They'd been blessed with only one child, although he suspected you'd need to have sex more than a couple of times a year to have a decent chance of a brood.

There had been no romance in their lives for quite a while, at least not for him. He took a large gulp of the amber liquid, fire rolling down his throat. When he'd last attempted to initiate sex, she'd told him her life was so hectic that she wasn't in the mood. A frown came over Rhys's face as he tried not to think of what was keeping her busy. Maybe his business partner. Screw Vijay. Rhys smiled grimly at his choice of words.

A divorce was the answer. He doubted Morwen would want one. For all her bluster, she lacked confidence and even the simplest of organisational skills. Heaven forbid she'd have to do anything around the house except let workmen and cleaners in and beautify herself.

It would cost him a small fortune, but half of a lot was still plenty. As long as he had a big brawny saloon car and some decent grog, he'd be fine. Maybe he could catch the eye of someone pleasant, who wasn't only after the lifestyle he provided. A lady who liked him. Wanted simple pleasures like bar snacks, museum visits and gentle walks.

Rhys was leaning back in his executive chair, beaming and imagining such a woman, when a loud rap came at the office door. He jolted upright, spilling his drink over his shirt.

'Yes,' he shouted, sounding guilty.

'I'm going up. Don't overdo it, or I'll hear you snoring from upstairs.'

'Okay, darling. Merely a nightcap. See you soon.'

'You sound hammered already.'

'Not drunk. Happy!'

He waited for a response, even though he knew one wouldn't come, and took another rebellious gulp. A further feeling of contentment embraced him as the burning sensation seeped into his stomach. Was that a sense of peace over the decision he'd just made?

The prospect of an argument in the morning with a hangover was unappealing, assuming he found the courage to ask for a separation. Better he waited a few days until he felt strong, and located a flat to rent, so he had somewhere to go when she furiously showed him to their door. Yes, that was a plan.

Another wave of relaxation spread through his body, radiating outwards to his fingertips and toes. He hadn't realised how tense he'd been, how tightly wound. Now, a blissful, calm cocoon enveloped him. The edges of his desk blurred, the cityscape painting of London on his wall dissolved into an impressionist scene.

His breathing slowed, each exhale longer, sweeter, but weaker than the last. As he gave a contented sigh, Rhys's eyelids fluttered closed.

9

DCI BARTON

Saturday

Barton awoke around nine o'clock after struggling to drop off the previous evening. He hadn't wanted to leave Holly downstairs, but she had shooed him out of the lounge, saying if he didn't clear off, she'd be demanding her own baby.

Even though it was early, shouts and howls could already be heard in the house, along with cries of 'don't kill me', but they were echoing from his youngest son's room. Luke, almost a teenager now, and his pals joined group WhatsApp calls and played Fortnite or Roblox for hours on end on their Xboxes and PlayStations. Barton thought of his own youth, cycling all over for miles, messing around in barns and haystacks, trees and fields, ponds and rivers, and worried again at a changing world.

A cup of steaming coffee sat on his bedside table, giving him further proof everything was normal. After finishing his drink, he got up and pulled on the supposedly oversized hoodie his eldest son, Lawrence, had bought him for his fifty-first birthday. He stared in the mirror. The garment fitted perfectly and wasn't too big at all.

After a quick wash and brush-up, Barton thundered downstairs and headed to the kitchen with his stomach rumbling. He could definitely smell sausages, and he could also detect laughter.

He opened the door, and three faces turned towards him. Holly rose and pecked him on the cheek.

'Lily, this enormous womble is my husband, John, who you met last night.'

Lily gave Barton a sheepish smile.

'Sorry about yesterday, and thank you. I was at my wits' end after my money ran out and—'

'Nice to be properly introduced,' interrupted Barton. 'And no problem. As the song says, "Life Is a Rollercoaster". I have to say, you look much better.'

Lily had more colour in her face, but she still seemed frail. She had prominent cheekbones and thick brown hair. Her son had inherited her big blue eyes, which tracked Barton entering the room. Tommy appeared capable of chewing bricks. He thudded his hand on the high chair, which Barton assumed had been fetched from Lily's, and made a loud, high-pitched cooing sound.

Holly reached over and stroked the soft down on Tommy's head.

'Lily's going to stay here until Monday, then I'll ring around and talk to the council and utility companies. Get her the right discounts and benefits now she's a single woman. Her boiler's fine. She was worried about money and had turned it off.'

The Bartons had converted their garage, so Lily and the boy would sleep down there. He held his wife's gaze for a moment before nodding.

'No worries.'

Holly beamed at him.

'Tommy's one very soon, so I'll buy a cake today. Are you still out with Mortis tonight?'

'Yeah, we're having a few beers at The Wonky Donkey in Fletton. He also wants to talk about something, which sounds ominous.'

'Doesn't everything he says sound that way?'

Barton chuckled. 'I suppose so.'

'As you can tell, we've collected more things from Lily's. I'll just show her the shower, then you and I will have that little chat.'

Barton curled his lip, but his mood improved when he glanced over at the hob and spied a tray of cooked sausages waiting for him. They were still warm enough, so he made himself a brown-bread sandwich with fruity HP sauce and sat down next to Tommy. The baby grinned, showing two white bottom teeth. Barton idly wondered at what size babies were referred to as toddlers. He assumed when they toddled.

Tommy grabbed a piece of sausage in his left hand and another in his right, then, while grinning triumphantly, he crushed them both and let the pieces fall onto the table.

'I know how you feel, pal,' replied Barton, licking his lips.

Layla, who was in her final year at school, breezed into the kitchen.

'Ooh, bangers.'

Barton smiled as she grabbed herself a plate. His daughter spent most of her time in what used to be called the garage and was now affectionately nicknamed the annexe.

'I take it you're aware we have a guest. Will you be all right staying in your bedroom for a few days?'

'Of course, Daddy dearest. Mum's already spoken to me. We did a deal.'

Barton resisted a groan. Layla often wanted expensive things, which she couldn't afford herself. Even so, she negotiated hard.

'Is that why you're in a good mood?' he asked. 'Or has your spell worked on the cowardly lion?'

Barton and Holly jokingly referred to their daughter as the Wicked Witch of the West due to the arrival of her unpredictable and volatile nature when she hit her teens. Layla liked the nickname. Her intellectual boyfriend, who was a quiet and gentle soul, had dumped her after a recent outburst, and she'd been trying to win him back.

'Yes. Eye of newt and a particularly short skirt did the trick last night. He's taking me to the cinema this evening, so I'm buzzing. Thanks for the advice.'

'Words of wisdom are what dads are for. That and paying for everything.'

'I know, and I do love you.' Layla cocked her head to one side. 'Have I told you that lately?'

'Not since you were about nine, so it's lovely to hear it.'

'Oh, I always do, I forget.'

'That's okay, sweetie. At your age, there's a lot of noise. Jobs, uni, guys, your future, friends, exams, but every once in a while, the clouds part and you see things clearly.'

Layla slowly and captivatingly raised an eyebrow. A trick she would no doubt use to her benefit for the rest of her days.

'What does that mean?'

'Try not to spend your whole life looking ahead. Now is where it's at. That's one of the reasons people meditate or pray at whatever their holy place is.'

'Don't you worship at McDonald's?'

'I attend as often as I'm able.'

Layla stood behind him and kissed the top of his head. She then did the same to Tommy.

'Babies smell so sweet,' she said. 'You? Not so much.'

Then she vanished and Luke arrived.

'You better have not eaten all the sausages. Ooh, what's this? Two chubby bald things at the table.'

Luke grabbed a bowl, slung three sausages in it, covered them in a horrendous amount of ketchup, then disappeared.

Barton tucked into his sandwich, but he didn't really taste it. He'd been used to banter around his weight all his life, ever since he went to junior school and was a head taller than all his friends. He had been a powerful young man, brilliant in the scrum, and an impressive police officer in uniform, but it seemed of late that the jokes were hitting home.

Holly appeared and frowned at Barton as he uncharacteristically pushed the last of his breakfast away.

'Okay, John. Time to talk.'

10
DCI BARTON

Barton raised a finger. He rose from his seat, switched on the kettle, which boiled quickly, made them both a coffee and sat down.

'Okay, hit me.'

'First up, I went to suss out that unit on Oundle Road that's up for rent.'

'The one that used to be a salon?'

'Yes. There was a shop attached selling gems and crystals. That's also vacant. The lease is reasonable. There's not much work needs doing, and there is plenty of space for what I've finally decided I plan to do.'

'Which is?'

'All this with Lily is a sign. When I raised our tribe, there were Sure Start centres, kids' clubs, church groups, you name it. I wasn't a single parent, but you worked such long hours, I often felt like one.'

'Sorry about that.'

'Don't be daft. You were doing an important part. Your promotions and salary, and pension when you take it, have put us in a strong financial position. Of course, I'm hoping my business makes a tidy profit, but I want something for the community, for women like Lily. Most of the mother and baby groups are gone, or others are forced to charge. Just heating the places is expensive nowadays.'

'Is this going to be a café or a mothers' club?'

'Both! A spot where mums can meet other mums, make friends. Enjoy a hot chocolate. Let their kids play in safe areas. I'll provide free nappies and wipes. It'll be warm. We'll sell great cake.'

'I thought you said there was no parking there. Won't that be a problem?'

'There isn't any, but I spoke to Raj over at the Nisa shop. His car park is huge, and rarely full, so he's offered to allow us to use it, guessing that if the mothers head in and enter their registrations, they'll probably buy something at the same time.'

'Sounds like you've given it a lot of consideration.'

'Yes, I have. I was leaning to it having a book theme. A quiet spot to read and maybe discuss fiction.'

Tommy threw a spoon at Barton, then roared with laughter when the big man pulled an over-the-top sad face.

'There won't be any peace when Tommy's tearing the place apart.'

Holly smiled at the lad.

'That's true, but last night's incident with Lily has made up my mind to put that on the back burner, but obviously I wanted to discuss it with you. If Lily had somewhere to go before she hit crisis, I'm sure what happened could have been avoided.'

'Makes sense.'

'She also told me about the worst things her husband did.'

'I bet it's a sad tale. I hadn't spoken to her before. You know, too busy doing my part.'

Holly chuckled. She came and perched on his knee. She was a little over five feet and slim, and he barely knew she was there. She squeezed one of his cheeks.

'Such a good boy.'

'You said he cleared off with another woman.'

'Yes, but he emptied the joint account first, and they only had his car, which he took. The credit card was in both names but near its limit, so he left that.'

'So, he did the dirty, then probably behaved as if everything was her fault and she needed punishing.'

'Exactly. I think that was part of her meltdown. The shock. It's like the father, Fraser, forgot he has a lovely little boy whose life has been turned upside down. Fraser has money, too. His business is doing well.'

'I saw marital arguments all the time when I was a response officer.

Women hammering on doors demanding help. If the ex is self-employed, it's hard for the Child Maintenance Service to assess their financial assets. I assume she's told him she's skint?'

'John, the fucker's not answering his phone. I would love to get my paws on his assets. I'd rip them off.'

'Okay, moving swiftly on. What else was on your mind?'

'I got a call from Debs Edyvane.'

Barton grinned. Debs was the wife of Steve Edyvane, aka Eddie. A fellow officer and a good laugh who'd joined at a similar time to Barton but moved to Lincolnshire to raise his family.

'Excellent. I've not heard from Eddie in a long while. How is he?'

'Dead.'

Barton's face fell.

'What?'

'I'm afraid so. Apparently, he asked her if she wanted anything from the shop and didn't return to the house. When she went outside to see if he was on his way back, she found him lying in a bush in the garden. Stone cold.'

'Shit. Heart attack?'

'Yep. Post-mortem found a blood clot, so it will be the usual. Life of stress, no exercise, and a poor diet.' Holly slipped off Barton's knee. 'Sound familiar?'

'I play tennis.'

'Yes, regularly. Once a year. What were your results like from your latest Well Man check?'

'Not bad.'

'How would you know? You haven't picked them up.'

Barton froze, caught out with his lie.

'I rang the GP, but they said I had to visit.'

'What did you reckon that was for, you fool? To present you with an award for the highest cholesterol?'

'I'll make an appointment.'

'Don't worry. I've made you one for Wednesday at midday. I was collecting my HRT prescription and asked the receptionist about your check-up.'

'That's a breach of data protection.'

'I'll breach something else if you fail to show up.'

Barton growled.

'Anything else?'

'I'm serious, John. The family don't want to lose you. We need to have a proper discussion about what happens now DCI Cox is back and you're surplus to requirements. You aren't forced to be at the brutal end of policing any more.'

'If not me, then who?'

Holly crossed her arms. 'Your job is killing you. Let someone else bear the load. How many other DIs are active at your age? You've done your bit. I read about the violence and death and horrific crimes in the local news. You never tell me the specifics, but you're obviously in the middle of it.'

Barton sighed as the weight of the imminent decision pressed down on him. It was more than just a job; it was his identity. Retirement felt like uncharted territory. A place where he'd have to redefine himself, which might not come easy.

Without the cases, the responsibility, the life lived as a senior police detective, who would he be?

11

DCI BARTON

After a relaxing day where he and Holly took Tommy for a walk and didn't do much else, Barton checked his watch. If he was going to stroll to The Wonky Donkey, he'd need to set off in five minutes, but he was thoroughly enjoying himself. Tommy had almost mastered walking but was only confident holding on to something. The joy on his face was infectious. Even Luke came to see what all the laughter was about.

Tommy reached the end of the sofa. Barton's armchair was a metre away. Tommy, wide-eyed, stared at the distance as though it were a gaping chasm. He conquered his fear and set off, stout legs tanking along, features tense with concentration and determination. He stumbled just after halfway. The ground raced to greet him; the crowd gasped. Barton swept him up and sat the child on his knee, where the lad waved victoriously at his adoring fans.

Barton kissed him on the head.

'He does smell nice.'

Holly came in with two glasses of wine and handed one to Lily. Holly took a sip of hers, then placed her glass on the coffee table and beckoned Luke over.

'I want a word with you.'

Barton chuckled, which made Tommy laugh.

'What?' asked Luke, with an innocent face.

'Who had a shower and dropped their dirty undies on the bathroom floor, then didn't flush the toilet after using up about four toilet rolls, *and* left the lid up?'

Luke's neck reddened.

'Oh, yeah, I forgot.'

'Again?' She glared at her son. 'Why are you still here? Get to it.'

Luke scoffed a retort but was wise enough to keep it inaudible. He trudged back upstairs. They heard the flush.

Barton passed Tommy over to Lily. He cringed as he recalled an incident the previous weekend.

'Last Saturday, Luke left a nasty mess in the toilet at the front of the house and didn't shut the lid or close the door. The Sainsbury's delivery woman arrived, and I began bringing it in. I failed to notice until I'd returned the final crate that the driver had a perfect view of the carnage. I realised and tried to explain, but by the expression on her face, I don't think she believed me.'

Lily couldn't help herself.

'Wow, fancy trying to blame your son.'

'Men, eh!' replied Holly, winking at her. 'Besides, John, you can't talk. You're always leaving your grotty pants on the floor.'

'Hey, you could eat your dinner off mine.'

'Yeah, right. Perhaps as an alternative to Dignitas.'

The sound of women laughing followed Barton as he headed outside. He turned at the door, a hint of a smile tugging at his lips.

'Have a wonderful evening, Tommy.'

He strode down the street with enthusiasm, but it was a longer walk to The Wonky Donkey than he'd remembered, and he had to pick up the pace.

Mortis gave him a weary shake of the head when he eventually burst through the pub door, sweaty faced and ten minutes late.

'Mr Barton. Tardiness is a lack of respect.'

'Lack of fitness, in my case.'

'I have to say, I've seen you in ruder health.'

Mortis could always be relied on to get straight to the cutting truth.

Barton sampled the pint waiting for him. 'Zander was saying the same thing.'

The owner came over to join them. 'How do, John?'

'Do I look rough, Dave?'

'No more than usual.'

'Cheers.'

Dave Williams was a former police officer. He also knew Edyvane and frowned when he heard of his demise. 'Bloody hell. Another retired copper dies too soon of a coronary.'

'You had the right idea, getting out early, running this place.'

Dave took a deep breath.

'I've kept this fairly quiet, but a year ago, I was mega rough. Absolutely awful. My missus was away, and I was so ropey, I drove to A & E at four in the morning. Got there and explained to the receptionist how bad I felt. She didn't seem too concerned and said to take a seat and wait. I staggered a few steps, then had a heart attack on the spot. They restarted me twice.'

'Blimey. Are you all right now?'

'Couple of stents, good as new, although I've stopped eating vindaloos, just in case.'

Mortis raised an eyebrow. 'Well, you can't be too careful.'

Barton and Mortis carried their drinks to a table. The pathologist analysed Barton. 'When I used to do standard hospital post-mortems at the start of my macabre career, I'd see someone your age and size every week.'

'Can we talk about something else?'

'Okay.' Mortis drank a mouthful of his beer. 'I'm retiring.'

Mortis, whose nickname had come from his fascination with the stages of death, had already dropped down to part-time.

'Completely?'

'Yes. There have been hardly any forensic pathology cases in the last few months. As horrifying as your rape spree investigation has been, nobody's ended up on my table, and it's given me an opportunity to think.'

'I suppose that's something to be thankful for. The bloke responsible was evil, but the girls survived.'

Mortis glugged the rest of his ale, then plonked his empty glass down.

'But it's more sadness. I've finally had my fill. That includes examining people's bodies. Cutting out hearts, weighing brains, breaking bones, removing eyeballs. It takes a toll.'

'You don't say.'

'I used to be able to put on my clinician's hat and focus on the science. It was the woman from The Village Killer case who first deeply moved me, after you said how full of life she was. Since then, I've begun to really see the individuals under my scalpel. Imagine their lives, the trauma of those left behind, even wondered about the victims' hopes and dreams. Not like me at all.'

'So, that's it? You're done?'

'Yes. I'll be around if I'm needed until Christmas Eve, but I'll probably go a few days before. After that, I'm going to be officially retired. Actually, talking of heart attacks, I've agreed to take on a case to ease the workload for the hospital pathologists.'

'Anything suspicious?'

'Nope. An overweight man in later life, from Stilton.'

Barton forced himself to swallow the gulp of beer he'd just taken.

'My age?'

'Not quite. Mid-sixties. I'd guess at a coronary event. He died suddenly in his office chair.'

12

THE BOOK CLUB KILLER

The news of Rhys's death rippled through the book club in a wave of phone calls and texts. What a great guy. Such a kind bloke. He'll be sorely missed. Taken too soon. The usual platitudes. Were they being sincere, or were they enjoying the drama?

I suppose Rhys didn't do too terribly in life. None of us are perfect. Only one major sin I'm aware of, but you don't get to be rich and successful as he was without cutting corners or trampling others underfoot, and a single unpleasant deed can be enough to deserve punishment.

His death was unexpected, though. I expected him to be extremely unwell, yes, but I hadn't anticipated him dying, even if it was always a possibility. Still, it's what people crave – excitement, commotion, a distraction from their own mundane lives. And Rhys's passing, with its air of mystery, gives everyone that.

Ironically, the novel we chose for the club, *The Slay Before Christmas*, starts off briskly in a similar vein. Atmospheric, suspenseful, with well-drawn characters. The title itself hints at a shocking killing, setting a tone of impending doom before anyone would have turned the first page.

The detective, however, is a cliché – a coke-snorting divorcee with a handgun. Implausible in the UK and, frankly, obnoxious. Perhaps the author will surprise me and knock him off unexpectedly, but, for now, it's a point against the book.

There is a peculiar thrill to a shocking demise, such as Rhys's. Like the woman getting skewered at the end of *Pitch Black*, or Murron's fate in *Braveheart*. The steady march of time at our age has done away with most thrills, but there's a shudder, a visceral reaction that transcends the normal responses when someone unexpectedly dies. I felt it when I heard Rhys had gone, as will have nearly everyone else.

The Slay Before Christmas might offer some inspiration, or at least some idea of what to expect if the police get involved. Although, unlike in real life, fiction demands a satisfying resolution. No loose ends, no unanswered questions. I, on the other hand, may escape the long arm of the law. Who knows how thorough, or busy, the mortuary is? Or how efficient, driven and experienced the detectives are?

It's always the characters that draw me in when I read. Their lives, their secrets, their motivations. Not to forget guilt, revenge, and regret. It's the way they react to trauma and bad news. With Rhys gone, the future is up in the air. Might the members yield to the siren call of rumour and speculation? Could The Tax Titans cease to be?

When all becomes clear, I expect the members to ponder over who could have done such a thing, and why.

When they should be worried who's next.

13

DCI BARTON

Wednesday

Wednesday morning came around fast, and Barton found himself at the doctor's surgery. He smiled to himself while he waited to be seen. Tommy's birthday party on Monday afternoon had been such genuinely innocent fun, even though a slice of cake hurled by Tommy had caught Holly a glancing blow to the temple. The little lad's laugh afterwards could have come out of The Joker's repertoire.

Barton's GP popped his head around the door and called his name. Barton gave the man a nervous nod as they sat down in the consulting room.

'Morning, Adam.'

'Hello, John. Always a pleasure.'

'Cheers. I was thinking outside that you've been my GP since before I joined the police.'

'Don't the years fly by? I've got eighteen months to go, then I'm off on an around-the-world cruise. All paid for. No changing my mind this time.'

'Nice. Space in your luggage for a small one?'

Adam laughed. 'My son asked the same thing, and he's twenty-nine. Right, let's take a quick blood-pressure reading, and I'll get to why I wanted a face-to-face appointment. Although, it's taken you a while. Been busy, or avoiding me?'

Adam's eyes crinkled. After nearly thirty years, he knew Barton well.

'Bit of both.'

Adam removed the cuff from Barton's arm. 'One-forty-three over eighty-eight.'

'Not too bad.'

'Not too bad for someone who isn't already on medication to bring it down. You also weigh over twenty stone.'

'I've been eighteen stone since I was about sixteen.'

The doctor sat back down and peered over his glasses.

'I'm aware of that, John. I've treated you all these years, broken fingers, twisted ankles, dislocated shoulder, but you've hit your fifties now. You'll have lost around 30 per cent of your muscle from your rugby days, which will have been replaced by one substance.'

'Brains?'

'Fat! And you're heavier than you were, so...'

'You're making me feel like a ball of Edam.'

'Your readings aren't outrageous, but, combined with your weight, they are a worry. The most concerning fact is the direction they're heading. Action is needed now.'

Barton mentioned his friend Eddie dying of a heart attack.

Adam nodded.

'I see it all the time in men similar to you. The lucky blokes have a medical incident, then make the necessary changes to their lifestyles and diets. The unlucky ones are buried. I assume you'll blame your occupation.'

'Of course.'

'Well, don't. It's *your* hand going to your mouth. Nobody else's. *Your* mind that argues against taking a long walk.'

'Aren't you docs supposed to have a gentler, non-judgemental manner nowadays?'

'We do, but I'm leaving, so I get to say it how it is. If the job genuinely is the problem, the answer is still within your hands.'

Barton nodded at hearing his own thoughts repeated. 'Right.'

'A new course of action has become available to us. We've been given some tirzepatide as a trial.'

'Isn't that the so-called fat jab for obese people?'

'Yes.'

'I see.'

Adam grinned back at him. 'Think about it. Perhaps it's a choice that might not involve quitting the job you love. Most people tolerate the medication well and go on to lose 20 per cent of their weight. That would make you a much healthier sixteen stone.'

'I'd be worried about blowing away.'

'The other method is to use willpower, which takes more planning and stronger commitment.'

Barton pulled a face.

'How does the treatment work?'

'Simply put, it makes you feel fuller for longer and decreases your appetite. Many skip meals because they aren't hungry. Some people are nauseous for a day or two after the injection, but the side effects lessen after a few months.'

Barton considered his own urges. He had to admit to being starving most of the time.

'When do I need to give you my decision by?'

'I'll give you a leaflet. Ring the surgery by the end of the week. If it's a no, then you should diet the normal way.'

Barton's phone rang.

Adam turned back to his computer. 'Answer it. Have a wonderful day.'

Barton stepped out of his consulting room. 'Morning, Mortis. What's up?'

'You remember the post-mortem I agreed to do for the potential heart attack?'

'Yes.'

'I'm beginning to suspect that it wasn't a simple myocardial infarction.'

'Hang on a minute. Let me get in my car.'

Barton walked to the car park with his mind whizzing through the possibilities. Mortis would only ring him if he suspected a crime could have been committed. As he opened his vehicle's door and got in, he prepared himself for Mortis's reasoning, which would no doubt include many medical terms.

'Okay, fire away.'

'With a possible coronary incident, us pathologists are quick to note certain details. Rhys Jones was in his sixties, had average musculature, but was overweight. He ticked a few boxes, although when I opened him up, his organs were surprisingly healthy. A thorough examination of his arteries revealed no major obstructions. No issues at all, in fact.'

'You've said before it could still be heart-related without obvious evidence.'

'True, but when I checked his NHS record, Rhys had no medical history of any significant problems whatsoever. That moves me from suspecting a simple cardiac event.'

'Okay, go on.'

'There was also severe pulmonary oedema present in Rhys.'

'Which is again?'

'Liquid in the lungs. If it builds up too quickly, the tiny air sacs are flooded, which are meant for air, not fluid. With no sacs available, the person can't breathe. It's common when a patient has heart disease.'

'Which he doesn't have in this case?'

'Correct. There are other potential causes, including kidney failure and altitude sickness.'

'Yet Rhys's organs were healthy, and him having hiked at extreme heights is unlikely considering the village where he lives is on the edge of the fens.'

'Yes. Last of all, my preliminary examination of the brain tissue indicated oxygen deprivation, which is usually present when there's been respiratory depression.'

Barton had read enough post-mortem results to have some guesses to where Mortis was heading. Barton listed the causes.

'Drowning. Choking. Overdose. Stroke.'

'Excellent. The chair he died in wasn't at the bottom of a swimming pool. There was nothing in his throat. My guess is something caused his blood pressure to drop so low he stopped breathing.'

'I'm assuming this guy didn't regularly dress in rags and sleep on cardboard down an underpass.'

'No. Obviously, people hide their addictions, but this man was a wealthy accountant. A quick search on Google shows he was a respected one, often being asked for his opinion on the latest taxation rules. I can't find any fresh injection sites, so if a substance caused his death it was likely ingested or inhaled.'

Barton didn't like the sound of that.

'How long for blood-test results?'

'I fast-tracked them while I examined the body parts, so hopefully tomorrow.'

'Could it be carbon monoxide poisoning?'

'This guy was white British so there would normally be cherry-red colouration of the blood, lips, nail bed and internal organs in that case, which isn't present. However, he died last week, so those factors might not still be visible. Elevated levels of carboxyhaemoglobin in the blood would be an indicator, but these also decrease after death. I suppose CO poisoning could be the cause.'

'A house call to the widow makes sense to check if they have a faulty fire. Thanks for thinking of me, but you could have referred this to Uniform, or is it the Mortis mind operating like the Barton belly?'

'I'm just covering my arse.'

Barton knew his friend was suspicious of something else. 'Send me the details through. What exactly are you suspecting?'

'What I'm saying, John, is the cause of death at this point is unexplained, and we scientists abhor that. This man is unlikely to have died in this manner by his own hand, so it needs a second look. Besides, you said on Saturday night you were winding down. I'd hate for you to be bored.'

'Thanks a bunch.'

Barton cut the call, then stared out of the window. Mortis was implying two things. One was that Rhys had been murdered. The other was that more people could be in danger. Barton would need to investigate immediately because five days had gone by.

That meant that if indeed there was a killer's trail, it would already be cold.

14

DCI BARTON

Barton drove to Thorpe Wood police station, deep in thought. He'd never been too bothered about ageing or his diet, so it wasn't a surprise both had got away from him.

Barton didn't usually notice the building as he turned into the entrance. Many of the modern stations had the same utilitarian design of brown and beige bricks, giving them a subdued and functional air. Peterborough had done some basic landscaping and added a few shrubs, but it was a grim place to leave at dawn on a grey morning after a night in the cells. He suspected that was how it should be.

Barton parked and almost walked straight into his office, but it now belonged to someone else. Detective Chief Inspector Cox, the officer Barton had been covering for, had Detective Chief Superintendent Troughton in there with her. Barton swiftly veered away from the entrance, but he was too late.

Cox's boss opened the door.

'Cracking timing, John. Come in.'

Barton painted a smile on his face, entered, and shook Troughton's hand. He nodded at Cox behind what had been his desk.

Troughton eyed him up and down.

'I hear the handover has gone smoothly. What are your plans for your last few weeks?'

As the DCI in Major Crimes, Barton would have been busy with meetings, community relations, training, assessments, disciplinaries, and end-of-year appraisals, but they were now Cox's concerns.

'I had planned to visit the skills centre in Huntingdon and talk to them about an opportunity, but I'm not now.'

'Why? You're an excellent trainer. Pass on your knowledge.'

'Teaching new detectives was okay, but it was like buying a nice ice cream and watching another person eat it.'

Troughton bobbed his head as though he understood.

'Fair enough. Listen. I've had it confirmed you'll retain your rank as DCI whatever you do next. Twice you've covered the role and done a fantastic job.'

'I appreciate that,' said Barton with feeling, but it would not stop what he was about to say even if part of his pension would be based on his final salary.

Troughton took a seat and gestured for Barton to do the same.

'Which way are you leaning, then?'

'I think I'm going to retire.'

Troughton's gaze stayed on Barton, but his expression remained neutral. He no doubt had expected the answer.

'We don't like losing people with your experience, John. There are plenty of departments who would jump at the chance to have you.'

Cox had stayed silent, her surprise evident. 'Do you mind me asking what's led you to that choice?'

Barton leaned back in his seat.

'You both know I love detective work, but these last twelve months have been challenging. Maybe those three years behind a desk softened me up, or perhaps I would have burnt out anyway, but frazzled is how I feel. My wife and I will discuss everything over the next few days, but it's time I focussed on my health for a while.'

Troughton folded his arms.

'Nobody's stopping you heading to the gym after work or at the weekends.'

Barton almost tutted. Typical higher rank forgetting what life was like on the front line, but he wasn't there for an argument, so he explained calmly.

'When a serious and swift-moving investigation begins, it becomes all-consuming. That's the only way to solve some cases. Meals are missed, fast food eaten, sleep suffers, stress and excitement can take over. It's the job.'

Cox nodded. 'He's right. The combination of enthusiasm and drive with knowing you're doing something beneficial takes hold. It's about protecting the public. Putting the worst criminals away for a long time, before anyone else gets hurt. There's nothing like it, and other concerns fall by the wayside.'

Her last sentence hung in the air. Barton knew that too well.

Troughton was a clever man and got to the nub of the issue.

'I take it you heard about Edyvane? Such a shame.'

'Yes, shocking. Give me a week to ponder everything. Carry on sending me other opportunities. I'd hate to miss out on helping set up a new team in the Maldives.'

Troughton's expression was unreadable. 'Nothing as lovely as that around at the moment, unfortunately, but I shall keep you posted. So, your immediate plans?'

'There was a death in Stilton last Friday evening. The pathologist called me with some concerns. I could pass it on to CID at this point, but I've got the time. I'll take a member of my old team and visit the deceased's home.'

Troughton nodded. 'Hoping for a final case?'

'Of course.'

'I was friendly with Rhys Jones. Played squash with him in the same league a few years back. Decent player. In fact, I never beat him. Like the rest of us, carrying a bit of timber, but not one I'd have down for a heart attack.'

Barton was unable to resist. 'Unlike myself?'

'Don't be daft, John. You'll live forever.'

Barton couldn't help himself and laughed out loud. 'Really?'

Troughton grinned back at him. It was clear he'd already been briefed about Rhys's post-mortem and untimely death and had planned to send Barton to investigate anyway. It would be a win-win, because Cox wouldn't want him sitting in the main office for weeks with nothing to do.

'I reckon it's worth a drive over, John. Word to the wise, his wife's a handful. Feisty Welshwoman called Morwen. Keep me in the loop.'

'I'll get on it now, sir.'

'Excellent. Before you leave, I was wondering why you haven't considered regulation thirty-three.'

Troughton might be a slippery eel, but he was an intelligent one. Barton hadn't thought of taking an extended break from his position. Regulation thirty-three included an option that meant he could leave, but the exit door would remain slightly ajar in case he wanted to return.

'Thanks for reminding me. I'll reflect on that carefully.'

Barton was smiling as he left the room.

15

DCI BARTON

Barton headed for the main office. DI Zander, DC Minton and DC Malik were watching DS Maria Zelensky and DC Kevin Hoffman having an intense discussion. DC Leicester was staring into space.

'Road trip, Leicester,' said Barton. 'Dodgy death in Stilton. You're driving.'

Their superior's appearance put an end to Zelensky and Hoffman's row. Both returned to their seats with annoyed faces. Barton would normally have asked what was up, but there had been anger between the pair of late. He'd inquired once already, receiving only denials in reply. They'd be having another chat with him shortly, but it was time to get on the road.

After they set off, Barton speculated as to whether Leicester would mention the tension in the office, but he was a quiet, consistent member of the team and rarely probed into other people's affairs. Barton had been searching for an opportunity for a low-key conversation with the ginger-haired officer because he'd sensed a thoughtful air about him.

'So, Leicester. How are you?'

'Is this work-related or a personal question?'

'Either's fine.'

'Work's ticking along. We've had some interesting cases, but I am considering what to do next. I passed the sergeants' exam twelve months ago, but I was happy to spend another year as DC under you and Zander. I've now decided I definitely want more responsibility, so promotion is the goal after Christmas.'

'You've been efficient and dependable as always.'

'Thank you, sir.'

Barton smiled. Leicester and he had enjoyed some good chats during The Santa Killer case, but he remained distantly polite and still insisted everyone call him by his surname. After another minute of silence, Barton couldn't help himself.

'How about your home life?'

'That's why my job needs to be worthwhile, because I don't have much away from it. No girlfriend. Malik and I were close, but he's busy with his offspring. Minton and I go for a run together sometimes or visit the gym.'

'Weren't you two getting friendly?'

'Different aspirations.'

Barton frowned. 'Does that mean one of you wanted to settle down and the other didn't?'

'Yeah, she wants to travel at some point. Maybe work abroad, or at least a new department.'

Barton wondered how to give Leicester a boost.

'Something will turn up for you. Mark my words.'

'I'd love what you have.'

'The body of a bulldozer?'

Leicester wasn't in the mood for jokes. 'A wife. Children. Shared lives. A family, I suppose.'

Barton was about to say no money, no sleep, no peace, but realised it would sound insensitive. Marriage and responsibilities had given him a solid base and purpose, not to mention an understanding of the issues other parents and couples had.

'You know what, Leicester? You're right. I'm a lucky guy, and I've been a bit grumpy recently, when I have no cause to be.'

'Haven't noticed, sir.'

Barton's eyes swept across to Leicester, who was failing to hide his smile.

'That's because I'm such a professional,' said Barton with a grin, 'but I have been focussing on some of the negatives. I'm fortunate, in lots of ways, and if my future isn't with the police, then so be it. By the way, Holly insists you come again on Christmas Day. Told me to ask you now, so you don't make other plans.'

'She's a kind lady. I thoroughly enjoyed it last year. Zander's twins were hilarious; so was Mortis after he got a taste for your sherry.'

Barton grinned at the memory of the taciturn man breaking into song at the table, then being horrified by his actions.

'Funny you should mention our pathologist. He's the reason why we're off to Stilton. To bring you up to speed, Mortis is suspicious of how Rhys Evans died. Rhys was a successful accountant who lived and worked in the village.'

Barton explained Mortis's deductions so far. Leicester cocked his head to one side as he considered the facts.

'Sounds as though it's worth a visit.'

'Agreed. Toxicology should be with us tomorrow, but I'd like a quick word with his widow beforehand. We'll come across as genuine because we don't know much. Sometimes this approach causes them to lower their guard, and they unintentionally disclose details that the upcoming results will contradict.'

'And nothing beats a surprise visit to spot suspicious behaviour.'

'Yes. Maybe there will be strobe lights and bunting when we arrive, or her beaming from ear to ear while dragging an enormous suitcase into her car.'

Barton turned off the A1 and drove by the now-derelict Stilton Cheese Inn.

'That used to be a fabulous location.'

'Another place shut because of the pandemic?'

'No, that one closed well beforehand. The Talbot and The Bell are still going, as is The S Bar over the road, which is great seeing as many of the other villages surrounding Peterborough have lost all of their pubs.'

He took a right just before Angel Spice.

'That's also a top-notch curry house. Next time you get a date, book a table. Can't go wrong.'

'Will do.'

They headed up past the lovely properties on Caldecote Road.

Leicester whistled. 'Not bad. Accountancy clearly pays handsomely.'

Barton parked up and got out. The imposing building certainly had a prime location on the raised western edge of the village. At the front of the home, a sweeping block-paved driveway provided off-street parking for multiple vehicles, and the integral double garage had a long up-and-over door. Probably five bedrooms, yet it wasn't super ostentatious.

The most striking feature was the Porsche 718 Cayman GTS perched on the centre of the drive. Barton tutted as he took in the bright Miami Blue colour and low profile.

'Look at that. Why would anyone spend so much on a car when there are more important things in life? I bet it drinks petrol, is shit to park, and I dread to think how expensive it is to insure.'

'I thought you were being upbeat.'

Barton shrugged. 'Well, I didn't say change was easy. At least it means someone's in. Let's take this casually. Leave the introductions to me but keep an eye out for nervousness or signs she's not too upset.'

'Which are?'

'Perfect make-up, tennis racquet on the kitchen table, big bin liners full of his clothes.'

Leicester laughed. 'You've taught me everyone acts differently at times of crisis.'

'That's right, but you also need to play the odds.'

Barton and Leicester hadn't quite reached the door when it swiftly opened. A slim, sharply dressed Asian man stepped outside. He flinched when he saw them. Barton tried to take in the man's expression.

It was hard to discern whether he wore a hunted look, or a guilty one.

16
DCI BARTON

The man departing from the house recovered quickly and held out his hand.

'Apologies, you startled me. Vijay Singh.'

Barton took the handshake offered and received a firm grip in reply.

'Detective Chief Inspector Barton and DC Leicester.'

'Pleased to meet you. How can I help?'

'We've come to have a chat with Mrs Jones.'

'Oh, is something up?'

'You mean apart from her husband's passing?'

Singh's face reddened.

'Sorry, I obviously know about that, and it's tragic, but why are the police interested?'

'Rhys's case is being passed to the coroner.'

'For a heart attack?'

Leicester had been with Major Crimes for over five years. He knew to switch roles, so Barton could concentrate on studying the subject.

'Why do you think that's how he died?'

Singh scratched his head. 'What else could it be?'

'Coronary issues would be the most likely cause, but it's standard procedure to ascertain the exact reason in the case of an unexpected death.'

'Well, he was on blood-pressure tablets.'

'It's still necessary if the deceased was not attended by a doctor during their last illness, or if they hadn't seen a doctor for the condition they died from within twenty-eight days of passing.'

Singh licked his lips at the detailed explanation.

'Okay. I just wouldn't want any unnecessary aggravation for Morwen.'

Barton had noticed the slightest sheen of sweat on Vijay's forehead. It was a cool afternoon, and Vijay might have been rushing around, but there was also a damp patch on his shirt at chest height.

He gave Vijay a commiserating smile.

'I assume you've been comforting the widow.'

'Yes. It's been a terrible shock for her. For all of us.'

'Are you a family friend?'

'Business partner and friend. I popped over to see if she needed help with the funeral and to bring some flowers. Offer support.'

'That's kind of you. We'll let you get on your way.'

'Thank you.'

'Do you have a business card?'

Barton wasn't surprised when the man brought a silver holder from his inside jacket pocket and passed him an embossed card. Barton reciprocated.

Vijay's leaving handshake was surprisingly weak, a fleeting, almost absent gesture. Yet he marched to his vehicle with a purpose. Bouffant, grey-flecked hair bouncing, and clothes that moulded to his body like a fluid shadow. A stark contrast to Barton's jacket, which clung in the manner of a drunken mugger wrapping himself around his frame.

Vijay slid into his sports car with a youthful ease that belied his years. The engine's purr was a low thrum of power, a soothing vibration that resonated deep within Barton. The accountant's parting wave was accompanied by a smile, a momentary curve of his mouth that never got close to his eyes. Then he was gone, a wisp of blueish smoke the only evidence he'd been there at all.

17
DCI BARTON

Leicester's gaze lingered on the road for a few seconds after Vijay had vanished. After a brief shake of his head, he turned to his boss.

'Do you sometimes think other people are living a different sort of life?'

'I know so. It's all superficial, though. Vijay's probably lonely, and miserable, and suffers from piles.'

'Yes, piles of cash. An ailment I'd welcome. Weird how he shook our hands before we introduced ourselves. We might have been flogging double glazing.'

Barton patted the younger man on the shoulder.

'It seems I can still teach you a few things. Rich businesspeople don't tend to be wealthy by luck. They're charming. If you treat everyone politely and with respect, any opportunities are yours for the taking. It's also a technique to control the conversation.'

'I suppose so.'

'Besides. I suspect the only way we could appear more like coppers would be if we were wearing custodian helmets and thwacking truncheons into our palms.'

Leicester smirked at the prospect of them arriving in their characteristic British, tall, black cylindrical head protection, but he was clearly still thinking of Vijay, who had obviously intrigued him.

'He had a Blake Mill shirt on and a Tom Ford suit. I bet his shoes cost as much as my car. Yet, despite all the style, poise and confidence, there was something shifty about him.'

'Agreed. I thought it was nerves, but it might be he was distracted. His business partner has just died.'

Barton pressed the Ring doorbell. A shadow swiftly approached the door, which opened to reveal a woman who could have passed for forty-five.

She coolly regarded them.

'Morning. How can I help?'

'Are you Morwen Jones?'

'I am.'

Barton and Leicester showed their warrant cards and Barton stated they were there as a courtesy.

Morwen took a keener interest in their ID than most did.

'Thank you, Officers. Do you want to come in for a coffee and explain what that means?'

'No to the drink, but we do need a quick word.'

Morwen had raven hair that appeared to cascade over her shoulders like a waterfall. Her figure, curvy yet slim, moved in a smooth and captivating way as she escorted them to a vast, modern kitchen. Barton suspected when Morwen walked down the street, heads turned and conversations paused, with even the most hardened of builders and workmen finding themselves stunned into silence.

'I'm sorry for your loss,' he said when they'd sat around an island in the centre of the room.

Morwen dipped her head but didn't reply. Up close, the few laughter lines etched around her eyes only served to pull the observer in. Barton explained about the interest of the coroner's office and asked her if she'd mind explaining the events of Rhys's final evening.

'We'd been out for the night. After I'd taken my make-up off, I noticed Rhys hadn't come to bed, so I came to fetch him. It's not uncommon for him to fall asleep downstairs.'

'Were you worried in any way at that point?'

'A little. He'd seemed quiet and withdrawn on the drive home.'

'And he was slumped in his office chair?'

'Yes. He wouldn't stir, even when I prodded him. I didn't know what to do, so I rang 999. They said to check his pulse, but I wasn't sure how. I tried, but I couldn't find one. He appeared not to be breathing. They told me to do CPR, but I never learned.' Morwen ran a hand through her hair. 'He was so heavy. I struggled to get him out of his seat.' She put a hand to her mouth. 'I apologise, but my memories are a panicked blur.'

Barton gave her a few seconds.

'Must have been a terrible few minutes.'

Morwen nodded, but her face was impassive.

'Kind of an out-of-body experience. Still feels vague now. The ambulance arrived at the same time as the police. The paramedics worked on him, but not for long. They suspected he died minutes before I came down. The officers were helpful. Asked me a bit about his health. I said our GP doesn't live far and would come out.'

'At that time of night?'

'He's a family friend. Rhys had the firm's employees signed up for private healthcare, and he was the GP who provided consultations. It was him who arranged for the funeral directors to pick up Rhys's body afterwards and mentioned there would be a post-mortem.'

'Was his doctor as surprised as you were?'

'Yes. They played padel together once a month until a few years ago when a back injury forced the man to quit. Rhys always thrashed him.'

'What's padel?'

'A racquet sport, a bit like tennis but simpler.'

Barton had taken a stool, but Leicester had been perusing the many photographs on the kitchen wall. He stopped and peered closely at a large frame.

'I assume this is you and Rhys?'

'Yes, on the left-hand side. It's of our book group last December. We take a picture every year.'

Barton ambled over and studied the photo. There were eight people in the photograph. Rhys stood straight and appeared relaxed.

'You look happy,' said Leicester.

Morwen nodded.

Barton hid his smile. Even from where he was sitting, he spotted Vijay was standing beside Morwen with a huge grin on his face, although Rhys was also smiling.

There were quite a few photographs of the book club members. Barton wandered down the line of them. They went back decades. Benjamin Button style, the individuals in the images became younger, slimmer, trendier, and more vibrant people. Except perhaps an older gentleman who stooped throughout, and the woman holding his hand, who appeared bookish even in the earlier pictures. The others looked pretty or handsome.

'Okay,' said Barton. 'The post-mortem results will be out shortly, then you'll be able to put him to rest. It's nice that you have friends to support you.'

She gave him a puzzled glance. 'Pardon?'

'Like Mr Singh.'

'What about him?'

Barton pointed at Vijay on one of the photographs.

'We saw him outside.'

Morwen's eyes momentarily widened. 'Oh, he only wanted to talk about what was happening with the business. Rhys and Vijay are joint partners, fifty-fifty.'

Barton sniffed. 'Seems a mite thoughtless, all things considered.'

'Oh, I don't know. He's a professional. Very commercially orientated, and other people's jobs are affected. I can understand that.'

'We popped around for a couple of reasons. Carbon monoxide poisoning is a possibility. Do you have open fires?'

Morwen shook her head.

'Not at all. We got a heat pump a few years back. Everything's electric. The environment is important to me.'

Barton wondered if it mattered to her husband, but he recalled the solar panels on their roof.

'Anything you'd like to tell us?'

Morwen folded her arms. 'Like what?'

'Chest pains. Anxiety. Headaches. Depression.'

'He used to wake up regularly in his sleep. Seemed to be in pain. I suspected it was angina, but he'd chew on a few Rennies and say it was heartburn.'

'Did he take any pills?'

'Not as far as I'm aware, except for his blood pressure.'

'Drink heavily or smoke?'

'He hated smoking but was partial to finishing his night off with a substantial whisky at home. I guess that would place him in binge-drinking territory. The spirits annoyed me. I could always smell the liquor on his breath the next day.'

Barton rose from his seat. 'We'll let you get on. Any questions?'

'No. Thank you for coming.'

When they were sitting in their car, the detectives shared a look.

Leicester glanced at the house as he pulled away. 'Aren't you concerned she's in there hiding evidence?'

'No, not with modern techniques. Besides, nothing says guilty like a thoroughly bleached interior.'

Barton tapped a finger against his chin.

'What are you thinking, sir?'

'We might not be screeching back to Stilton with handcuffs, but I'll be amazed if we don't have words with Morwen and Vijay again.'

18

DCI BARTON

Thursday

Barton deliberately took a leisurely breakfast with Holly the next morning. He'd imagined more of them in the future if he retired, but after hearing of her plans for the café, he suspected he would be having them on his own.

As they were eating, she was beaming.

'It's all coming together. I struggled to sleep last night with my mind going over the details.'

Barton reached over and squeezed her hand.

'Have some confidence. The café will be great.'

He told her about the weight-loss injections and that he was considering taking a lengthy spell away from the role.

Holly frowned.

'What do you mean by lengthy?'

'It's fair to say I've been struggling of late, but retiring from a job I love is tough to consider. Saying that, having a few months off to pull myself together probably wouldn't be enough.'

'There's no shame in having a hard time, John.'

Barton ignored the comment.

'Regulation thirty-three deals with career breaks. People mostly use it for maternity leave, but travelling is another option, as is a health gap.'

'How long can you take off?'

'The maximum is five years.'

Holly sipped her coffee.

'What if you can't face returning afterwards?'

'I wouldn't have to.'

Holly got up and hugged him.

'Sounds perfect, although resuming a position that had been making you ill would need careful consideration.'

'Perhaps it would be more of a reset. At least it wouldn't feel like the end, even if it was. I could help you at the café in the meantime.'

Holly scoffed at him as she sat down.

'Yes, a large, hungry male police officer, bored out of his mind, is exactly what I need in my cake and sandwich shop aimed at supporting women with young children.'

'I meant with painting, cleaning, getting the place ready. You said it doesn't need much, so maybe we could tart everywhere up ourselves instead of paying for professionals.'

Holly giggled. 'Oh, sorry. I had visions of opening the walk-in fridge and finding you asleep in there after putting the delivery away, surrounded by empty boxes.'

'Healthy living from now on, remember? Well, after Christmas.'

'Of course. We'll both have a rewarding year of change. Today's the day if I want to formally make an offer on the rent, but they've agreed to the terms in principle. My solicitor reckoned a month for the paperwork to progress and to officially receive the keys, but the owners are happy to allow access before completion so I can order any equipment or furniture we need. Shall I go for it?'

'Sounds like you're ready. You'll be an enormous success. I'm certain.'

Holly took a deep breath.

'We'd still be taking a risk. I know we've had the money ringfenced for years, but you out of work and not drawing your pension would make funds tighter.'

'We have our savings. That's what they're there for. As long as I delay buying the Ferrari I so obviously deserve, and throw away my Florida-condominium catalogue, we should be okay. Don't forget, I'll be eating less. We'll save thousands.'

Holly rose from the table and put their dishes in the sink.

'You seem relaxed. Is it the lifting of the sword of Damocles?'

'I guess so. You know, when I first started out in life, I simply got on with things. It's only later, with a reputation and scores of others relying on me, that the stress has ratcheted up.'

'What are you saying?'

'Perhaps I've hoisted most of the pressure on my own shoulders. Now I can feel myself pushing it off.'

'I'd say you've just had enough.'

'Well, it seems we have a final case. If so, I'm going to enjoy myself. Take the opportunity to thank people for their efforts over the years as I go about my business. A chance to do my best, perhaps for one last time. Then golf.'

Holly folded her arms. 'Mortis finally persuaded you to give the sport another whirl?'

'Said he'll teach me. Apparently, I need to get my own clubs, because he doesn't want me bending his.'

'Practice makes perfect.'

Holly kissed him on the cheek, then draped a pair of Marigolds over his shoulder.

'You can start by being the best washer-upper in the land.'

Barton was pressed for time and ended up breaking a mug in his haste to leave the house. His phone rang as he was battling with his seat belt.

'Morning, Mortis. Case or no case?'

'Definitely a case, John. These results are damning, yet they are also strange.'

19

DCI BARTON

Barton couldn't recall a recent occasion when Mortis had said results were strange. He turned the car's engine off.

'I'm listening.'

'The blood test found heroin, ketamine, baby powder, paracetamol and three other unidentified compounds.'

'Wow. The secret life of an accountant, eh?'

'Normally I'd think the same, but remember, I couldn't find any injection sites.'

'His wife said he didn't smoke either. Hated it, in fact.'

'That really is concerning then, although I doubt if it would have made any difference regardless of whether he had injected or smoked the heroin or ketamine.'

'Sorry, I'm not following.'

'The presence of those two drugs is low. I don't believe we're in the realms of overdose territory even if the person had no tolerance for it. I suppose some people react badly to small amounts, especially if, as in this case, alcohol was consumed.'

Barton's mind whirred as he tried to catch up. 'Assuming the heart attack wasn't from natural causes, then something else caused the respiratory depression. One of the unknown substances.'

'Exactly.'

'Got to be fentanyl.'

'No. That's so common now, the test would have identified its presence.'

Barton took a moment to consider what the drug could be. 'Whatever it was had to be strong.'

'Yes. His stomach was half full, and the small intestine packed with digesting food, so he'd had a large meal that evening, which makes it less likely he ingested anything lethal.'

'You reckon he snorted the compound that killed him?'

'I do now you've mentioned he hated smoking, although I couldn't see anything in his nostrils. Samples of the material in his stomach were sent over as well, so they'll also be analysed. If a drug was hidden in something he ate, then I should hear by tomorrow morning.'

'I assume with the substance being unknown, the results will take time.'

'Probably not. The lab knows what to test for. Various cleaning and laundry detergents are likely to show up as mixer agents, but the technicians narrow their search down to chemicals that could swiftly kill.'

'Like what?'

'Arsenic, deadly nightshade, methanol, Polonium-210.'

Barton tutted. 'Don't even joke about that.'

'There have been some incidents where carfentanil has been found in street drugs. That drug is to elephants and other huge animals what ketamine is to horses. It's much more dangerous to be purchasing a wrap of heroin or cocaine than it used to be. Twenty years ago, a user might have received a few side effects from snorting baking soda, but it wouldn't kill them. Nowadays, imagine what a substance that tranquillises rhinos would do to a human heart.'

Barton winced at the prospect.

'Yeah, but the picture we're already forming of Rhys Jones is not of a man acquiring his hits from dealers at the roadside in the arse-end of town to snort off a mirror at home.'

'I guess he could have been desperate, but I would agree that seems unlikely. So how did he die? Would he eat anything dangerous willingly? I suspect the conclusion of my post-mortem won't be that it was an accidental or deliberate overdose.'

The pathologist didn't need to state the obvious to Barton.

Mortis suspected Rhys had been poisoned.

20

DCI BARTON

Barton said goodbye to Mortis, drove to Thorpe Wood, then strode to DCI Cox's office. As he approached the room, he realised he'd referred to it as her office all the way through this latest covering tenure. It had never once felt like his.

Her door was open, so he knocked and marched in.

Smartly dressed, in an immaculate navy-blue suit and cream blouse, she stopped typing but didn't bother to smile.

'That's what I'd call a purposeful entry, John. What's up?'

'To echo the pathologist's words, something strange.'

'Would you care to explain?'

'Are you busy?'

'I am, but the teams aren't. I've never known it so quiet. No doubt it's the lull before the storm, but I've got people getting the filing shipshape, revisiting past cases, booked out on training and updating development plans. I even allowed a member of your old gang to have today as time off in lieu.'

'Do I need to ring for a doctor?'

Cox smiled at him, but she wasn't one for letting a joke run.

'Does that mean you found Rhys Jones's death problematic?'

'I've just spoken to Mortis. There's a possibility he was poisoned. Leicester and I visited the widow yesterday, and, while nothing was obvious, there was something out of kilter. A business partner was leaving when we arrived, and he appeared shifty. There were contradictions in his and Morwen's replies as to why he'd popped around.'

'So, alarm bells are ringing. What do you want to do?'

'Return to Stilton with Leicester, now we've received preliminary PM results, and take a statement from the widow.'

'With her being the most likely one to have knocked him off.'

'That's usually the scenario, but the method of killing may be street heroin.'

Cox frowned. Barton watched her roll some theories around her head before she appeared to decide not to get involved in the intricacies.

'Well, Leicester was the officer having the day off, but, by all means, take one of the others.'

'I'll chat to my old team. Twenty minutes to bring them up to speed. Just in case I call in the troops at short notice.'

Cox drummed her fingers on her desk.

'Do you reckon it might come to that?'

Barton took a moment to consider.

'Mortis should find out tomorrow how the poison entered Rhys's system. If it's as we think, I'll reach out to the drug unit. Hopefully, there isn't a dangerous batch of heroin going around. If there is, Rhys won't be the only victim.'

'That's true. Maybe they'll take the investigation, and Zander can get the Domestos out and tackle the office kitchen.'

Barton took a deep breath. 'One last thing, the regulation thirty-three break that was mentioned. My mind's made up on it.'

'Right. As per Troughton's suggestion. It's a clever idea. Changes and development in policing are like the movement of a mountain. Progress is glacial until there's an avalanche. Who knows what opportunities might be available in a year or two?' Cox leaned back in her chair. 'If this is to be your last case in Major Crimes, better make certain you solve it.'

Barton nodded.

'I'd appreciate the guys hearing my decision from me.'

'Tell them. Just so you know, I have news about your people.' Cox rested back in her chair. 'I suppose they're Zander's guys now. They'll be absorbed into other units in the new year.'

It wasn't a shock to Barton. Nobody had specifically told him, but he'd heard rumours.

'Is Zander aware?'

'He will be when you next talk to him, but keep it quiet. There'll be an announcement for those affected when it's 100 per cent confirmed. Another DI is moving out of county in January, so Zander should slot in that vacancy nicely. Most of the other teams are light, so the rest of his crew can probably pick where they'd like to go.'

'I'll let him know.'

'John, it seems this really will be an opportunity to work with your friends and colleagues for the last time. Enjoy yourselves, if that's the right phrase, and make sure I'm kept in the loop.'

Cox returned to her computer, so Barton plodded back to his desk. He had an email address as the primary point of contact for the drug unit. Sending a message as opposed to ringing also left a record and therefore covered his arse. After firing off a quick query as to whether there had been any recent overdoses in Cambridgeshire, he went to gather the officers who he still considered his people.

Zander, Hoffman, Minton, Zelensky and Malik followed him into a meeting room where he would drop his supposed bombshell.

Barton took a deep breath.

'I'm leaving the department to take an extended break. Focus on my health and really consider how I want to spend the end of my career.'

He was met with a sea of blank stares.

'Good luck for the future, sir,' said Minton after a heavy pause.

The others murmured their agreement, with Zander smiling at him. Barton figured he'd been their DCI for twelve months, not their DI, so they hadn't seen loads of him.

After a few more seconds of silence, he rubbed his hands together. That was the way of it. Life moved on, so it was back to business. They had a case to solve.

He updated them on Rhys's death and watched frowns spread through the room.

Hoffman was a smart but cheeky member of the team. 'Ooh, juicy. The wife has been having an affair with the other partner. They've eliminated him so they can finally be together and have all the cash as well.'

Barton considered him a fresh face, but it had been four years since he'd joined Major Crimes. The first flecks of grey had appeared in his hair, and the beginnings of bags under his eyes.

'That's our starting point, but how often is it that obvious?'

Hoffman stared around at the others, almost challenging them.

'It was clear-cut in the Hendry killing. The guy was caught, had confessed and was serving life before we could come up with a decent moniker for him.'

Barton barely remembered the brief investigation eight months ago when a landlord murdered his lodger. The killer had walked into the police station, a week after a missing person article had been issued in the local press, and admitted to losing his temper over the central heating.

'I guess that's true,' he said.

'What's the plan, then, boss?' asked Zander.

'Minton and I will formally interview Rhys's wife and his business partner. Take statements. She should be at home, and the company office is minutes away on the main street. Let's see where that leaves us. Hoffman, ring CSI for me. We're going to need a search on the Joneses' residence for traces of drugs. Arrange for them to arrive at midday when I'll have had a chance to quiz her.'

Barton let his comments sink in.

'Any initial thoughts from anyone?'

Malik hadn't appeared fully engaged, but it was he who spoke.

'Sounds messy. There could be numerous angles of interest from his work and domestic life. We might need to dive deeply into both.'

Zander nodded. 'The pivotal piece of information will be how the drugs got into his system.'

'Agreed,' said Barton. 'Mortis should know that tomorrow morning. It could have been with his dinner, or chocolate, or a person appeared and fooled him into taking it. Bear in mind there were no bruises or signs of forced entry, yet the two people closest to him were economical with the truth when questioned.'

Zelensky hummed. 'You mean the two we think are the closest.'

'Good point.'

'We should start with that. Where was Rhys during the day he died? Did he go out that night? Who was he with and why?'

As the team discussed the case, Barton observed and smiled, fully confident in their combined ability to solve it. And yet a nagging worry lingered that further considerable complications lay ahead.

21

DCI BARTON

Barton and DC Caroline Minton arrived at High Street, Stilton, at eleven.

'Drive past Angel Spice,' said Barton. 'We'll check out Rhys's business premises, which are just beyond it.'

With no vehicles behind them, Minton slowed the car. She drove by a row of residential buildings, the Indian restaurant and then The Ten Salon, a chic women's hairdressers. Minton turned in the wide street and stopped outside a two-storey building with a gabled roof.

The neat brick façade, with its white-trimmed windows, striking door and prominent chimney, was a picture of classic English charm, fitting seamlessly into the historic village. A small gold plaque was pinned to the wall.

Minton read it.

'Jones and Singh Accountants.'

'Okay, appears low-key but professional. Good to see they have parking. Pull away, take the next left and follow the road up. I'll let you know when we're at the Joneses' place. You can lead with Morwen, or she'll use her feminine charms on me.'

'Is she a looker?'

'Striking.'

'What's your gut feeling?'

'Probably not directly involved, but she's a cool customer. The thing is, I can usually resist beautiful women due to generally being a bit lazy, but not all men are the same. Some are driven crazy by them.'

'Is that quality dating advice? Avoid lethargic blokes.'

'It is if you want an exciting, romantic relationship. Flowers in the post from Pepé Le Pew, or to get blindfolded and whisked away on mystery holidays.'

'I'd settle for a Ferrero Rocher and a soggy day trip to Hunstanton.'

Minton's face hardened as she slammed on the brakes to let an oncoming van pass when she had the right of way. Barton waited for her to comment, or more likely curse, but no response came.

Caroline Minton had joined from CID a little before he'd returned a year ago. She was a bright woman, easy-going and hard to ruffle. Perfect for Major Crimes, but he couldn't remember seeing her appearing happy of late. More someone going through the motions. A person who had allowed themselves to sink into the background.

As she accelerated away, the moment for probing had arrived.

'You all right?'

'Everything's fine.'

'Just fine? You were enjoying the job the last time I spoke to you.'

'Yeah, I was.'

Barton considered leaving it there but wondered if he could help with anything.

'Work or play on your mind?'

'Both. I'm jaded. My love life is non-existent. God knows where you find a decent man nowadays.'

Barton frowned. He had suspected she had been the one to break up with Leicester but wasn't sure why.

'I've always liked Leicester.'

'You try dating him.'

'I'm too old for an affair.'

Minton laughed.

'Poor Leicester, so close to heaven. Maybe that's the answer. I should have an illicit dalliance. Create some crisis in my life.' She bit her lip for a moment. 'To be fair, Leicester *is* lovely, *and* we got on well. We enjoy the same hobbies and interests. Never argued. The physical stuff was nice.'

'Nice is okay.'

'Pah! It was all too bloody pleasant. We were so incredibly boring together. Our combined dullness had me convinced we were shuffling off to our diamond-wedding-anniversary dinner every time we had a date. I want fireworks and drama, worry and thrills. Leicester and I went to the seaside and had fish and chips at eleven in the morning because the queues are shorter then. He took me to the Saturday matinee at the pictures because it was two quid cheaper than the evening slot.'

Barton smiled. He sometimes got lunch early when he visited the coast for that reason, and he loved leaving the cinema when it was still light. It always felt surreal.

'Hoffman's about your age.'

'I don't want you investigating *me* for murder. Work's not what I expected either.'

Barton knew she'd initially been underwhelmed with the role, having spent time with her during The Village Killer case, but she had seemed energised with the resolution of that case.

'Surely solving major crimes is the equivalent of the Premier League. What's tiresome about that?'

'But is it, though? We live in a digital world. Our job is to pore over computer reports, or number-plate-camera printouts. Scour CCTV, read medical findings, check dashboard cams, and trawl the bloody internet.'

'Ah, you want to be in *Hawaii Five-O*. Sprinting down streets, then loosing off rounds at the bad guys.'

'I can do without the gunplay, but yes, I would have preferred detecting in the seventies.'

'If you'd like more aggravation, become a prison officer.'

Minton again didn't reply, which suggested she'd at least thought about it.

Barton pointed at the house, and she drew in to the side of the road. He got out and pulled his coat around him. A grey, blustery day would do little to lift Minton's spirits. Despite the empty drive, the lounge light was on, so they left the car and rang the doorbell.

Barton realised he'd returned sooner than he'd anticipated. The investigation had moved beyond mere formalities. It was time to dig deep and uncover the truth, no matter the cost. Barton steeled himself.

The most significant part of his last case was about to commence.

22

DCI BARTON

Barton had barely removed his finger from the doorbell when Morwen appeared, without make-up and dressed in an ill-fitting T-shirt above baggy jeans. Her thick hair had been scraped into a tight ponytail.

Her eyes flicked to Barton.

'Can't keep away?'

'Hello, again. How are you?'

'Still kind of stunned and not expecting guests.'

'Apologies at what must be a sad time. This is Detective Constable Caroline Minton. The post-mortem results have returned, and there's an anomaly we need to discuss.'

'Did you find a heart?'

Barton wasn't sure what to say to that unexpected comment.

Morwen briefly covered her face with her hands.

'Sorry. I've no idea why I said that.'

'Don't worry,' replied Minton. 'Shock does strange things.'

'Come in, please. Would you like a cup of coffee? I was about to pour the water into the cafetière.'

Both the officers agreed, then followed Morwen into the spacious kitchen, where they sat on tall chairs around a granite island. Minton took out her laptop.

'I'll take a statement as we talk.'

'Why?'

'We're concerned your husband's death may not have been from natural causes.'

Morwen appeared to busy herself with collecting cups, pouring milk into a small jug and selecting spoons. She brought everything over with the now full cafetière, sitting next to Minton and opposite Barton.

Morwen frowned at Minton.

'I don't understand. What other reason could there be?'

'We believe someone may have wished him harm. Can you think of anyone?'

The seconds ticked by while Morwen stared out of the window, as though there was a large list of individuals to choose from. She turned back to the female officer.

'No. My husband was a decent man. He lived to work, without doing much else. Besides, do accountants offend people?'

Minton gave her a disarming smile. 'Dodgy ones might.'

'That wasn't Rhys.'

'Was your relationship solid?'

Morwen pouted. 'Surely you don't suspect me of anything?'

'We need to speak to those who were involved in his life. It's your turn today.'

Morwen took a deep breath. She pulled her hairband off and tossed her locks.

'If I'm honest, Rhys and I weren't close any more. He was always laser-focussed on his company and had become more so. We met shortly before he set it up. I'd come out of an unhealthy relationship with a man called Blake who cheated on me. In fact, did everything terrible you can do to a woman, apart from he knew not to leave marks.'

'I'm sorry to hear that,' said Barton.

'Thank you. From the outside, Blake and I appeared happy, but I was stuck in his house with no money. He kept my friends and family distant and called me names one minute but was kind the next. Always mean then apologising, and saying we'd get married soon, but coming up with excuses as time passed.'

'Kids?'

'I have a condition which meant I probably needed IVF. Blake kept saying he was saving and was close, but he never had enough. Rhys and I were lucky enough to have a child naturally. She lives abroad.'

Barton was struggling to garner much sympathy for Morwen, but he knew trauma affected people in myriad ways, assuming she was telling the truth. Her answers were delivered without passion and as if she'd been repeating those words for decades. He suspected Minton felt the same by her next question.

'Why didn't you leave Blake?'

'I just told you. I didn't work. He wouldn't let me, so I had to ask him for money when I needed some.'

'What about those friends and family?'

Morwen scoffed her reply. 'As I said, he isolated me.'

After hearing Minton's comments on the journey over, Barton could see she wasn't in the right mindset for questioning someone like Morwen. She'd only irritate her, which probably wouldn't help.

Some women considered themselves home-makers, even if they didn't have children. A rich man might want a woman at his beck and call, taking care of his needs, waiting for him whenever he finished at the office, and be more than willing to pay for her to live the high life. Sometimes it worked and both partners were happy, but what Morwen had mentioned was a tick box for a coercive and controlling relationship.

He cleared his throat.

'That must have been tough, but you did eventually get out.'

'Yes. Ironically, he shagged a slapper from the Happy Eater, or was it the Little Chef? Anyway, she fell pregnant, he threw me out. I saw her a week later driving the car he'd supposedly bought me for my birthday. He'd registered it in his own name, so I never owned it.'

Barton studied the photographs on the walls, which were mostly of Morwen, as he considered her history. He spotted an old picture at what he assumed was the Joneses' wedding. She could have stepped out of a bridal magazine, whereas Rhys, suit buttons straining, might have been giving her away. Barton imagined Morwen's confidence and pride took a hit when her previous relationship failed.

'Then you luckily met Rhys.'

Morwen's cool gaze fell on Barton, but she surprised him when a solitary tear trickled down her cheek.

'Yes. He was the exact opposite of my previous partner. Rhys was enthusiastic and unashamedly complimentary, at least at the beginning. Generous, kind, trusting, and he took me on the most amazing holidays.'

'Fairy-tale ending,' said Barton, knowing it was not.

A dark shadow came across Morwen's face. Her jaw set. 'How did Rhys die, then? I didn't see any injuries.'

'We're concerned he may have taken something.'

'Like drugs?' Morwen tipped her head back and a brittle laugh came out. 'If only. We may have had more fun. He liked a meal out most Friday nights, then he used to read the newspapers on Saturday evening while I watched TV. If I was entertaining friends here, he'd sit in his office. That was our champagne lifestyle together.'

'You said you were out last Friday night.'

'Yes.'

There had been an almost imperceptible pause before Morwen answered. Minton picked up on it.

'Where did you go?'

'We had dinner at The Bell, here in Stilton. Lovely food. Great wine. It's a relaxing and cosy place. Have you been?'

'No,' replied Minton. 'Could he have eaten something there that upset him?'

'I think booze was probably the problem. He was floppy when we got back, which isn't like him. Rhys believed he had a reputation as a man of the community, so he only tended to get plastered at home.'

'And he wasn't feeling down or out of sorts?'

'No, not at all. Surprisingly, he seemed rather upbeat until the drive home, although he may just have been drunk. He told me we'd enjoy lots of time together when he retired.'

Barton almost chuckled. Her lack of enthusiasm at the prospect was evident even after her husband's passing.

'Was that going to be soon?' he asked.

'Yes. The business was consuming all his time. Rhys wanted to spend more time travelling.'

The detectives carried on skirting around the topic of him being poisoned, but they received little of any value back from Morwen. Barton checked his watch and saw it was nearly midday. CSI would arrive shortly.

The Joneses had clearly developed problems between them, but they weren't too far out of the ordinary.

The moment for more direct questions had arrived.

'How would you describe your marriage?'

'Convenient. Don't misunderstand me. Our partnership lacked in passion, but I got what I wanted. The good life. No hassle. Money, cars, status, commitment, support. I have no regrets.'

'No arguments, bad words or resentment?'

'Not from him.' Morwen tapped her perfect fingernails on the table surface. 'I'm not daft. You obviously think someone killed him. You're wondering if it was me.' Her gaze flashed between the two officers. 'My God! You haven't got a clue who's responsible.'

'It's early days,' said Minton firmly.

Again, Morwen surprised Barton. Surely she was clever enough to understand their investigation was only beginning. Even so, her manicured finger pierced the air as she jabbed it in his direction.

'If he's been murdered and you don't know why, perhaps it's time to consider whether I need protecting.'

23

DCI BARTON

Barton was saved from making a swift reply when there was a strong knock at Morwen's front door.

She huffed. 'Who the hell is that going to be?'

Minton leapt from her seat. 'It will be the crime scene investigators. I'll let them in. Where is your husband's office?'

'Back of the property on the right.' Morwen's stony gaze flicked around to Barton. 'What on earth are they doing here?'

'Your husband died in this house. We have to process the scene. Do you have somewhere to go while they do their jobs?'

'How long for?'

'They should be finished by the weekend.'

Morwen's eyes blazed. 'You're kidding.'

'Sadly not. They'll need to take a swab from you to confirm your presence in the building against any other evidence.'

'Are you saying someone broke in?'

'It's possible. How is your security?'

'Tight. We have a state-of-the-art alarm system linked to a monitoring company and CCTV throughout the home.'

'Excellent. We'll need the recordings from Friday night. Where will you go?'

Morwen shook her head. 'A friend's. Kasia lives around the corner and she's not at work today. Don't worry, my mobile is always on, and I'll be ringing you if I'm worried. Maybe I'll be safer there than here.'

Barton knew Minton would be briefing CSI, so he took the opportunity to probe further.

'Where does your child live?'

'New Zealand. Alice couldn't have put any more distance between us, short of pitching her tent in Antarctica. Probably says a lot about our parenting styles.'

'Do you miss her?'

Morwen squinted as she considered the question.

'I grieve the kid she used to be. All the way up to her A levels, when she became incredibly woke and lecturing. She transitioned into a vegan with an obsession over sustainability, which is all admirable, but I like a Lamb Garlic Chilli Saagwala from the Angel and won't apologise for it.'

Barton smiled. 'Sounds tasty. Will she come back with what happened?'

'No, I shouldn't think so. She and her father weren't close because he worked so hard. The one ritual they had before the veggie thing began was KFC on a Saturday afternoon, but another crusade was her being anti-corporate. That put an end to Bargain Buckets. She lives on an organic farm with other like-minded souls, no doubt dressed in hemp dungarees, stinking of cabbage and patchouli, while lecturing the sheep about ethical consumerism.'

Barton couldn't help chuckling.

'I guess it's reassuring she's found her place and her tribe. Surely it is a noble quest not to leave a mark on the planet.'

'Yes, well, when my mother died five years ago, I sent Alice two grand to cover the travel costs. She caught the flu a day before she was due to fly home.'

'That's a shame.'

'Actually, the shame was her not returning the money.'

'Maybe there was no cancellation policy.'

'I told her to change the departure to a month later. She'd miss the funeral, but we could still catch up, show her the grave, reconnect. Alice and she got on well. You know how some old people often have a connection with the youngsters. My mum was the only person who was able to tell her to, and I quote, "shut up with that bollocks", and not get a death stare in reply.'

Barton grinned.

'The power of grandparents. I take it your daughter didn't alter her flight.'

'She reckoned the type of ticket made it impossible. I guessed she was lying, so I said that doesn't sound right, email me the ticket information and I'll check the small print. We never heard from her for four years until she needed eight hundred quid to pay for some tooth-saving private dental care.'

'Kids, eh?'

'Yeah. I still sent it.'

Minton returned with two CSIs, who began bringing their equipment in. Minton printed off a statement for Morwen to sign, which she did without reading the contents. Barton made her go over it.

'We require his mobile phone and laptop, please,' he said.

'Good luck getting in them. I never could.'

Barton and Minton exchanged a glance while Morwen fetched both and handed them over.

Barton walked the widow outside to her car.

'Will you be okay?'

'Kasia should be fine with me staying, but I'll need to return for clothes and toiletries. My valuables are in the safe.'

'No problem, come back late afternoon and the investigation team will let you in. Leave them a set of keys, access to the safe, and explain about your security system. There'll be a presence here tonight, so the place will be protected. Please give the crime scene manager the CCTV for the last few weeks, or however long you have.'

Barton watched as the garage door opened. Morwen expertly reversed a bright-red Volvo XC90 out of the garage. She pointed a small remote at the garage door, then hit her steering wheel when nothing happened. She got out and stamped inside to shut the door from within. On returning to her vehicle, she gave him a sarcastic wave before pulling off the drive, but she didn't appear overly furious about the inconvenience.

Whether that was because she felt certain she would be proven innocent, or simply confident nothing incriminating would be found, it was hard to say.

When she'd gone, Minton drove Barton away from the property.

'We still going to the company address?'

'Yes.'

Minton cursed softly. 'I forgot to ask Morwen about what happens with the business now her husband is dead.'

'That's not the end of the world. I think we can both conclude that Morwen's deliberately withholding information. Vijay will hopefully reveal everything about the firm. He'll know it all in glorious Technicolor.'

'Ah, clever. We'll be able to catch Morwen out if she lies to us.'

'Exactly. I wouldn't be surprised if she acts a bit scatterbrained as a ruse.'

'Agreed. She's not stupid,' said Minton, eyes narrowing. 'We would be fools to underestimate her.'

24

THE BOOK CLUB KILLER

The toughest thing about death is the finality of it. I reckon death's irrevocability is what those left behind struggle to comprehend. The bereaved grapple with the understanding that there are no second chances, no opportunities to try again, to rewrite what has been written. No time for apologies or making amends. No encore after the final curtain. It's over. The end.

We're cushioned through life from extremes such as that, and we don't like to imagine the unimaginable. I used to fear the bony fingers of my demise resting on my shoulder, but only in an abstract way. There was too much life ahead of me for any genuine concern. The good times would happen. Goals met. Victories enjoyed. That, perhaps, is the ultimate tragedy. Having been granted plenty of time, the value of it was diminished, so what I had, I wasted.

When life's conclusion approaches, the end can come in a rush. Not everyone is able to enjoy a final few pleasures, nor has the strength to do what they should have done before their drive failed and their reserves were spent.

We should all take more risks. Who wants to be last, anyway? I remember someone telling me long ago, when maudlin after too many whiskies in The Bell, that one of us would see all of our funerals, whereas one of us would see none. But that first person would have none of us to witness theirs.

They would die alone.

25
DCI BARTON

Barton spent the short journey contemplating Morwen's personality. Killing your own husband was a bold move, considering that the spouse was usually the first suspect to be questioned. While Morwen had little love left for her partner, she didn't strike him as someone who'd take that kind of risk. At least not on her own.

Minton parked in one of the spaces at the front of Jones and Singh Accountants. Barton led the way and pushed the door open. While the building clearly once served as a residence, its interior had been transformed. A long oak desk with a young receptionist seated behind it dominated the large hall.

'Good morning. How may I help you?'

'We're here to speak with Vijay Singh.'

'I'm sorry to say he specifically asked not to be disturbed this afternoon. He has a complicated return to complete.'

Minton showed the woman her warrant card, receiving a wide-eyed look in return. 'I'm afraid we must insist.'

'Ooh, is it about Rhys?'

Minton seemed ready to give the girl a stern reply, but Barton smiled at her.

'I bet it's quiet working in a place like this. Sorry, I didn't get your name.'

The girl peered up the stairs before she replied.

'Leah. Yes, quiet as a tomb most of the time.'

Barton suspected Leah would reply honestly to anything he asked.

'Would you describe Vijay and Rhys as nice bosses?'

'I guess. This is my first job, which means they're the best so far.'

Barton chuckled, charmed by the receptionist's vibrant personality.

'I suppose being partners, Vijay and Rhys had a fantastic relationship.'

Leah put a hand next to her mouth and spoke in a hushed voice, which reminded Barton of young kids playing whispering games. He supposed she must have only recently left school.

'They were always having heated arguments, but it's like when your parents have a row, and they don't want you to know. Saying that, Rhys and Vijay had a few bigger ones lately. Proper shouting. Never when Katarzyna is about, though, but it's as though I don't exist.'

'Argue about what?'

'I guess it's kinda sad, really. Like, there used to be loads of accountants here, even an admin person at one point. But then it was just four of them, and now Bernie's sick. Vijay wanted to, like, rebuild and stuff, but I don't reckon Rhys was feeling it any more.'

'So, there was Rhys, Vijay, Bernie and...?'

'Katarzyna. She only does three days. I stay because of her. She's funny and laughs at the other two.'

Barton was a little surprised at the comment. 'About what?'

'They can be a little serious.'

'Okay, which office is Vijay's?'

'Top of the stairs, looking out onto the street.'

'We'll go up and see him.'

Leah's eyebrows shot up towards her hairline, her lips forming a small 'o' of surprise.

'He won't appreciate that.'

'It's okay. We saw him yesterday at Morwen's house, and he insisted we speak to him about anything connected to the case. Vijay was determined to help.'

A suspicious expression passed over the receptionist's face. Minton was quick to distract her.

'Do you like Morwen? She must pop in every now and again.'

The girl dismissively bobbed her head from side to side. 'She's okay. I don't see her much.'

Minton leaned towards Leah and murmured just above a whisper. 'Can you do me a favour? Make sure nobody disturbs us.'

'Yeah, all right.'

'We'll talk to you when we're finished.'

A smiling Barton and Minton left a blinking Leah behind her desk and stepped up the stairs. The thick carpet masked their approach. Barton knocked on what he guessed would be the right door and marched inside. Weak winter sunlight filtered through the tall window, reflecting off the sleek glass and chrome of the modern desk. A minimalist bookshelf held a wide selection of accounting texts and financial journals. Arranged neatly, they echoed the large room's contemporary design.

The furniture had been set out so the desk was in the middle of the space, almost like a throne. It faced towards the street, enabling Barton to see Vijay's computer screen, which had a complex-looking graph on it. A subtle aroma of freshly brewed coffee filled the air.

Vijay's head snapped up from whatever he was perusing, his expression a mix of shock and wariness, like a fox caught in a sudden spotlight with a bird in his mouth. He plastered a wide, overly bright smile on his face and boomed, 'Well, Officers, to what do I owe the pleasure?'

Yet Vijay couldn't quite hold Barton's gaze.

26

DCI BARTON

Vijay got up and strode over to enthusiastically pump both their hands. Barton had to admit it was another swift recovery.

'Would either of you like a coffee? I've just bought one, but I can send Leah back to Ali's Coffee Box. They do a fabulous cappuccino.'

'We're okay, thanks,' replied Barton.

'How may I help?'

'There have been a few discrepancies around Rhys's passing. Is it okay to take a few minutes and chat about them?'

'Of course, of course.'

Vijay ushered them over to two seats in front of his desk, then he sat back in his larger chair.

Minton took out her laptop. 'I'll prepare a statement from what we've discussed.'

Vijay bridged his hands and rested his chin on them. 'Do you think his death is suspicious?'

Minton gave him a restrained nod. 'We aren't sure what's occurred at this point, so we're having conversations with those close to him, in case they have any information that might be deemed important further down the line.'

Barton imagined Vijay's neurons firing as he absorbed and processed the ambiguous details Minton had given him. The accountant made himself comfortable in his seat, no doubt a ploy to get his head straight.

'Am I a suspect?'

Barton smiled neutrally at him. 'I suppose everyone is at the beginning, but, at this point, we have no concrete evidence to indicate it's a murder.'

'Ask away. I have nothing to hide.'

'Excellent. Tell me how you and he came to be in business.'

'My wife and I moved to Stilton over thirty years ago. We were much more outgoing then and socialised in the village. Rhys and Morwen were on the next table one night when we were having a meal at The Bell and, with us being bean counters, we got chatting and became friends. Six months later, Rhys told me he was setting up an accountancy firm. He offered 50 per cent of the business to us, and we accepted. He had a special golden share though, on expansion or selling the company.'

'Which meant he kept control.'

'Yes, although Rhys said it wasn't about that. It was just we were two to his one, so it made sense for him to have the advantage. He was always a smart chap. It was so clever the way he played that aspect down, but I suppose we couldn't have known where we'd end up. We all worked like stink on a low wage to build the organisation up.'

Barton could understand why a lack of control might cause some hard feelings.

'Shouldn't he have given you 33 per cent each but kept a commanding edge?'

'Perhaps, although it was his idea, and he put down the initial investment, which was substantial. But there were two of us, and only one of him, doing the work. It was incredibly demanding at the beginning. I often wonder if the stress was what made my wife ill. A year later, we expanded and brought in Bernie Goodman, and soon after Charlie and Katarzyna McGrath joined, all of whom had experience and contacts. We hired an accounts clerk to do our admin and jokingly referred to ourselves as The Tax Titans. If we did a pub quiz, that was our moniker. We even set up a book club with the same name.'

Barton remembered the photograph he'd seen on the wall when they'd spoken to Morwen.

'So, you socialised outside work?'

'Yes. Five couples all bonding, having fun, connecting over wine, great food and literature. Back then, the company was more than just a business; we were a family. Those were golden days.'

'Did your wife leave the firm?'

'Died. Cancer. Slow, then sudden. You know how it goes. That's around the time when it all went wrong – 1999 was a tough year for us. We lost two huge accounts to a bigger accountancy firm, then a few more defected not long after. We had a high wage bill, and our finances appeared precarious. Rhys struggled with the responsibility and didn't want to take any risks after that, so we remained a small nimble operation, doing a great service to loyal local businesses.'

Barton noticed Vijay's eyes slide to the side.

'Was his lack of ambition a subject you two argued about?'

Vijay's reply was half a second too slow to be a natural response. 'We got on well. Barely a bad word.'

Barton glanced over at Minton, whose posture had stiffened. Vijay picked up on her response and huffed out a breath.

'Bloody hell. That little minx out there has a big mouth.'

Minton tutted. 'That's out of order, referring to a young female member of staff with such a derogatory term.'

'If I had my way, she'd have been let go. It's not completely her fault. She does have a head for numbers and is confident with people, and she can type like the wind, but she's bored and mischievous. If you peered under her desk now, you'd notice she has Crocs on, but if anyone interesting pops in, she puts on a pair of stilettos. A new postman nearly had a coronary earlier this year, although the episode did at least guarantee us a delivery every day afterwards.'

Barton could see they were going off at a tangent.

'Did Rhys have any enemies?'

Vijay paused, no doubt taking time to think.

'Occasionally you get a director who doesn't like the figures we come up with, but they're hardly likely to charge down here with murderous intentions.'

Barton wouldn't dismiss that, but he had other questions.

'With Rhys gone, what happens to the business? I assume as a director he was insured. Who gets that money?'

'The life insurance was cancelled when we reached fifty. It was getting expensive, and we didn't need it by then. Our partnership was set up in trust. If I or my wife died, the surviving spouse inherited their share. If Rhys passed on, his wife would receive his portion.'

'His 50 per cent and the golden share?'

Vijay paused, seemingly waging a brief war on whether to explain further. Barton tipped the scales.

'I find it's better to be upfront about what you know. If I later discover you've been keeping information from me, I'll be suspicious.'

Vijay's Adam's apple shuttled up and down.

'The golden share would be passed on to me.'

'Which would cede control of the company to you.'

Minton paused her typing and glanced up. Vijay's face flushed before he answered.

'Yes, that's right. Rhys only announced his retirement on Friday night. It was a bit of a surprise, but not totally unexpected. Things were up in the air. No decisions had been made. Look, there's no way I had anything to do with it. We worked so well together.'

'Apart from the arguments?' asked Minton.

'They were healthy, heated discussions around important matters. They weren't bitter disputes. Honest conversations like those have kept the business solvent all this time. We go out for dinner. We're friends.'

Minton pursed her lips. 'Where were you on Friday?'

'I was at work, with Rhys. He seemed fine.'

'What were you doing Friday night?'

Vijay gasped as if the question were a drowning man thrown a lifeline. He practically choked on his own relief. He sat upright.

'Yes, I was at The Bell. Morwen and Rhys were there as well.'

'They saw you?' asked Minton.

At Minton's sceptical face, he blurted out the facts.

'No, I was with them. The Tax Titans. Our book club. We were all present.'

'And what time was that from?'

'Seven until gone ten.'

Barton immediately recalled Morwen failing to offer up that piece of information. He needed some peace and quiet to contemplate everything they'd heard. Wracking his brains for what he should ask right then, he considered whether Rhys had fallen ill in the pub or at home.

'Was Rhys in good form?'

'Yes, very. In fact, he was merrier than usual.' Vijay appeared to consider adding something, then paused. 'Book club night is always a fun occasion. We all love reading.'

Barton suspected that wasn't what the man in front of him had been going to say.

'Would you mind giving us the names of everyone there and their contact details?'

'Of course, of course.'

Barton watched him write a list on a piece of printer paper, then a column of mobile numbers, which he took off his phone, next to the respective names.

'Addresses, too, please.'

Vijay did as he was asked.

'I don't know Eric and Mary Thwaite's address since they left Stilton, but the rest are correct. Might be Paston or Gunthorpe.'

Barton rose to leave. Minton and he shook the proffered hand again. It was she who paused at the door.

'This golden share that passes to you...'

'Yes?'

'Is his wife aware of that?'

Vijay bared his teeth in a grimace, his voice only just audible.

'I don't think so.'

27

DCI BARTON

Barton and Minton went back downstairs, passing Leah, who had come out from behind her desk in high heels to talk to a middle-aged delivery man. Barton kept his eyes on Leah's face and thanked her.

When they had both got in the car, Minton chuckled. 'Okay, I will admit that was a minx-like tiny skirt.'

'She was helpful with us catching out Vijay.'

'There's that phrase again. Catch out. Why aren't people being honest?'

Barton peered up at Vijay's window. 'Did you know some Japanese believe we have three hearts?'

'Nope.'

'One for the public, which is polite and respectful, but usually hides their true feelings. A heart for close friends and family, which is more genuine, where they can relax and be open with people they trust. The last one is an innermost heart, just for themselves. It holds their deepest thoughts and feelings and is rarely revealed to anyone.'

'You're saying people, perhaps especially as they age, carry shame and regrets, or hopes and dreams, and have secrets from family and friends, never mind the police?'

'Precisely. It's either that or Vijay and Morwen are a pair of sneaky bastards who killed her husband for romantic and financial gain.'

Minton laughed. 'Any inklings?'

'It's wise not to jump to conclusions when you're dealing with clever people. If one or both are implicated, they won't have done it without careful consideration about how to not get caught.'

'So him announcing his retirement isn't likely to have been the trigger.'

'Poisoning is rarely an impulsive act.'

Minton waved Vijay's piece of paper in the air. 'At least we have a cast list of who might be responsible or involved.'

'Yes, but my guess is the cause of death will be how we solve this.'

'Street heroin?'

'If that's what the final results come back as. They'll be testing Rhys's hair to see if drugs are present, which would indicate a longer habit, or at least him having imbibed at a reasonable level recently.'

Follicle tests could detect drug use for up to three months, but it might take a week for them to be detectable in the hair after intake.

'So,' said Minton. 'If it's in his hair, he's a regular user and this perhaps becomes not murder but manslaughter.'

'I suppose, but unlikely, considering the two performances we've witnessed this morning. The Bell will be finishing the lunchtime rush soon. We'll head down there and check if the staff who worked Friday night are prepared to corroborate that part of the story. Piecing together the sequence of events will help the investigation.'

Minton had been studying the list of names. 'There are only eight here. Weren't there five couples?'

'Vijay's wife died of cancer. Perhaps one of the others did or there was a divorce.'

'That's assuming his wife did have cancer and didn't OD on heroin.'

Barton smiled. 'Yes, well, Vijay lying about that really would be daft. We can easily check.'

'Records back then might be incomplete.'

Barton gave a slow nod. 'Fair point, but the other accountants will know if she was genuinely ill.'

Minton drove around to the rear of The Bell and took the last remaining space. She smiled appreciatively at the line of cars, which indicated that, despite it being a Thursday, the pub was thriving and the customers were wealthy.

Barton's phone rang as they walked past the tables in the pub's courtyard.

'DCI Barton.'

'Good afternoon, sir. My name is PC Kiara Parveen from the drug unit. I'm calling regards your email concerning dangerous heroin circulating in the area. I've been tasked with your query and can confirm there have been two suspected overdoses within the last week. I've checked the details. Both victims have significant criminal pasts for acquisitive crime and possession of class A drugs, which points to substance abuse.'

Barton knew there would still be a coroner's inquiry to ascertain the exact cause of death with the victim's histories for public health records.

'Are your post-mortems complete?'

'Not yet. I rang the pathology department. It's obviously a busy time of year, but they had already bumped both cases to tomorrow at the request of a Dr Monteith, the forensic pathologist.'

Barton grinned. Mortis had got there first. 'How many overdoses do we normally get in the county each week?'

'About thirty a year. Most of which are opioids and painkillers, but poly-drug overdoses are increasingly common.'

Barton frowned at the term. 'What's a polydrug?'

'Deaths involving the use of multiple substances, for example heroin and Valium. Opioids and alcohol. Cocaine and alcohol. Not to mention dissociative anaesthetics with the aforementioned.'

Parveen spoke in a formal tone as though she were delivering a lecture. He wondered if she was nervous, or if it was simply her style. She reminded him of Mortis.

'Dissociative anaesthetics?'

'For example, ketamine causes dissociation and hallucinations but can offer pain relief and sedation.'

'Do most of the victims die of respiratory depression?'

'Correct.'

'So, one a fortnight normally means two occurrences within a week may suggest a problem with the batch.'

'They sometimes come along like buses, sir, but we appreciate your reaching out. My partner and I will be heading to Peterborough this afternoon to speak to users in the city centre and various squats we're aware of.

There are around twenty-five rough sleepers at any one time, but we have an idea where some of the hidden homeless are.'

'I assume they won't be keen on giving up their dealers.'

'They're more forthcoming if there's a lethal supply circulating. They will all have lost friends and acquaintances that way, although the majority of homeless addicts are alcohol dependent as opposed to drug users. We'll head out early evening too, as some may be out begging during daylight. I should be able to report back to you first thing tomorrow with our findings.'

'How about known dealers?'

'We tend to arrest them.'

Barton couldn't help laughing. Until that point, the conversation had felt closer to an interaction with AI than a chat between colleagues, which he hoped wasn't a disquieting glimpse into the future.

'Is Jeff Crenwick still around?'

'He was off long-term sick, but he returned on Monday.'

Parveen didn't offer any details, although Barton knew Crenwick had been suffering with a bad back from his time in uniform, hence the move to the drug unit.

'The identity of the supplier is going to be important.'

'We do have suspicions of where the drugs are coming from and who's involved, sir. It's not as simple as heading there, because we may be at the intel and evidence gathering stage, or there's the possibility of CHIS involvement.'

Barton understood that, but he still had a sense of being lectured to. CHIS was an acronym for Covert Human Intelligence Source. Undercover workers.

'I take it a pile of dead bodies would lead to adjustments in your strategy?'

'Yes, sir. Will there be anything else?'

'No, thank you.'

Barton put his phone away. Parveen at least sounded efficient, which he supposed was one of the most important qualities for an officer.

He and Minton took a left in The Bell courtyard and headed to the restaurant and bar door. Barton held it open for Minton.

'There may have been two more overdoses.'

Minton hesitated, then drew Vijay's list from her pocket. Her eyes skimmed the names.

'Eight people,' she said, her voice low. 'Take out Vijay, Rhys and Morwen, and that leaves five.' Her gaze met Barton's. A grim understanding passed between them.

It was Barton who stated the obvious.

'Assuming they're all still alive.'

28

DCI BARTON

Barton followed Minton into the building. The restaurant's tables were mostly occupied, with the clink of cutlery and hushed conversation filtering out of the room. Minton headed to the bar on the right. Barton set off to follow but was distracted by the see-through fridge cabinet just before it, which was stacked with cheese.

He crouched down and read the labels. Real Stilton and a Coachman's Cheddar. He still had some port left over from Christmas back at home. Barton gritted his teeth and dragged himself away, earning him a guarded look from a couple who passed him as they were leaving.

Minton was deep in conversation with the two staff members behind the bar, dressed in de rigueur white shirts and black trousers. Minton had impressed him a year ago, the first time he'd worked with her. She had a no-nonsense style. One that stated, *I'm doing important work, so please be helpful.* Being six feet tall helped, but she generally got what she wanted by being firm and persuasive.

She turned to him as he approached.

'This is Detective Chief Inspector Barton,' she said as an introduction. 'Neither of these two were working that Friday night, so they can't confirm the book club was here. They both do Thursdays and Saturdays. The guys from Friday should be on tomorrow again, if you want to return and talk to them then.'

Barton nodded and scanned the cosy space. The decor had been spruced up since he'd last visited. An old fellow had pulled his seat up near the open fire and was taking little sips from dark liquid in a small glass. He had a faraway expression. Barton felt an urge to buy himself a rum and join him.

He turned back to the staff members.

'Could you check if they're definitely on the rota tomorrow?'

'Sure,' said the woman. 'I'm Sally. Come with me to the office.'

The officers followed the blonde, who appeared a little older than Barton. With styled hair, a slim figure and a winning smile, she oozed good health. She escorted them back across the courtyard, through a heavy door to the hotel reception desk.

'Wait here, please,' she said, disappearing through a doorway behind her.

Thirty seconds later, Sally returned.

'Yes, Helen and Matt are both on for the lunch session tomorrow.'

'That's great,' replied Barton. 'Have you worked here long?'

'It will be forty years soon, if you can believe that.'

'You don't look old enough.'

'Thank you.'

'Although that should make you aware of The Tax Titans.'

Sally smiled in agreement. 'Yes, but I'm more on the weddings and hospitality side of things. Helen knows the book club well. She's been here as much time as I have.'

A shorter, younger woman appeared through the doorway.

'Hi. I'm the manager, Alishia. You can return to the bar, Sally. I'll assist the officers.'

Alishia waited for Sally to leave, then came around the counter and stood in front of him.

'Can I help at all?'

Barton introduced himself and Minton. He considered what he was going to say, but the woman didn't seem the type to fall for a tall tale.

While he was thinking, she folded her arms and got straight to the point.

'You've come because of Rhys Jones, who was here on Friday night. The rumour mill in Stilton, which I believe has no equal, said it was natural causes, but now a chief inspector shows up. Should we be alarmed?'

Barton puffed out a breath. It seemed the village folk were a sharp bunch.

'We've not had confirmation of the cause of death, but we do know he was here in high spirits less than an hour beforehand.'

'What are you saying?'

'Judging by you being pretty busy now, I suspect Friday evening was heaving.'

'We weren't fully booked all night, but not far off.'

'Anyone else fall ill?'

'Are you suggesting he passed away at our hands?'

'Just making inquiries. I take it that's a no.'

'Of course. We had a large wedding celebration Saturday afternoon, so I spent most of the weekend here. Everyone left of their own accord on Friday, even if some were wobbling. Wait! If you're saying that, you must believe he was poisoned.'

Barton felt hemmed in for a moment. Minton cleared her throat.

'I'm sure that's not something you'd like to consider, Alishia, but it's a possibility. We're here to rule your business out. We wouldn't be doing our job otherwise. There are any number of ways he could have consumed a substance that upset his system. A hazardous lobster thermidor, too many Martinis, or perhaps his heart stopped because his time was up.'

Alishia looked up and held the much taller woman's stare. She bobbed her head as if to say she appreciated the forthright response.

'Let me show you around. Explain about our operation. Help rule this establishment out. Follow me.'

Alishia guided them to a medium-sized hall full of chairs with white covers and ribbons.

'These are ready for this Saturday. We have a wedding most weekends, which fills up all of our twenty-two bedrooms. During the week, business-people and tourists keep us busy. We have a lot of repeat custom. The recent refurb has accentuated our finer points, with new furniture, carpets, flooring and fresh paint throughout.'

They followed her up a flight of stairs to the next floor.

'These are the bedrooms, which have also been updated.'

'Nice,' said Barton, peering through an open doorway.

'We pride ourselves on our plump pillows, soft linens and comfortable mattresses. All the rooms are unique in shape, size and decoration, adding a touch of mystique to every visit. It's modern living in a historic setting.'

Barton was happy for her to keep talking while he got a feel for the place, even if it did feel he was part of an advert. Alishia was clearly proud of her workplace.

She took them through another door.

'This is my favourite spot. The snug.'

Barton stared longingly at five comfy-looking chairs parked opposite an open fire. The flames licked upward, bathing the room in a cosy glow.

They carried on to another seating area, and finally there was a raised section ideal for smaller celebrations of around twenty guests.

Alishia exchanged a bit of banter with a group dressed like ramblers. There were plenty of empties, so they'd clearly worked up quite a thirst. She collected the used glasses, then returned to Minton and Barton.

'We run a tight ship here. Most of our employees have been with us for over ten years. Stilton is a place people move to and never leave, not if they can help it. There's still a real sense of community here.'

'I'm learning that,' said Barton.

'All those visiting The Bell notice what everyone who works here has in common. Our employees genuinely love their job. As a proud family company, we welcome our team members in with open arms and look after them.'

When neither officer responded, she took them through another door to a corridor.

'My chef is brilliant. He could work anywhere he liked, but he chooses to be here. For those who join The Bell, the hours are long, and it can be stressful, but we're a family. Nobody would jeopardise that.'

She pushed open the next door, and they entered a spacious, busy kitchen. The stainless-steel surfaces gleamed under the bright lights, reflecting the smiles of the staff in their crisp white jackets as they greeted their manager.

A gentle hum of activity filled the air, punctuated by the rhythmic chopping of vegetables and the sizzle of onions hitting the hot stove. Aromas of garlic, herbs and simmering sauces mingled tantalisingly, a testament to the culinary magic still underway. Steam curled from the dishwasher, hinting at the lunchtime rush, but now a calm efficiency reigned.

'Are you hungry?' asked Alishia.

Barton's mouth watered. He grinned at Minton and licked his lips.

'I'd be prepared to risk it.'

29
DCI BARTON

Alishia showed them how the food was delivered to the restaurant downstairs, meaning customers couldn't tamper with it, then took them back to the courtyard. She smiled warmly, shook their hands, and offered any assistance they might need.

After she'd gone, Barton and Minton headed to the car park in silence. Minton piped up first.

'Lovely place. To think I've been frequenting KFC.'

'Nothing wrong with the Colonel's secret recipe.'

'Not as many fireplaces, though. Okay, what's the plan?'

'We return to Thorpe Wood. Write up what we have. Alishia's probably helped us there.'

'In what way?'

'It seems unlikely to be a staff member. And even less probable that a customer sprinkled deadly nightshade beside the parsley.'

'People often leave drinks on bars while they're chatting.'

Barton considered that.

'It sounds like they were sitting down together. If whatever killed him was administered not long before he died, it's a small window, meaning there should be fewer suspects.'

'Assuming he didn't OD himself.'

'Right. Tomorrow might be busy, so we'll make sure the others on the team are up to speed when we return.'

'What about the risk to the other book club members?'

'The five we haven't spoken to?'

'Yes.'

'Two are couples. The Goodmans and the Thwaites. Give them a ring, confirm they're not sparko in their armchairs, and tell them to expect a visit at eleven and twelve tomorrow.' Barton checked the list of names Vijay had provided. 'Katarzyna is the final one. She's the part-time member who still works at Jones and Singh.'

'That's an unusual name. Russian?'

'Wait a minute.' Barton took his phone out as Minton pulled onto the A1. 'Katarzyna is the Polish version of Catherine, and Kah-sha, spelt Kasia, is a diminutive of Katarzyna.'

Minton clicked her fingers. 'Which was the person Morwen said she was going to stay with.'

'Well, at least we know she's still alive.'

'Interesting she was the first person Morwen thought of and felt it was okay to turn up unannounced.'

'Yeah,' replied Barton, filing the fact in his head. 'Unless Morwen is drinking a cup of tea sitting on the sofa next to her dead body. I'll call into the office and let whoever's there know that there'll be a discussion when we return.'

They jumped in their car and drove to the station, heading directly to the meeting room. Minton revealed what they'd uncovered to the team.

Zander, sharp in a new black suit and waistcoat, looked like a different man. The weariness that had plagued him since the twins' arrival appeared to have vanished, replaced by a focussed energy.

'Let's hope they aren't too tight knit a group.'

Most of those present nodded, but Hoffman appeared distracted. He was one of the newer members of the team and had only recently turned thirty.

'Why might that be a problem, DC Hoffman?' asked Barton.

Hoffman was always fashionably dressed, but in a more casual suit style than Zander's.

'Loyalty can run deep. If the club's a tight unit, will they close ranks? We might get given shady alibis. There may even be a special method of communication. It's also possible the group or some within it are working together.'

'Well done.'

Barton hid his grin. Hoffman was a cocky git, but if he could take the role more seriously, he would go far.

'The statements we've taken today were generally relaxed affairs. Depending on what's uncovered tomorrow, that's likely to change. To successfully gather evidence, you need to create rapport, decipher subtle cues, and consider complex social dynamics. Obviously, there's another way of saying that.'

'Find out who's lying,' replied Malik.

'Exactly. Zelensky, you can come with me in the morning to speak with the two couples. The rest of you be ready, because you might be needed to visit the others. We'll probably need people escorted here and interviewed under caution. That will be the time to further ratchet up the pressure. Any thoughts?'

Those present shook their heads, so Barton brought the meeting to a close and headed to his desk. There was a note to ring Detective Inspector Jeff Crenwick from the drug unit. He still had the man's number in his phone, and Crenwick answered immediately.

'Afternoon, John.'

'It's been a while, Jeff. How are you?'

'So-so. I have to endure regular injections for slipped discs, but I'm good to go for a few months afterwards.'

'Excellent. It's good to have you back. I take it you have some information for me.'

'Yes. You spoke to DC Parveen. She's been checking on the known rough sleepers and unfortunately, we've got another body. Parveen also dropped in to Peterborough and Hinchingbrooke HDUs. There's an overdose in there, although he should make it.'

HDU was the high dependency unit, the stepdown from ICU, which indicated a lower level of concern.

'Jeez. That's worrying, but at least the survivor can give us details of where he purchased his drugs and who from.'

'Parveen's on it. As soon as he's out of danger, she'll be there.'

'She has an interesting style.'

Crenwick laughed down the line.

'She said you'd had a chat. Robotic? Yes. Impressive? Very.'

'I'll be having a meeting tomorrow here at ten, so if she's around, ask her to attend.'

'That's a sound idea.'

'I assume these more recent victims weren't upstanding citizens?'

'The bloke who survived has a bit of previous, but mostly petty theft for food from being homeless. He's likely one of those who lost his job and home, hit rock bottom. We're seeing more and more of them. The other bloke was a nasty thieving dope-head.'

'I bet Parveen would have something to say about that terminology.'

'I rarely use that type of language nowadays, but this guy took a knife and a syringe into a newsagent's and threatened to inject his HIV+ blood into the eighteen-year-old behind the counter if she didn't hand over the till contents.'

'That kind of thing's also getting more common. I suppose karma caught up with him.'

'Seems so. I'll email you the case numbers and my mobile number. We need to find whoever's been flogging this heroin, or we'll have a disaster on our hands. Whatever's in it dropped the guy so quick he still had the needle in his arm.'

'That's the sort of potent stuff Rhys Jones had in him. Before you go, I've got a possible new recruit for you.'

'Not you, is it? This department only has room for one diplodocus.'

'No, it's a DC on our team. Bright, keen. She wants a faster pace. I could send her over to you in Huntingdon for a day to see what you're about.'

'Sure thing, especially if this case turns out to be ours. We're always short, and people with potential aren't easy to come by.'

'Chat soon, Jeff.'

Barton smiled as he put his phone down. He fondly recalled some of the laughs he and Jeff used to have, but his mind swiftly shifted back to their dead accountant.

Addicts, shoplifters, armed robbers, the homeless and Rhys Jones. It just didn't make sense.

30
DCI BARTON

Frustration clouded Barton's face all afternoon as he grappled with the mystery of Rhys's death. He considered a few possible motivations and methods, but the significant risk of getting caught weakened their plausibility.

His gloom lifted as he left the office, replaced by a sense of purpose. Peterborough's drug unit was big enough to handle the case if it turned out simply to be a bad batch, but his gut told him something sinister was up. Tomorrow, he would start to unravel the truth.

When he reached home, Kelly Strange's car was parked on his driveway. She'd been a brilliant sergeant in his team before she had twins with Zander, but had decided to quit instead of returning, wanting to try something new. The couple had finally got around to focussing on the wedding now the fog of early parenthood was dissipating, so Barton suspected she was on a planning visit.

Shouting and squawking from the kitchen were the first sounds to greet him on stepping through the front door. He heard his wife urge someone not to throw the Play-Doh, which meant the twins were there. Barton veered off to the lounge. Strange was perched on the sofa with Lily. Tommy was sitting on the carpet, seemingly showing a cautious-looking Gizmo his teddy.

Barton dropped into an armchair and smiled at the lad. The two women had coffee and a cake.

'Evening, ladies. Putting the world to rights?'

Lily put her hand over her mouth as she tried to eat and talk.

'Kelly was telling me about how she met Zander. It's a romantic story. She's invited me to the wedding.'

'Ah, brilliant.' Barton turned to Kelly. 'Holly told me you'd set a date. Have you chosen a location?'

'Down the road at the Orton Hall hotel. Everyone can walk or get taxis. The food is top-notch, the grounds and building are beautiful. Holly and I are going to Stamford to try some dresses on. We've found a cheesy disco guy for the evening, an entertainer for the kids in the afternoon doing balloons and face painting, and there's plenty of space for a bouncy castle outside.'

He grinned.

'That's me sorted for the day. Sounds as though everything's in hand.'

'There's only one unresolved aspect. My name.'

'Eh?'

'Shawn wants me to take his surname, but I'm not keen. Kelly Zander makes me sound like a subspecies of newt.'

Barton's shoulders shook as he laughed. The pressure of the investigation faded away, especially when Tommy giggled as well. The boy dragged himself to his feet, then staggered and weaved his way across the carpet to Barton, putting his hands up at the finish.

Barton hauled him onto his knee.

'Woah! He is such a solid little man.'

'Tommy's always been a bit of a bruiser,' replied Lily, 'which means he's enjoyed playing with Zane and Zack. He copies everything they do.'

Holly appeared at the door. 'I'm not sure that's a positive. Zane has managed to get two direct Play-Doh hits in my spaghetti bolognese.'

Barton was distracted by the jiggling being on his lap. He began singing an adapted version of one of his favourite songs to him.

> 'Every morning at the nursery, you could see him arrive.
> He stood two-feet-six, weight twenty-five.
> Kinda narrow at the shoulder and chubby at the hip.
> And everybody knew ya didn't give no lip to big Tom.
> Big Tom, Big T-o-o-o-m, Big Bad Tom!'

Tommy screeched at the top of his voice, grinning wildly.

Holly shook her head. 'I'm not sure who's the most childish out of you pair.'

Barton rose and handed Tommy to Holly. 'Maybe we *should* have another one,' he said with an impish grin.

'No way, but I could hide some of your daughter's birth-control pills.'

Barton covered his ears and pretended to gag.

'Not funny! You know that topic is taboo. I'll put a shift in with the boys before you say something else to upset me.'

Barton trod in some green Play-Doh the moment he walked into the kitchen to start his babysitting duties. It was everywhere. One bit was even stuck to the ceiling. He went to the cutlery drawer and selected a slotted spoon.

Holly's bolognese was worth saving.

31

DCI BARTON

Friday

Barton had only just sat down at his desk the next morning with a coffee when he received a text from Mortis. It simply told him to check his email. Barton logged on to his laptop, praying the substance wasn't going to be elephant anaesthetic, and found the message from the pathologist. He scanned the report.

> Substances identified – linear alkylbenzene sulfonate, sodium carbonate, isotonitazene. See additional notes.

Barton located the section. The first two compounds were materials used in laundry powder. One being a surfactant to remove the dirt, the other to soften the water so the cleaning products worked better. Common cutting ingredients in powdered drugs.

It was the third on the list that mattered.

> Isotonitazene, a class A drug in the UK, is a relatively new type of nitazene or synthetic opioid to appear in the drug chain, having first been noticed around 2020. Similar to fentanyl, but often much stronger, it's frequently found in combination with other opioids, benzodiazepines, and

even stimulants, increasing the risk of overdose and unpredictable effects.

Isotonitazene may not be included in standard drug screenings, making it harder to identify in overdose cases. Isotonitazene binds strongly to the opioid receptors in the brain, which are responsible for pain relief and euphoria. This contributes to its high potency and addictive potential.

Respiratory depression begins with slower and shallow breathing, impeding the intake of oxygen and expulsion of carbon dioxide. Lack of oxygen quickly affects vital organs by impairing their function. Simultaneously, the build-up of carbon dioxide establishes an acidic environment in the blood, further interrupting cellular processes. Without treatment, this combined assault leads to organ failure, potentially shutting down the brain or stopping the heart.

Barton wondered whether it was a peaceful way to go. Some seemed to believe that about drowning, but Mortis had told him the truth. There was often an instinctive struggle for survival, accompanied by panic and intense physical discomfort. As the drowning process continued, the individual became dizzy, confused and might experience hallucinations. Sounded terrifying and not at all like drifting off to sleep.

Barton carried on reading the report.

Primary location of substance likely to have caused death: isotonitazene was discovered in microscopic quantities in the large intestine and slightly larger amounts in the stomach. Other material was present in both areas including mushrooms, potatoes, kale, leek, liver, red wine, whisky and lager. However, the most isotonitazene was discovered in a dessert product, which had been eaten in large bites and was partially intact. It appears to be a cake with icing. My best conclusion is the substance was placed within this product and given to Rhys.

There is no evidence of a pill having been taken.

Barton rang Mortis, who picked up after the second ring.

'Morning, John. You took your time. Was the font a bit small for you?'

'Yes, I had to hunt for my magnifying glass. Is this a preliminary report?'

'No, the actual one, but I'm nowhere near finished. It's become more complicated with the sort of drug identified. A lot of people will end up reading the minutiae, so I need to get it perfect.'

'So, what the hell is a nitazene?'

'They're compounds created by scientists in the 1950s in research for new medication. They hoped the developed drugs would be cheaper than morphine and have fewer side effects. Initially, they showed potential. Nitazenes result in prolonged receptor activation in the brain, but this amplified and extended stimulation caused the drug to have a highly addictive nature.'

'Any chance of that in English?'

'You get a mega buzz, but it's super addictive.'

'And isotonitazene is one of these nitazenes.'

'Yes, a particularly powerful type. Like all opioids, they flood the brain with dopamine, creating an intense high. Over time, the brain adapts to this surge of dopamine, making it less sensitive to the drug. You then need more to achieve the same effect and experience significant withdrawal symptoms when you stop using it.'

'The more powerful it is, the bigger and longer the high, with worse withdrawal.'

'Correct. And this is one of the big daddies of the family. Consider heroin as the baseline with a score of one. We've had encounters with fentanyl already, which is around fifty times stronger. Isotonitazene is around five times more potent than fentanyl. Next to a natural opioid like morphine, gram for gram, that's about seven hundred and fifty times stronger.'

Barton whistled. 'A man-made monster.'

'Yes. The aforementioned hippo-snoozer, carfentanil, is the winner, being ten thousand times more potent than morphine.'

'Who the blazes would mix isotonitazene into a drug? Putting some in a street deal would be idiotic if it killed all your customers.'

'Let me explain. As you're aware, most of the heroin in Europe comes from Afghanistan. The Taliban recently prohibited the cultivation of opium, which led to a dramatic decline in production. The subsequent gap in the market has resulted in other drugs being used as replacements to boost the strength. Dealers only put in a tiny amount of these types of compounds for the reason you stated. It can be fatal, but the chains of supply are long. Who knows what's added at various stages? The person who included this may be relatively untouchable.'

'We have a drug unit now, which deals with this type of crime, but usually I've heard of the names of the substances.'

'America has a worse overdose problem than us, with around a hundred thousand souls perishing from drugs each year – 75 per cent of that is down to opioids. We're at around seven thousand cases, so, even though we have a smaller population, it's not anywhere near as bad. However, if you consider our trajectory, it's fair to say we're catching up. Even so, I suspect we've only had a handful of deaths from isotonitazene over here.'

Barton's mind had been creating the sequence of events while he listened.

'In summary, Rhys heads out for dinner with the book club. He eats and drinks well, finishing his meal with a cake. That dessert contains, amongst other things, heroin, which has been mixed with this nitazene. He goes home, where the effects of the drug kick in as his system absorbs everything he's eaten.'

'A plausible theory.'

'It takes hours for the body to process a dense meal, but a sugary cake would break down swiftly.'

'That's right. Nitazenes can be in powder form or dissolved in liquids. My guess is this was in powder form, but it just shows the strength, with him dying quite quickly after having consumed it.'

Barton considered the swiftness of Rhys's passing.

'So, even though there was barely a trace, the little that was absorbed still overwhelmed his system. The drug was that powerful.'

'Yes. Rhys's hair tests came back with no evidence of illicit compounds. He was not an addict or an occasional user. This was likely a one-off. The poor guy would have had no tolerance for opioids at all.'

'Not only that, but he'd have been sleepy after a huge meal and the added impact of a considerable amount of alcohol meant he literally went to sleep in his chair and his heart stopped. The drug was so potent that, even ingested as opposed to injected, he didn't stand a chance.'

'Right. The drug would still be many times stronger than heroin, despite some being metabolised in the liver before reaching the bloodstream. If anyone was unlucky enough to inject this, the drug would immediately bypass the digestive system, resulting in higher bioavailability. So, far more of the drug would hit the brain in a much shorter period of time.'

'Like the addict who died?'

'Yes. I did the first post-mortem last night, and it strongly indicated an overdose. Obviously, we'll test for isotonitazene now.'

Barton nodded respectfully, even though Mortis couldn't see him.

'You were right to be suspicious. We can make rapid progress on the case now.'

'We are a dream team, John. The Barton belly and the Mortis mind. Your hunches – or should I say haunches? – and my guile, but all remarkable unions sadly come to an end.'

Barton was surprised. His friend was not one to reminisce, even though they'd worked together for nearly two decades. He wasn't sure exactly what age Mortis was, but he had to be around seventy.

'You talk as if we're elderly men.'

'I am an old man.'

'What makes you think I've made up my mind about leaving?'

'Because you're clever.'

Barton briefly closed his eyes.

'Actually, I'm going to take a sabbatical.'

'Sounds like a smart choice. Perhaps your fight will resume one day, but it's the right time for me to exit the battlefield.'

'And enjoy a long and happy retirement.'

'That's the plan, but fate has given us a leaving gift.'

'The thrill of another puzzle?'

'Yes! We live once more! Speak to you soon.'

Barton cut the call. He closed his laptop with a click, which echoed in the quiet of the office. The smile that had lit up his face moments before melted away, replaced by a grim recall of what the results meant.

Their worst fears had been confirmed.

32

THE BOOK CLUB KILLER

A tin of ravioli on toast for breakfast, and why not? One of the joys of ageing is the realisation you're no longer beholden to anyone. I can do what I like, when I like. It's a shame I didn't realise that when I was younger, when I might have taken advantage of the freedom.

My appetite was healthy once. I used to have a large can, not these half-size things. Three rounds of bread, whereas now I only need one, and occasionally some of that single slice remains uneaten. Everything is diminishing. My food, my energy, my looks, my hunger, even my ability to sleep. Nothing as fast as my dreams. Who knew God's waiting room was so bleak?

As the song goes, I could eat my dinner in a fancy restaurant. Get a late booking holiday. Spend a weekend away in a castle or go up in a hot-air balloon. What about a ride on a steam train on the Nene Valley Railway? Yet, I don't.

To the world, I put on a brave front. Laugh at jokes. Talk about subjects others will find interesting, which is mostly *their* lives or *their* children. Feign an interest I do not have. Paint my face with a smile, when inside I'm doing anything but. Over the years, I've become an expert at masking my true feelings. I doubt anybody has a clue about the depths to which I plunge. The total darkness.

Yet, something has shifted this last week. A light has come on. Excitement, intrigue, gossip. I struggled to put my finger on it at first, but I suppose the word is fun. I'm enjoying myself.

Yes, I know what I've done. All things considered, that makes me a bit of a devil, but I had forgotten what it meant to feel alive. If this is what it takes, then so be it.

Which means it's time for the next chapter. Will it be someone's last?

33

DCI BARTON

Barton hadn't noticed Parveen from the drug unit entering the office earlier in the morning, but she was in the meeting room when he arrived. She sat quietly at the back, wearing smart dark blue trousers and a red kurta, which was a shorter version of the kameez, a long tunic-type shirt.

When everyone had taken their seats, Barton repeated what Mortis had told him. He then introduced DC Kiara Parveen. To his surprise, she confidently stood up and joined him at the front.

'Thank you for inviting me here. As you're aware, there was another death yesterday, making three in all. There's also the individual who survived. He's out of imminent danger but under close watch. The hospital has permitted a short interview with him this afternoon considering the need to stop the flow of deadly drugs.'

Barton pointed at Minton.

'You buddy up with Parveen. Spend the day with her. You can both be the link between our teams. What are your team's findings so far, Parveen?'

'There is clearly some dangerous heroin around, but we suspect it's not all contaminated with this nitazene, or, if it is, the quantities are much reduced. We spoke to a man yesterday evening who bought some last week and reckoned it was the best night of his life.'

'What about who sold it to him?'

'The dealer was a stranger, but he knew enough to head under the bridge on Oundle Road where some of the homeless congregate.'

'No description?'

'Said he was white, furtive, with sharp teeth and a furry coat.'

Barton rolled his eyes.

'Sounds like he scored off an Arctic fox.'

Parveen didn't crack a smile.

'Yes, well, the witness stank of drink and slurred his words.'

Barton groaned. 'Let's hope the case doesn't hinge on his evidence. I take it you're spending today visiting some of the other addicts and more flophouses?'

'Yes. We picked up two of the people we have suspicions of being dealers, but neither had anything on them. No comment interviews. It does ruin our investigation into their affairs because they'll be super cautious now. Other members of my team are checking CCTV in the city centre. It's a laborious process, especially if he came via a route with few cameras.'

Parveen sat down, which Barton assumed meant she'd finished.

'Thanks, Parveen. I'd say three dead people are more worrying than any surveillance concerns. Okay. This is the plan for today. Zelensky and I will visit the two couples at eleven and twelve, as mentioned yesterday. Malik and Hoffman, bring Morwen in by midday. She's staying at the house of a lady called Katarzyna McGrath, who could be at work. If Katarzyna's also present, ask her to come in with you to help with our inquiries. Zander, you and Leicester head to Jones and Singh Accountants and fetch Vijay.'

'Who do you want for the interviews?' he asked.

'I'll sort that out later. I suspect after today we'll have a much better idea of what's occurred, even if it's just to rule people out. Bank accounts and phone records are likely to be telling. Anyone who refuses us the opportunity to check either of theirs will find themselves moving to the top of the suspects list. It's time for Morwen and Vijay in particular to face harder questions as to their involvement. At this point, they appear to have the most to gain, but I want them cautioned and their responses on video. Any thoughts?'

Zander nodded. 'Let me get this right. You're saying that some of the wraps of heroin sold out of the same batch might be more potent than others.'

Barton looked over at Parveen.

'Yes,' she replied. 'It's pot luck, or Russian roulette, if you prefer. It's so strong, not much would have been put in. Even a few micrograms would be harmful to some people.'

Zander had more questions.

'Could this have been purchased off the internet?'

'That's right, well done. A regular supplier in an established chain, perhaps coming in bulk through Holland, would be unlikely to mix such a strong nitazene in his product due to the potential for multiple overdoses. They wouldn't want it affecting their business relationships, never mind the interest from the authorities. Our unreliable informant said he didn't know the dealer, so the drugs may have been ordered online.'

Barton smiled at Zander, who was also amused at Parveen's compliment.

'From the dark web?' asked Hoffman.

'Perhaps, but people don't even need to use that nowadays. Substantial amounts of pills, including illicit opioids and stimulants, are smuggled into the UK using the postal system from Europe, with the sheer volume of mail making interception challenging. The amount we do seize would indicate a growing problem.'

Hoffman's eyes narrowed. 'Surely it's only a matter of time before someone doing that is caught. You have their address for a start.'

'There are some idiots who send it to their own house, or a family member's or a pal's, but other people get cuckolded into accepting it. Abandoned houses or business premises are also used. The only deterrent is the significant custodial sentences waiting for those who are convicted, but, as experienced detectives such as you know, many criminals don't plan far ahead or consider failure. Some of the smart ones only use an address once. And because the drug is so potent, the package would be small, making the possible earnings significantly higher than trying to smuggle something bulky like marijuana, or even heroin itself.'

Barton had to admit Jeff had been right. Parveen couldn't have been more than twenty-five-years old, yet she held a room of hardened detectives in the palm of her hand.

Barton rose to his feet. 'Let's be sharp today. Rhys Jones's demise in this manner doesn't make sense to me. From what Parveen has said, the dose he ingested in the cake might not have killed him.'

Parveen tipped her head in his direction. 'That's true, although the poisoner may not have known that. What is possible is that there was no real emotion to the killings.'

Barton frowned, as did most of the others in the room.

'Please explain.'

'The person supplying the drugs didn't care about the plight of the people they were dealing to. That indicates a naivety, or a high level of carelessness and ruthlessness. The individual who slipped the heroin to Rhys also wasn't particularly concerned if he died. If he was supposed to perish, there are significantly more effective methods.'

Barton rubbed his hands together.

'That's a valid point. Rhys's wasn't a vengeful, pain-filled death. He probably drifted into a sleep without even realising he was dying. If you combine that with nobody being aware of the presence of a nitazene, it makes me suspect the idea was not for Rhys to die, but to suffer.'

34
DCI BARTON

Zelensky drove Barton to Paston with neither saying much on the way. Barton enjoyed working with Major Crimes' newest sergeant. She reminded him of Kelly Strange. A pocket-rocket blonde, tough, no-nonsense, who had overcome many challenges in life, but she was another one who hadn't quite been at the top of her game.

Barton had considered whether to break the silence, but he wanted to prepare the questions for Eric and Mary Thwaite in his head. Vijay had said the couple used to live in Stilton but they moved. Paston was a working-class area of Peterborough with a completely different vibe from a village like Stilton. Eric or Mary had to have worked for the firm at some point, or they wouldn't have been in the book club.

Zelensky took the slip road off the parkway for Paston Ridings.

'Did you say Stowehill Road?'

'That's the one,' replied Barton. 'It's not too bad there compared to around the shops.'

She chuckled. 'Yeah, I know the area well. What was the name of the pub at the centre?'

'The Postillion.'

'That's it. I'd only been in Uniform a little while and got called there to sort out a disturbance. It was reggae night. Music blaring, folk dancing, and while local kids were fighting outside, their parents were scrapping inside.'

'Sounds about right, but those types of pubs played a part in community cohesion. Yeah, there were punch-ups every now and again, but they'd be back drinking together the following weekend. Makes you wonder where everyone goes to let off steam with so many shutting.'

'Boozing at home.'

'Most likely, which has to be worse. Look at the recent rises in domestic abuse.'

Barton pictured the pub. 'The Postillion was about as different from The Bell as it's possible to be.'

'Maybe Mr and Mrs Thwaite were regulars before it shut. Might tell us a bit about the type of people they are.'

Zelensky parked outside the property, and she and Barton strode up the path. A dirty ten-year-old Kia sat on the driveway. Rusty hinges on a sagging low gate groaned a mournful protest as he pushed it open. The squat bungalow seemed to cower under the eaves of the two-storey houses on either side. Yet its rendered façade, though weathered by time, had a sturdy charm.

The shiny PVC door, which appeared a recent addition, opened as Barton raised a meaty finger to press the buzzer.

A mature woman in a charcoal skirt suit, face scrubbed clean and framed by a practical grey bob, appeared. She reminded Barton of Detective Chief Superintendent Troughton's brisk and efficient secretary.

'Sorry to startle you, but the gate is better than a guard dog. My husband's not as productive as he used to be at getting around to those little jobs. Must be three years for that one.'

Barton chuckled when he saw her eyes crinkle. Her gaze, warm and appraising behind rimless glasses, met his with confidence. Even without a trace of make-up, her strong bone structure and soft cornflower-blue eyes grabbed attention.

'I like to build myself up to those jobs, too.'

'I'm Mary Thwaite. My husband's waiting out the back.'

Barton introduced himself and Zelensky, and was invited in. The bungalow felt fairly homely if not a little sparse. They followed the lady through a narrow clutter-free hall, to a sparkling kitchen, then into a large conservatory, which took up half of the garden. A man with a bald head covered in liver spots, much older than Mary, was lying back on a recliner, seemingly asleep.

Mary stood beside him.

'Nap number two, I think.'

She pulled over a chair, perched on it, then gently shook Eric's shoulder.

'Wake up! The police are here.'

Eric's eyelids fluttered open, but they were immediately focussed and sharp.

'Morning,' he said, struggling to sit up straight.

'You can stay where you are,' said Barton. 'This isn't quite an informal chat, because we'll be taking a statement, but consider it background for our investigation.'

Eric nodded. His voice was not frail, but surprisingly deep and melodic.

'We heard Rhys's death is being treated as suspicious. He was in top form on Friday evening. Seems strange he died shortly after.'

The officers sat on a solid-looking double rattan seat opposite Eric.

'So, you were both there that night?' asked Barton.

'Yes, yes. They're always great evenings. I tend to watch the action unfold, although it's harder to keep up nowadays. All the little swipes amuse me no end.'

Mary still had her hand on his shoulder. She squeezed it again, but not as gently.

'Come now, Eric. We all get along.'

Zelensky had been taking notes, but her fingers froze. Eric's expression clearly conveyed that he didn't agree.

35

DCI BARTON

Barton smiled at Eric.

'There's some antagonism within the group?'

The elderly man licked his lips, keeping his gaze away from his wife.

'Well, not loads. I'll be honest, life's a bit of a drag when you get to my age. You've got to find joy in the small things. And who hasn't had a falling-out with a friend or two along the way?'

'Do you mind telling me how old you are?' asked Zelensky.

'Eighty-nine. At least, I think that's right. I might have napped through a couple of birthdays.'

Mary patted his shoulder. 'And marvellous for it he is, too.'

Zelensky glanced over at the younger woman, waiting for her to say her age. Mary got the hint.

'I'm sixty-four. Retirement beckons, but Eric's been finished a long time.'

Barton took over so Zelensky could carry on with her notes.

'Which one of you worked for Jones and Singh?'

'Eric did. I'm a librarian at Central Library, and a real book fiend. That's how we met. Eric used to come into town because Stilton doesn't have a library. He loves Peter James and Val McDermid, so I held them behind the counter for him. We got chatting, although I prefer cosy crime. Richard Osman's books are fantastic.'

Barton had enough of police in his day job without reading detective novels, but he knew how popular they were.

'When did you retire from the accountants, Eric?'

'Around twenty-five years ago. We lost a few big accounts, but it was computers that did it for me. That's why I left.'

'Bless him,' said Mary. 'When I was at school, we learned to type, but the boys didn't. It's hard to get to grips with the latest technology once you've hit sixty. I struggled with new android phones at first. Still miss my old Nokias, but they do so much more nowadays. Even make your shopping cheaper with all these apps.'

Barton's ears had pricked up at another reference to twenty-five years ago.

'One of the others mentioned that period being a troubling time for the firm. Vijay's wife dying. Redundancies. The business teetering.'

Eric coughed. 'Not to mention Charlie's accident.'

'Charlie?'

'Charlie McGrath. Another employee. Not that he was missed.'

'Eric!' chastised Mary with what appeared another firm squeeze. 'He was ambitious and driven, that's all.'

Eric looked down, but Barton detected mischief under his bushy eyebrows.

'How did he die?'

'Crashed his car while off his face.'

'Now, Eric, we don't know that's true. It was an open verdict.'

Troubled time indeed, thought Barton. 'Was he an alcoholic?'

Mary vehemently shook her head.

'It might have been due to an issue with some prescription medicine. A mistake, I'm sure.'

Mary nodded firmly, while Eric continued to peer out of the window.

Barton paused while Zelensky caught up. He'd decided to be upfront about the cause of death, but not the substance or the delivery method.

'Any opinions as to why someone would poison Rhys?'

Mary opened her mouth, then shut it. Her eyes shifted to the side. Whether that was to think or prepare a lie, Barton wasn't sure. He suspected Mary liked to see the best in everyone, but she also overshadowed her husband. That could have been down to his age, but Barton reckoned Eric had full control of his faculties.

They had both obviously heard from other members of the club about the police visits.

'Not at all,' said Mary. 'Like Charlie, he was a successful businessman who lived to work. We both thought a lot of him, didn't we, Eric?'

'Of course.'

Eric was far from convincing. Barton asked the next question suspecting Mary was going to dominate.

'Tell me about last Friday night.'

Mary shifted forward in her seat. 'The usual. We meet the first Friday of December for a meal. Lovely, it was. Picked an interesting book, didn't we, Eric?'

'Great choice. Amazon delivered it Wednesday, so I'll get started soon.'

'What was the title?' asked Zelensky.

'*The Slay Before Christmas.*'

'Not a rom-com, then?'

Eric softly whistled. 'We've had a few of those in the past. Time-slip historical twaddle, you name it. We don't mind a bit of variety, though, do we, Mary?'

Barton was struggling to figure out the exact dynamics of the relationship but decided to move on.

'How is the book selected?'

Eric's gaze had sharpened. 'We all put our suggestions in, then we vote. I think this novel was Bernie's idea.'

Barton waited for Zelensky to record that information, then smiled at Eric. 'What did you both have to eat that night?'

Again, Mary cut in. 'Eric had fish and chips. He can't eat steak nowadays. I had the venison. It's nice to try food I don't cook at home.'

'What about dessert?'

'We don't tend to have them, but, without going out much nowadays, we shared a crème brûlée.'

Barton nodded. 'I'm an apple-pie man, or perhaps a big slice of gateau.'

'Your appetite will be bigger than ours.'

Barton didn't detect any malice in Mary's response. She smiled at him, while Eric was gawping out of the window again. Barton turned to his sergeant.

'Anything you want to ask?'

'Perhaps the Thwaites could describe Rhys's mood.'

Barton was surprised when Eric swiftly answered. 'Top form. Like the Rhys we used to know and love.'

Mary's smile faltered. She clasped her hands together. 'We all had a smashing meeting.'

Zelensky tapped away on her laptop, then abruptly glanced up. Barton suspected she was about to bark out a pertinent question, so he kept his eyes on the couple.

'Why move here? It's hardly Stilton.'

Mary's reply was as swift as Eric's had been.

'We wanted a bungalow. They were too expensive in the village. My sister lived here as well, but she's in a home now, with Alzheimer's.'

'Yet you still carried on attending the club meetings?'

'Absolutely. We're part of the team.'

Barton got out of his seat and peered around at his surroundings. Something was bugging him, but he couldn't think what.

'Thanks for talking to us. Can I use your toilet before I go?'

'Of course,' said Mary. 'I'll show you.'

As Barton followed her through the kitchen, he realised what was different in the property. There were no photographs and only one painting. A nondescript view of a farmhouse. He supposed some people preferred a minimalist home. He took a quick wee, even though he didn't really need to go, while realising the discussion he'd just been involved in was similar to the ones with Vijay and Morwen.

They were conversations where some of the truth had been twisted, and what Barton actually wanted to hear was hidden in the silences.

36

DCI BARTON

Zelensky printed off a statement on a small portable printer and had the couple sign at the bottom.

Mary showed them to the door. She bit her bottom lip. 'Should we be worried?'

Barton didn't have a clue. 'I'd be vigilant until we understand what happened to Rhys.'

'How long will that be?'

'Soon. We'll be in touch.'

When they were on their way to Stilton, Barton asked Zelensky what she thought.

Zelensky shrugged before she answered. 'I found it difficult to read either of them, but I reckon we'll later revisit their replies and consider why they didn't mention something obviously important.'

Barton tilted his head in agreement. Zelensky had grown into a competent and industrious sergeant who proactively managed and developed her team, or she had until recently. He guessed she would suspect he had noticed her dip in performance. She'd also understand there was no escape when they were stuck in a car together.

'How are things, Maria?'

She smiled. 'The famous Barton technique, eh? Grill 'em while they're driving.'

'You got it.'

'Is my behaviour so obvious?'

'Only to me. I'm guessing it's to do with Hoffman.'

She nodded.

'You know what? When you said to come with you today, I guessed you'd give me the Spanish Inquisition, but I do want to talk to someone. Your advice is generally sound.'

'Generally?'

Zelensky cracked a smile. When they next reached a junction, she turned to him.

'So, you're really leaving.'

'Well, a sabbatical. I'm probably fooling myself that I'll return, but it's making it easier to let go.'

She pulled away and indicated onto the parkway.

'The job's a big part of you. Won't you miss it?'

'I'll take up word searches. So, what about Hoffman? I heard you'd split up again.'

Barton noticed the vehicle's speed creep up as Zelensky's focus switched to her colleague.

'We've been on and off for over a year, ever since I cheated on Leicester with him.'

'Do you regret that?'

'No, not particularly, which shows what a dung ball I am, but Hoffman and I are like two circling planets, slowly being pulled together by gravity. It feels inevitable.'

'I take it you're hoping for a key-sliding-into-a-lock sort of union as opposed to a black-hole-supernova type of event?'

'Yes, but we're so similar. We can be cold, hard, calculating, and as aggressive and sarcastic as each other, but thoughtful and considerate. I reckon we thrive on being on the edge, which makes the sex brilliant.'

'Sounds tiring.'

'It's a bit like you and Zander.'

Barton gave her a snooty look. 'I'm pretty sure Zander's and my relationship is quite different.' They shared a glance and laughed. Barton couldn't help himself. 'Zander's crap in bed.'

'I meant you spark off each other and enjoy spending time together.'

'That's actually the key to a happy marriage. Perhaps the most important aspect. You need to be able to find pleasure in doing the humdrum. Still have a chuckle while mopping the floor or hoovering.'

'We do, although we often end up getting distracted.'

'I see. It might be hard to believe, but the romance fades. Before you can blink, there'll be a huge pile of his baggy Y-fronts to iron.'

'Do I seem the type to be putting creases in his work shirts?'

Barton chuckled. 'No, probably not, but you might be surprised. It's a bit of an old-fashioned view, but, often, one person in a couple is more inclined towards domestic chores. And to be honest, I'd rather take on tasks like staining a hundred metres of fencing, or changing a puncture in the rain, than spend hours on the ironing. Which means I've often peered through the window, drenched, to see my wife with her feet up watching *EastEnders*, having finished the ironing hours beforehand.'

'Or she's on her fifth load of washing while you're snoozing on the sofa.'

'Swings and roundabouts.'

'I suppose that's true. The problem is if we go public and give it a proper crack, it would be sensible for one of us to move teams.'

'Are you ready to settle down?'

'I think so, or is that wrong? Should I know so?'

'Life often doesn't pan out how you imagine,' replied Barton with emphasis. 'I believe there will be fresh opportunities in the new year.'

Zelensky turned right at the roundabout to Stilton and entered the village.

'I appreciate you telling me that. I've suspected one of the teams might get closed down. Makes sense with ours being understaffed. It'll be the end of an era.'

'And the start of the next. Embrace it.'

Zelensky parked outside Bernie and Beryl Goodman's house. She admired the large executive detached property.

'How do you want to play this?'

'Same as the Thwaites. Let's keep them talking, hopefully cooperating. Perhaps they'll drop the others in it.'

Barton assessed the location. It was middle-class suburbia, but the houses were pretty. The Goodmans lived around the corner from Vijay and one road over from Katarzyna. In fact, even the Joneses' property was just a few minutes' walk away. With the office the same distance away on High Street, none of them needed to drive.

The door wasn't answered on the first knock. A full minute crawled by until a lady in a loose twinset with bouffant grey hair appeared. Carefully applied lipstick, a defiant slash of crimson against the pallor of her skin, couldn't mask the devastation etched into her features. A shaky hand rested on the door frame for support. Her eyes, red-rimmed and swollen, spoke volumes of a pain so profound it had hollowed her out from within.

It was a face that whispered of a tragedy too terrible to bear.

37

DCI BARTON

Barton took a stride forward and held the lady's arm, worried she might fall.

'What's happened?'

The woman steadied herself on the wall, then removed a piece of folded-up toilet paper from her front pocket and dabbed her eyes.

'I'm sorry. It's only a bed, but it's made everything seem so imminent. I'll be all right. I assume you're the police.'

'That's right.'

Barton and Zelensky gave each other a puzzled look, then showed their warrant cards. No doubt, everything would soon become clear.

'I'm Beryl Goodman. Come in, please.'

They entered a large hall with a lovely staircase leading up to a wide landing, then walked through a pair of double doors into a dated kitchen consisting of oak units. Barton felt the heat from a radiator as he strolled past it. After the cool of outside, the shift in temperature almost choked him. He unzipped his coat as she opened a door to the side, which led into the lounge.

Barton paused at the doorway. The polished steel of an adjustable bed gleamed under the lights at the front of the room. Its sturdy modern structure was a stark contrast to the frail person who lay upon it. His form seemed to barely depress the mattress. Yet, despite the obvious frailty, a calm smile played on his lips. His eyes held a hint of his spirit, one determined to hang on. Barton recognised a man who was living a life of quiet defiance against the inevitable.

'That's perfect timing, big guy. Can you push me a touch so I'm not too close to the television?'

'Sure.'

Barton nudged the bed back half a metre, then put the brake on. He had seen plenty of hospital beds brought in for the final stages of a terminal illness while he'd been in uniform. Bernie was clearly the ill one, but, like many others in the same situation, Beryl was suffering, too. The bed arriving was a grim reminder that the end was nigh.

Bernie patted the mattress. 'It's a strange thing when at last it happens.' He smiled over at his wife.

'Stop that, Bernie.'

Barton raised his eyebrows but let the comment pass. 'We have a few questions for you both.'

Bernie clambered off the bed as though he were a hundred, not around sixty. 'You'd better be quick.'

'I said stop it,' cried Beryl, who rushed from the lounge as tears flowed again.

When she'd gone, Bernie sat gingerly in a comfy-looking armchair. 'Please, sit down. I've found humour is the best way to keep me from dwelling on what's approaching, but my wife struggles. She reckons I've changed. More sarcastic, crude, even callow.'

'I'm sorry to hear that. What was the "strange thing" about?'

'It's actually a nice memory I'm ruining. That's a line from our favourite film, which we saw on one of our first dates.'

'Hugh Grant,' blurted out Zelensky. 'He says those words to Fiona at the Scottish castle in *Four Weddings and a Funeral*. It's about finally meeting the person you truly love, even though in Hugh's case she'd just married someone else.'

Zelensky seemed as surprised as Barton by her comment.

'It's one of my favourite films, too. I enjoy a bit of heated passion.' She waggled a finger at him. 'Don't you dare let that fact slip out.'

Barton mimed zipping his mouth shut. He sat on the sofa next to her but paused before he spoke. The elephant in the room was Bernie's illness. It could be important. 'Do you mind telling me what's wrong with you?'

'A blood cancer came back. Spread to my bones and will leach out from there. They told me I'd probably make the summer if I took the medicine, Easter otherwise, but I won't reach either. I couldn't tolerate the chemo again, and it's moving fast. I'm not even sure I'll reach Christmas at this point.'

'You seem to be handling things stoically. It's what I would hope to do.'

The half-smile slipped from Bernie's face. 'There are times when I feel short-changed. Why me? But I've reached sixty-four. We have a lovely, successful son who runs a charming restaurant in Cornwall. Our lives have been full of laughter. I'd have liked grandchildren, but we don't get everything we want, do we?'

Barton shook his head.

Bernie stared into the ornate fireplace and shivered in spite of the temperature.

'Funnily enough, that line from *Four Weddings* applies to the cancer. It's a strange thing when at last it happens. I've often pondered how I might die, but now I'm staring my mortality in the face, I'd rather not know. I try to focus on beauty and nature, and being a tiny part of this vast ecosystem, but it isn't always easy. Even my favourite memories trigger sadness. I have guilt and remorse, comments I wish I hadn't made, and those I wish I had. Mistakes as well but mostly regrets.'

'Even Frank Sinatra had a few of those.'

Bernie gave him a tired smirk.

'Can you guess what my biggest disappointment is?'

'No.'

'Not following my dreams. I hoped to be a songwriter when I was young. Be in a band. I wasn't cool at school, and my parents couldn't afford music lessons, so I put my ambition on hold. Then I fancied being in the police. I've always been interested in crime, and I enjoy puzzles. That kind of challenge. Books are how I've got my fix over the years, but I think what I wanted most for my life was to be remembered. Some days, I believe all I did was spend my career buried in ledgers, and that I've wasted the time.'

Barton had heard similar from other people close to death.

'Your wife and son wouldn't feel that way, nor would your work colleagues and everyone else whose lives you've touched.'

Bernie's focus left the fireplace and found Barton's. He held his gaze. 'Thank you. That's helpful.'

Beryl returned and took a seat in the other armchair, her gaze drifting between the conversation and the hospital bed. The couple confirmed the details about the book-group gathering the previous Friday.

Zelensky had barely said a word until they got to Rhys Jones.

'Did you like and respect your boss?'

Bernie took a moment.

'I suppose so. He's a clever guy. Paid me just enough to stay all those years. Beryl thought I should have earned more, but we've always been comfortable.'

Zelensky scratched her chin before replying.

'You worked at that place a long while, but it remained a small business. There was no chance for advancement.'

Bernie bobbed his head.

'There you have it. I wasn't a risk-taker. I wrote songs all my life and kept them in a volume of books upstairs. Might as well stick them in my casket with me, because I was scared to fail. Like Rhys, I'm a pretty decent bloke, but we're wussies. He never quite recovered from the business almost failing. Sacking poor old Eric Thwaite back then deeply affected him.'

38

DCI BARTON

Barton managed to keep a straight face. He raised his hand slightly to let Zelensky know not to comment, then took a quick moment to consider how to phrase his next question.

'Eric's older than the rest of you, so he'd have been near to retirement back then, anyway. Why was it such a big deal?'

Bernie spoke confidently. 'Eric loved work. He found home life boring, so he was furious when Rhys let him go.'

'Redundancy can be brutal at any age, but it's often worse when you're older.'

'It wasn't only the loss of some important accounts which were his downfall. Eric always blamed computers and recent technology, but he was slow with the paperwork anyway. Rhys should have got rid of him years before that, but the soft sod didn't.'

'Interesting.'

'I'm sure you'll be speaking to Eric.' Bernie rubbed his chin. 'You being here means it must be an intriguing mystery. Are you allowed to tell us how Rhys died?'

'Perhaps poison or he ingested something toxic.'

Bernie's face didn't seem to register the answer, so Barton carried on.

'Were you both all right after the meal?'

Beryl finally contributed. 'Yes, it was a lovely dinner. Bernie and I chose an appetiser, then I had the glazed gammon. Bernie had the Caesar salad with extra chilli flakes. The chemotherapy first time around affected his sense of taste, so he prefers spicy, crunchy food.'

'Dessert?'

'We're always too full. I don't remember anyone having one.'

The Thwaites had said they'd shared a pudding, but he supposed Beryl could have forgotten. She had a lot on her mind. Barton was starting to suspect Rhys had eaten the cake when he got home.

'Not even Rhys?'

'A few of us used to when we were younger and had bigger appetites, but there are always the cupcakes if you fancy something sweet.'

'The Bell sells those, do they?'

Beryl snapped out her reply. 'No, they're supposed to be home-made, but the icing is too professional. Morwen must think we're stupid, bringing them in and lying to us.'

Barton's eyes narrowed, both at the switch in Beryl's temperament and the revelation. She looked away from him, put her hand over her mouth, and again ran from the room. Zelensky rose to follow her.

'No,' said Bernie. 'Leave her be.'

Zelensky sat down. 'It's hard on the partners, too.'

'Yes, sometimes she's terribly sad, but other times she can be incredibly angry.'

39

DCI BARTON

Barton attempted to carry on talking to the couple when Beryl returned a few minutes later, but she was barely present. Bernie's eyelids had drooped, and his replies became monosyllabic.

Zelensky had one final question.

'Can you think of why somebody might want to hurt Rhys?'

Bernie blinked slowly.

'He wasn't the type to inspire strong feelings in anyone. We had a modelling agency a few years back who were furious after we did their annual returns. They were more or less bankrupt. Speak to Katarzyna. The firm was her client. The lady who ran it stormed into Rhys's office, pursued by her partner, and went nuclear. I almost rang the police, but the husband managed to calm her down. They'd spent ridiculous amounts of money on entertainment. She said they needed to be seen around town. Partying, in effect, without enough bookings coming in.'

'Were drugs involved?'

'She might have been on them, the way she behaved, or perhaps she should have been prescribed some.' Bernie smirked at his little joke. 'It's rare to have that kind of response from a client. We deal in numbers. Facts. I suppose some people choose to shoot the messenger.'

Or drug him, thought Barton.

'Okay, we'll leave you. Thanks for talking to us.'

Bernie didn't get out of his seat. He slowly held his hand out. As Barton gently shook it, an unusual look came across the sick man's face.

'Please come back and visit. If I'm honest, I'm enjoying the distraction. Perhaps someone up there is giving me one last bit of excitement.'

Barton's gut twisted with the urge to reprimand him for his flippancy when a man had died, but the morning's relentless contradictory onslaught had left him reeling. Besides, Barton gave people in Bernie's position a lot of latitude, assuming, of course, he wasn't responsible. And hadn't Barton been pleased with a final puzzle to solve?

Outside, Zelensky hauled in the cool air before getting inside their vehicle.

'Is your brain about to explode?'

'Pretty much. We need to visit The Bell now, which could prove a dangerous situation. The smell of well-kept beers, that rich, malty aroma, might be irresistible to us in our weakened states.'

'I bet you had a few liquid lunches back in the day.'

'How dare you? I've always been the consummate professional. Actually, even I missed out on those halcyon days. There were a few officers who liked a pub lunch when I first put on the uniform, but I wasn't one of them. The prospect of chasing down a shoplifter with the remnants of a steak and kidney pudding and a couple of pints of Carling Black Label sloshing around inside me never sounded tempting. If I had that now, I'd be asleep before we reached the A1. You'd have to carry me into the office.'

'No beer or pie for you, then.'

They were soon parked at the back of The Bell, again taking one of the last available slots. Barton received a text from Zander during the drive, informing him that Vijay, Morwen and Katarzyna had already been escorted to Thorpe Wood police station.

Barton led the way into the inn and stopped at the cheese and coffee counter near the door. The waitress smiled at the customer she was serving and gave him his change. She turned to Barton.

'Good morning. What can I get you?'

'Is Helen in?'

'You've found her.'

Barton guessed the woman was in her mid-fifties, but she moved with confident grace, and her manner still held a youthful spark. Her slim figure was accentuated by a black pencil skirt and practical flat shoes. A crisp white blouse completed her attire.

He showed his warrant card.

'We're here to talk to you about last Friday evening.'

'Ah, the police. Yes. Alishia rang me. How can I help you?'

Barton supposed it was fair enough for the manager to have forewarned her, but he'd have preferred to have arrived without her having prepared for his visit.

'Can you tell me about how well you know The Tax Titans' members?'

'I chat with all of them. We're not what I'd describe as close friends, but some of them have been coming here since soon after I got the job, which was when I was still at school. I joke with them, light conversation, that sort of thing. The book club must have been created nearly thirty years ago. I felt a little jealous back then. They appeared to be having a brilliant time together until there was some...'

Barton paused his questions when a customer came to buy some Stilton.

Helen served the woman, then waited until she was out of earshot before she spoke again.

'Sorry about that.'

'No problem. What were you going to say?'

She shouted out to the barman.

'I'm going to be five minutes, Matt.'

'No worries.'

Helen turned back to the officers. 'Come through to the far room. We've got quite a few booked for lunch, but the bigger groups aren't due in just yet.'

Barton and Zelensky wandered after her, taking a right after the bar. There were three tables with reserved signs on. A man in a suit with a coffee was sitting in a seat nearest the fire, but otherwise they had the room to themselves. The biggest reserved table, which was large and round, would fit eight people. Helen pointed at it.

'This is where they were that night. They seemed in decent spirits, although a few of them are getting on a bit now. I didn't hear any arguments. Rhys seemed to be giving a speech at one point, but I don't know what about.'

'Did they have desserts?'

Helen squinted as she tried to remember. 'I can't recall for sure. I think so.

It was busy, but I recall someone asking for two spoons, so I assume they were sharing something. Possibly a crème brûlée.'

'Do you sell cupcakes or other types of cake with icing?'

'Are you referring to layer cakes? Like for birthdays or weddings?'

'Anything cakey.'

'No. We do sticky toffee puddings, sundaes, tarts and the just-mentioned crème brûlées. Most who come for a specific celebration bring their own cake. In fact, the book club does similar. There was a box containing cupcakes, which was theirs, on that wooden shelf all night.'

She pointed at a large hole in the thick brick wall separating the lounge from the bar area.

'What type of container?'

'A white cardboard one. The type you get doughnuts in.'

Barton wondered how to probe without giving the game away.

Zelensky walked over to the gap and peered through into the bar beyond. She raised an eyebrow and gestured towards the exit.

'That was risky. Someone could have run off with them.'

Helen smiled. 'It's not that type of establishment, or village, really. There's some petty crime, but not much.'

Matt appeared at the end of the bar.

'Sorry, Helen, but I need you back. The family of eight have arrived early.'

Zelensky quickly took Helen's contact details.

'Couple of final points,' said Barton. 'Are there any other details you can think of that might help our investigation?'

'Into Rhys being killed?'

'We're not certain of anything at the moment.'

'That's what the gossip is implying.'

Barton still wanted to hear what Helen had been about to comment on before the customer had interrupted her.

'What happened years ago?'

'Look, the club members were a tight bunch. The period when they lost two members was tough for them.' Helen cocked her head to one side. 'A few rumours circulated at the time.'

'What sort of rumours?'

'That Vijay had put his wife out of her misery. There was a strange detail about the car accident as well, but I can't remember what.'

Helen appeared as though she was about to say something else.

'Go on,' urged Barton.

'It was decades ago, and I was never certain, but you know what happens when a large group of young people meet on regular occasions and alcohol is added to the mix.'

'Risque behaviour?' asked Zelensky.

Helen had walked away, but she turned and peered through the gap at them with a mischievous expression on her face.

'Trouble!'

She had reminded Barton of where the cupcakes had been sitting. He supposed they could have been tampered with in situ or arrived containing the drugs, but there was still a final hurdle for the poisoner to target Rhys.

'Helen. Did you see who handed round the cupcakes?'

'I did actually, because Rhys had called me over to give me a tip in cash. It was Morwen.'

40

DCI BARTON

Barton tried to order his thoughts, but he needed to visibly see the interconnections of the people they'd spoken to. A meeting room whiteboard would do the trick.

It seemed Zelensky felt similarly, because she remained quiet and gently shook her head from time to time throughout the journey.

'I want time to study all this intel when we get back, sir. At least if I have the details clear in my mind, I can start to analyse the undercurrents that clearly exist.'

'That's a good idea. I'll take one of the others in to question Katarzyna. We'll take a break to eat after, then I'll convene a meeting where we link these characters together. I reckon something nasty is lurking in the background from years ago. Several incidents might be involved but determining the facts after so much time will be difficult.'

'Because most of them are accountants?'

Barton chuckled, but that was partly the truth.

'In a way, yes. If you asked someone for a stereotypical description of a bean counter, they'd most likely say organised, boring, sensible, clever and diligent.'

'Which means there could be significant planning and a lack of emotion in any decision-making.'

'Right. The hardest kind of killer to investigate.'

'Possibly even ruthlessness and cunning.'

'Perhaps. When you return to the office, instruct Leicester to look into Charlie McGrath's car accident. Get Hoffman to find out what he can about Avani Singh's death. Maybe both incidents were in the newspapers. I can't request an authorisation for her patient records without much stronger suspicions around Vijay.'

'We could ask him for consent.'

'True. Morwen, on the other hand, didn't mention either the cupcakes or the book club meeting. I'd describe her as evasive or perhaps distant, which is understandable in the circumstances, but she knowingly kept vital information from us. I'll check if she'll volunteer her bank and phone records, but I can authorise permission for access otherwise.'

Back in the office, Barton had a quick word with Zander and headed to an interview room with him. He explained why he wanted a chat with Katarzyna before the team meeting.

Zander fiddled with his watch while he thought. 'Sounds as if we have another complex investigation on our hands where the facts and what we're told don't align, but I do have some decent news for you. I'm pretty sure I know who the Arctic fox is.'

Barton scowled for a moment. 'Ah, you mean the drug dealer?'

'Yep. It came to me about thirty minutes ago. I'm certain you and I arrested this particular fox once, for his involvement in a pub fight, back when we were in uniform, but you'd joined Major Crimes by the time he went up in the world. His dad was a thief who dabbled in dealing. Mostly insignificant amounts to fund his own habit, but the son got involved with a serious operation. He didn't have particularly sharp teeth, just surprisingly gappy teeth.'

Barton attempted to drag the faces of the thousands of villains he'd met over the decades through his mind, but nobody appeared.

'Still not ringing any bells.'

'Okay, that's not surprising. He disappeared for years to Spain and immersed himself in gangland violence, which was rampant at the time.'

Barton recalled the period. 'That spell when the Spanish had trouble shutting down the bulk transportation of heroin and cocaine?'

'Yes, it got vicious. Lots of deaths, even car bombs. He then returned to Peterborough, where I nicked him for possession, but I couldn't ever get intent to supply.'

'So, he's dangerous, but not an idiot.'

'Still a little daft. Being richer from his spell in Puerto Banús, his signature piece of clothing was a shearling.'

'Is that something to do with sheep?'

'Yes. They're luxurious coats, crafted from soft sheepskin with a fleece interior. Warm and stylish and they also have a large, thick furry collar.'

'Sounds like a woman's coat.'

'I could carry it off, but you'd resemble a half-shaven polar bear.'

'Thanks.'

'No problem. Anyway, he vanished, assumed moved to London. I happened to spot him on the news years later. It was the coat I recognised. The numpty had turned up for his court case in it, looking exactly like a drug dealer.'

'Maybe it was his lucky jacket.'

'Wasn't fortunate for him because he was sentenced to twelve years for manslaughter.'

Barton tutted.

'Let me guess, he was recently released.'

'Yep. Six months ago.'

'Even though you never got him for selling drugs, were you sure he was?'

'Various addicts pointed the finger at him, but I think he had realised there was more money through being a muscle for hire. The guy could be vicious. I'd say he enjoyed it.'

Barton had been frowning as he searched his memory banks, but finally, his face relaxed. 'That does register. Was he short? Not much over five feet, but muscular. Mark Kirby.'

Zander theatrically clapped his hands together. 'Nice to see you have some functioning grey matter remaining. It's actually Mark Kilby. He later got on the steroids big time, which possibly made him more volatile than he already was. He went down because a guy he fought with died from stab wounds. I assume Kilby pleaded self-defence, but clearly the jury didn't completely believe him. I suppose at least he escaped a murder charge.'

'Well done. Let's track him down.'

'Malik's on it.'

Katarzyna was brought down to the interview room and took a seat. She wore a tailored dove-grey suit, the lines clean and classic. Her make-up was subtle, emphasizing her green eyes. A single strand of pearls added quiet elegance.

She extended a hand across the table, shaking both of theirs in turn.

Barton noted the cool, calm confidence in her touch.

'Thanks for voluntarily coming in.'

'Did I really have much choice?'

Zander gave her one of his most charming smiles. 'You have the right to legal representation if you think you want it, but it shouldn't be necessary since you're only assisting us in forming a picture. It's easier to do it here where we can record our conversation.'

'Easier for you.'

Zander nodded. 'For both of us. Your answers can't be misrepresented. Rhys seems to have been poisoned, so we need to check every aspect of his life until we find the person or persons responsible.'

'You'd like me to tittle-tattle on my friends.'

Zander's eyebrows rose briefly, signalling that he clearly expected her to be more submissive. 'We're after background details.'

Barton leaned forward. 'You must want to help.'

'I do, but I read too many crime novels to trust the police implicitly. What is it you wish to know? Did I do it?'

'A confession would shorten my day,' replied Barton.

'Sadly, no can do. Rhys and I weren't close out of work. His office interactions were always polite and efficient, strictly business and little more. The book club was a rare occasion where he still let his hair down. He was more fun when the company was in the early stages. It was exciting. The accountancy field seemed ripe for conquest until our world came crashing down.'

Barton felt the atmosphere shift in the room.

'Yes. I'm sorry to hear about your husband's car accident. What with the loss of the big accounts and Avani's cancer, it must have been a tough period, especially for you and Vijay.'

'Well, it's said the most devastating thing you can ever do in life is bury your child, so I would say Eric and Mary had the worst of it.'

Barton tried to stop his eyebrows from hitting the ceiling but failed. The Thwaites had definitely not mentioned that. He thought back to Eric and Mary's house. The quiet. The blank walls. Their interactions. Their energy.

Katarzyna's focus had remained on him.

'Seems like there's a lot you don't know. With that in mind, I will speak to a solicitor.'

41

DCI BARTON

Barton paused the interview and rang the custody desk. When an officer arrived to introduce Katarzyna to the duty solicitor, Barton and Zander left and marched back to the office to gather the team for a meeting. After a detailed conversation where everyone got up to speed, Malik offered a concise and helpful summary.

'That's an unlucky book club.'

'Yes,' replied Barton. 'A BASE jumping society would probably be safer. We can only guess that something untoward occurred years ago, but it's fair to say Rhys was murdered. Hopefully Katarzyna will give us more after she's spoken to the duty. My hunch is her asking to speak to one is an act of caution rather than an admission of guilt, but she's sharp and calm, and another person not to underestimate.'

Malik had an intent expression on his face. 'This is intriguing. The club members seem to love crime novels, so they'll be aware of police procedure, interviews, investigations, and to a certain degree what we're thinking. Which begs the question, if any one of them were involved, wouldn't they worry we'd solve it sooner or later?'

'What are you saying?'

'We usually come out on top, so would Morwen poison her own husband with her own cupcake?'

'Not unless she believed she could shift the blame elsewhere.' Barton peered around the room and found a sea of puzzled faces. 'Right. Let's sum up with what we have.'

Barton grabbed a pen and moved to the whiteboard. He drew a circle and wrote Rhys in the middle, then the other members of the club's names in spokes coming off it. To the left of that, he made a list comprising the angry business couple with the modelling business, Mark Kilby, and the waitress, Helen.

'Okay. These people on the left I don't like for it. Helen seems highly unlikely even though she was present, and how would the other two administer the heroin?'

Malik was the first to reply. 'Couldn't any of the three have sneaked over to the wooden shelf and perhaps injected the cupcake?'

'They could, but it doesn't seem probable.'

Zander ran his hand over his bald head. 'I'm not sure anyone on that board is likely to be a killer at this point.'

Barton, whose own brow was furrowing like a ploughed field, surveyed the faces of his team. Minton avoided his gaze, fiddling with a pen, while Leicester's usually sharp eyes were clouded with confusion. Even the normally boisterous Hoffman had lost his spark.

Barton pointed his marker at the names of Bernie and Beryl.

'Let's start with these two. The only angles I can see for their involvement is if Bernie, who is coming to the final few months of his life, decided to hit back at Rhys for a transgression in the past. He seemed engaged with the mystery and the shock around Rhys's passing, and possibly the excitement.'

Hoffman sat up straighter. 'Perhaps he did it for the distraction. You said he regrets his career as an accountant.'

'That's putting it a little strong, but he certainly had dreams he didn't pursue.'

'Do cancer meds send you crazy?' asked Hoffman.

Barton shrugged. 'I don't think so. They're often incredibly debilitating, but Bernie implied he wasn't taking any of his medication. Saying that, I had the feeling he wouldn't want to put his wife through more trauma, and where would he have purchased the drugs?'

Minton stopped looking at the table. 'It's not too hard to guess where narcotics can be purchased in Peterborough. Millfield and various places in the Ortons. Any of the homeless or street beggars in the centre would probably know how to acquire them. Users themselves would have no qualms sorting out a deal for a kickback.'

Malik shook his head. 'Those types would be more likely to take the money and disappear.'

Barton played a trick he'd learned over the years. 'Who's to say they got the drugs recently? If it's to do with the book group, someone might have had a long time to harbour a grudge and get their hands on some.'

Leicester fell for the bait. 'No, that doesn't fit. This rogue batch is new. The overdoses occurred in the last week, so it has to be a recent purchase. If whoever sold the heroin talks, then we can follow the trail.'

Barton focussed on Parveen. He knew the answer but wanted her to engage as the others were beginning to.

'Considering your experience in the drug unit, do dealers fold when they're caught?'

'No, generally not. Especially if someone's died. They sometimes admit their guilt if we capture them red-handed possessing the controlled substance, as well as hard evidence of them supplying it, such as scales and baggies. That's because the third off for a guilty plea is meaningful when the sentence for class A distribution is so substantial.'

Barton realised Parveen's way of talking meant he would need to concentrate every time she spoke, in the way he often did with Mortis.

'Malik. Did you make any progress with the whereabouts of Kilby?'

'The system says he was released on licence to an approved premises over six months ago, which means he will have moved on from there. He'll still be under Probation, who should know his latest address, but I couldn't get through to anyone when I called.'

Seeing as Malik was the most engaged, Barton wanted him to do Katarzyna's follow-up interview with him, so he gave out the other tasks.

'Minton and Parveen, I'm going to leave the Kilby angle up to you. Chase that guy down. I want him found by this evening. Having a description of him will help when you speak to the overdose survivor later. I'm guessing the dealer responsible will have vanished. It's been a week now, so his customers would normally have needed to score again. If he returned to sell more, he'd have heard about any deaths because they'd be public knowledge in their community.'

Barton smiled at them as the women bobbed their heads. He then drew a line under Vijay's name on the board.

'Zander and Leicester. Interview Vijay. Might be the time for the gloves to come off with him, depending on how helpful he is. With Rhys gone, he becomes the controlling partner in the firm, with Morwen the only other shareholder. He wanted to expand the business, but Rhys wasn't interested. There's conflict, and he appears to be holding a candle for Morwen, even if nothing's going on.'

Leicester had a pained expression on his face. 'Are you thinking he scores some heroin and slips it into a cupcake at the pub?'

Barton held his hands out. 'Someone tampered with that cupcake. You might as well ask him about the cakes, because Morwen is next for interview.'

Barton underlined her name.

'We need to ask her everything about those cakes. It seems a few of the members regularly communicate with each other, which is natural if you consider what's gone on, so their mobile records will show texts and calls between them. Zelensky and Hoffman, she's yours.'

'We've had a chance to check Morwen's security footage,' said Zander. 'Nobody broke in.'

Barton nodded, then circled Katarzyna.

'Malik and I will grill this lady. Her husband died in a car accident. I've got a feeling that won't be something as simple as him hitting a lorry. Of the rest, that only leaves the Thwaites. He's old, but not doddery. I detected a shrewdness about him, despite his domineering wife.'

Zander rose from the table to get everyone's attention.

'Eric implied his retirement was due to him being unable to cope with changes in technology, but it appears Rhys sacked him when the business was struggling because he wasn't great at his job. Not only that, but we hear the Thwaites' only child died around that time. That's two facts they kept from us, and there's another detail you should contemplate. Nobody has been completely upfront. We could be looking for a couple, or more than one person working in tandem. We'll meet here at five o'clock to discuss the progress we've made.'

Barton had a final comment to roust the troops.

'Let's energise ourselves. Consider this. I've done this job for many a year, and I can't think of an investigation where I've been so confounded by the people involved. But we do what we always do. Whittle away at alibis. Uncover backgrounds. Wait for mistakes. I want the best from you, because if this is to be my last case, I don't want to go out on a failure.'

Some of Barton's team departed with determined faces, but others left scratching their heads.

42
DCI BARTON

Barton took Malik to prepare in the interview room for when Katarzyna had finished talking to her appointed solicitor. They discussed their approach, with Malik taking the lead, but concluded the direction would depend on what she said. The phone rang to inform them Katarzyna would be there in five minutes.

Malik put his pen down. 'I'm sorry to hear you're leaving again, sir. You've been a...'

'Father? Monster? Inspiration?'

Malik chuckled. 'All the above.'

Barton laughed. 'Cheers.'

'I guess a mentor would be the most suitable label. I'd been an officer eight years when I joined your team but still felt like an impostor as a detective until I'd worked under you for twelve months. There was no drama. We simply got on with the job.'

'Do you plan to stay in Major Crimes even without my guiding light?'

'For the time being. I'm confident I could contribute to any department now. But what matters is the role makes me feel like I'm having a real impact. Major Crimes has been the making of me. And you've played a large part in that.'

'What a lovely thing to tell me. Nicer than anything Zander has said.'

'I suspect he feels the same way.' Malik's voice dropped to a whisper. 'I am struggling, though.'

Barton shifted in his seat to stare at the younger man. 'Babies!'

Despite the heavy bags under Malik's eyes, a weary grin tugged at the corners of his mouth.

'My God, I'm so tired.'

'Ah,' said Barton. 'I heard you have your third bun almost out of the oven, so to speak.'

'Yes. Please say it gets easier.'

'You know, I pleaded with my mother using those same words when my kids were young. Life does get easier, but don't wish any of it away. You'll look back and realise it was the best of times. That's assuming you survive.'

Barton felt a pang of melancholy as a memory surfaced of racing home, utterly exhausted, but excited to read to his third child.

The door opened and Katarzyna walked in with her solicitor. They both appeared relaxed. Barton waited for them to sit.

'Afternoon, Katarzyna. Or do you prefer Kasia?'

'My friends call me Kasia. You can use whichever you like because neither name killed Rhys.'

'Good to hear.'

Malik cautioned the woman and explained the interview was being recorded. As agreed, he began.

'Do you mind me asking why you took counsel, Kasia?'

'There's a natural caution with the authorities for my people. I'm old enough to remember communism.'

'How long have you been in the UK?'

'Forty years.'

'Feel British?'

'My heart is in Poland, but I'm so happy in Stilton and have been since I moved there.'

Barton slipped in a blade to bring her back to the challenging time the firm and its employees had.

'Even twenty-five years ago?'

He was sufficiently close to see Kasia's pupils dilate.

'I would say content for twenty-four years. My husband's death was quite a shock.'

Barton knew some people coped with bereavement swiftly, others never got over it.

'Did you move on after a year?'

Katarzyna pouted for a moment. 'That question is the reason I wanted advice. There are gossips and, I suspect, even bad actors in our book club.'

She had Barton's attention. Eric had implied antagonism, but this was the first evidence they'd heard of proper disquiet amongst the members. He considered why she was being honest and quickly understood.

'I think you realise the seriousness of what's happened, which I suspect some of the others don't. Rhys may not be the only one of your group who gets harmed. You also understand if you fail to tell us something, the culprit might spread misinformation, leaving you exposed and looking guilty.'

'Exactly.'

Malik was confident enough to ask, 'What do you mean by bad actor?'

The solicitor answered. 'It essentially means someone who behaves poorly or unethically.'

Malik steepled his fingers. 'Who are these wrongdoers?'

Katarzyna stared at the ceiling for a few seconds. 'I'm not sure. Rumours and gossip flow between the members of the book club. Who exactly is adding fuel or taking it away? I have no idea.'

'You and Morwen must be good friends.'

'We're close enough.'

Barton could tell again that what was not being said would be important. 'Keep your friends close?' he asked.

'We get on well. I have the perfect work-life balance at the moment. Hopefully she'll just leave it to me and Vijay to run the place.'

Barton nodded as a new pairing was introduced. Perhaps they had plans to take over the business.

'Tell me about the Thwaites' child.'

'I only met Walter on a few occasions but could see he was a little different. Lack of eye contact, shifty, nothing to say.'

'Sounds like he might have been neurodivergent.'

'I thought he was a criminal, wondering what was worth nicking.'

Barton guessed they were about to listen to a sad tale. 'What happened?'

'Two years after my husband and Avani died, Walter walked into the lake opposite the gift shop at Ferry Meadows. Someone had observed him, suspecting he had gone for a late swim, but Walter kept walking until he was under the water. They called 999, but...'

'I assume Mary and Eric suffered afterwards.'

'Oh, yes. Not long beforehand, Mary had finally told him to move out. He'd been stealing from them. They both felt such guilt over that.'

'Would she blame anyone else for him taking his own life?'

Katarzyna barked a short laugh. 'Heaven, no. She was happy to leave the village, because he'd stolen everything that hadn't been nailed down.'

Malik probed further. 'Are you saying they wouldn't have been angry with Rhys for dismissing Eric and forcing them to live somewhere more affordable?'

'The only person who blamed Rhys was Rhys. Eric knew he wasn't great at his job. He accepted he couldn't cope with the change of pace. It's just that Eric enjoyed the office banter so much. I got on well with him, and Avani, Bernie and he had a strong connection. You know how sometimes quiet people tickle each other. Bernie and Avani used to make each other snigger, which set Eric off. I missed their laughter longer than I missed my husband.'

Barton made a mental note of that.

'How did Charlie die?' asked Malik.

'Drink driving. A little over the limit. Sleeping pills involved.'

Malik hesitated, clearly struggling how to phrase his next question. Barton took over.

'Were you close?'

'Did I love him? Yes, but he was a complicated man. I got a big payout from his company's death in service, and the life assurance cleared the mortgage on our property. Perhaps that lessened death's sting. I've had no money worries since, neither have our children.'

'Where are they?'

'Both in Cambridge. Doing well. They don't return much, but that's mostly because I love going there to visit them. We're a tightly knit family.'

Barton got to the crux of the matter. 'Who might want to hurt Rhys?'

'Vijay has the most to gain. Maybe he has form for knocking off Avani.'

Katarzyna didn't pause for thought.

'Sorry?'

'Ignore me. There were rumours she died quickly at the end and perhaps he was responsible, but he's never had any balls. I suppose it's possible he grew a spine and took out Rhys.'

Barton couldn't help frowning. 'What does that mean?'

'He and Morwen always enjoyed each other's company. Often sat next to each other. Flirted.'

'Do you think they were having an affair?'

'That's the opposite of what I'm saying. He wouldn't have dared. Vijay was scared of Rhys.'

'Frightened?'

'Not of violence. Scared by his intelligence. Rhys was the genius. Both at business and accountancy. Don't get me wrong. We're all clever people, but Rhys was the man. Vijay probably won't admit it, but I reckon he hated that.'

Barton let the comment hang in the air before asking his final question. 'Who else might want Rhys dead?'

Katarzyna's breathing slowed as she pondered, then shook her head. 'Nobody.'

43

DI ZANDER

DI Zander had stayed in the office with the others until Barton finished with Katarzyna, then was told what the big guy had uncovered. The most salient point being there was disharmony amongst the book club members.

Zander took Leicester down to an interview room and waited for Vijay to be brought in. The accountant had at least come to the station when asked.

Leicester made sure everything was ready to record, then perched in the seat next to his inspector.

'It's been a while since you did one of these, sir.'

Zander smiled. 'I don't need to when I've so expertly trained my team to do them.'

'Ooh, splendid answer.'

'No, I'm serious. You're not the finished article, but there's huge potential. It might be an idea to gain experience elsewhere to develop your career.'

'Trying to get rid of me?'

'You can all see what's happening. We're under-manned. Another team's DI is leaving. Zelensky and Hoffman need to be on different teams.'

'Are you saying I can go where I like now because you'd probably be losing me anyway? If you weren't, you wouldn't have mentioned it.'

'Pretty much.' He shook his head slightly to confirm he was joking. 'Barton's meeting earlier took me right back to when he was first promoted to inspector, and I became his sergeant. Crazy how time flies.'

Leicester nodded. 'I suppose, but think how these accountants feel. They're all approaching retirement. Three of them never got to enjoy theirs, and another is in the same boat.'

'Getting older can be scary. When you're in your teens and twenties, you barely consider death, then the thirties come along and parents start to die. From your mid-forties, people your own age develop cancer, then men you've worked with are dropping dead in the street or on the golf course at fifty.'

'Maybe Eric or Bernie have realised time's running out, and they had to strike now, before it's too late.'

'Perhaps they left it too long, but their partners are taking revenge for however they feel they've been wronged instead.'

'Beryl and Mary, eh? The masked avengers.'

Zander raised his eyebrows. 'Maybe, but my money's on Vijay.'

Leicester didn't look so sure. 'It's interesting they're turning on each other.'

'Yeah, they'll be wondering who might be responsible. I suppose it's possible more than one person is involved.'

'A conspiracy?'

'Yeah.'

'Shall I start the interview with unsettling him?'

'Go for it.'

Zander did the preliminaries with Vijay, who he had to admit appeared calm and confident. He wore an uncrumpled black three-piece suit. Zander knew Leicester, with his fresh face and ginger hair, was often underestimated, but he possessed a talent for throwing people off balance.

Leicester began in that vein.

'We've heard from the other members of your book club that some of you don't get on.'

Vijay's hands flinched open as if he'd touched an electric fence.

'Who said so?'

'I can't divulge that. They told me in utmost confidence. It was interesting, though, and surprising. Tell me, will you miss Bernie? It seems he doesn't have long.'

Vijay's eyes shifted from side to side. He seemed disarmed by how the questions had been phrased.

'Yeah, I like Bernie. He had a few run-ins with Rhys about pay and hours, but that's it. His wife's pretty unstable. Crazy cow came in ranting and raging that Rhys was taking advantage of Bernie's better nature.'

'You and Rhys are equal partners. Why didn't she complain to you?'

'Even though that's true, somehow Bernie, Eric and Kasia knew about the golden share, so he was considered the senior partner. I'm not sure who told everyone. Probably Rhys.'

'Wasn't that annoying?'

Zander had noticed that Vijay's gaze tended to wander as he concentrated. He was clearly trying to be careful.

'Sometimes. Although not when that psycho came in, shouting and ranting. I used to hide in my office, chuckling to myself. Rhys was like me, you see. He hated confrontation. Poor Bernie was the same. A peaceful type.'

'How about Katarzyna and Charlie McGrath?'

'Kasia and I function well together. She has clear boundaries at work. I respect them.'

Zander cleared his throat. 'What do you mean, boundaries?'

Vijay answered swiftly, but his face had flushed. Maybe he'd tried it on with her, but wouldn't she have mentioned that to Barton?

'She works her hours. No more, no less. Brings in a lot of business and keeps our receptionist in check.'

Leicester resumed his questioning.

'Charlie's death must have been a shock.'

Vijay shrugged. 'More a relief for her. He was a player. A ladies' man. Dalliances all over. I never put him down for a pill popper, though. Shows you never really know someone. Perhaps all his affairs stressed him out.'

Leicester took his time making notes on his pad, which Vijay's eyes strained to read. Zander simply watched the man, leaving him to simmer in the silence. It wasn't warm in the room, but Vijay had begun to fiddle with his collar.

'How about the Thwaites?' asked Leicester. 'So sad when a child dies.'

'Don't think me heartless, but he was a troubled kid. They did everything for him. Booked psychologists, and he wouldn't show, or ignored them for the hour. It was the main reason why they moved, in the hope of getting him away from his friends and other bad influences here. Eric couldn't cope with the demands of the job by then, anyway, but they both worked so hard together for Walter. Eric was particularly cut up afterwards. Walter had been gone eight months when I next saw him at our book club meet, and he was still in pieces.'

Leicester's expression suggested that eight months after losing a child was no time at all, but he continued with his line of questioning.

'Whose idea was it to change the monthly meetings to once a year?'

'I'm not sure. Morwen suggested a break after Charlie died so soon after Avani. Nobody ever mentioned changing it back.'

'Do you like Morwen?'

Vijay's reply was too quick and sounded prepared. 'Morwen's a lovely person. We're not close, but we understand each other.'

'Will you be working closely together now Rhys has gone?'

'That's what I was referring to. I reckon she'll take a back seat. Be a silent partner.'

Leicester looked across at Zander, who'd been waiting with his own bombs to unsettle their interviewee.

Zander nodded supportively at Vijay.

'Can we see your phone and bank accounts? To rule you out as a suspect in Rhys's death?'

Vijay's eyes rattled around the room like a ball in a squash game.

'Yes, of course.'

'Thank you. Morwen's an incredibly attractive woman. I was just thinking you're both single now.'

Vijay barked out a brittle laugh.

'Too complicated. I get the impression she likes me, but she's not my type.'

Zander let Vijay stew for a few seconds.

'I'd have thought she's everyone's type.'

'Not me. I prefer the quiet ones. Cerebral. Scholarly even.'

The interview ended with Vijay attempting, and failing, to show them a convincing smile.

44

DS ZELENSKY

Zelensky and Hoffman entered the interview room together. He gave her a certain look as the door closed behind them, one she knew well, letting her realise without a shadow of doubt she would ask for different teams next year, whether they were together or not. The relationship had become a distraction.

Morwen arrived and dropped into a seat. She stared at them blankly while she was cautioned and offered legal advice.

'Just get on with it.'

Zelensky took the lead. 'I'm sorry for your loss.'

Morwen tossed her hair. 'Why am I here? I volunteered to attend, but when I became annoyed with waiting and tried to leave, they said I shouldn't.'

'I do have some positive news. You can return to your house.'

'Whoopy-do. Let me guess, nothing incriminating was found.'

'That's right.' Zelensky decided to shift focus. 'It was kind of Katarzyna to allow you to stay.'

'Yes, although she's probably trying to keep me sweet, with Rhys's share of the business becoming mine.'

Zelensky offered a conspiratorial smile, then nailed Morwen with the million-dollar statement.

'She'd have been smarter buttering up Vijay, with Rhys's golden share passing to him.'

Morwen's eyes glittered. 'What are you on about?'

Zelensky explained, which led to seconds of silence stretching out. Hoffman twiddled his thumbs while Morwen imitated a fish out of water.

She eventually managed to speak. 'I didn't know that.'

'Does it put you in a precarious position?'

Morwen's voice quietened as her brash attitude deserted her. 'I'm not sure what it means, but I would want to sell the firm. Maybe Vijay will buy me out.'

Hoffman took over to further disorientate their suspect. 'It's sad about Bernie.'

'Yes, I like him. They're a nice couple.'

'I heard Beryl could be difficult.'

'No, not particularly. She spoke her mind. Once, after Bernie's diagnosis, she charged into the office, all upset, because Bernie was still at his desk when he was clearly unwell.'

'What happened?'

'Well, nothing much. Rhys said he'd told Bernie to go home whenever he liked, if he felt rough. Beryl seemed to think Bernie should be off work completely with his condition, but Bernie had run out of sick pay, and he had accounts that needed working on. Rhys could get a locum to come in, but he couldn't afford the salary of both.'

'How did she take that?'

'She called him a miser, but she rang to apologise the same evening. I answered the phone.'

'It's tough that the members of your club have been through a lot of turmoil.'

Morwen stared daggers at Hoffman. 'What are you getting at?'

'Walter and Charlie dying.'

'Ancient history. Yes, Walter's death was sad, but he was a drunkard, staring through people's windows. Staggering through the streets, pie eyed. Stilton's a small place. Everybody knew him. It was difficult for Eric and Mary, though, who are a pleasant couple. Rhys was fond of them, too. He was wracked with guilt about dismissing Eric, but she was probably relieved to move away and be out of sight of everyone's judgement. Charlie, on the other hand, will be polishing the devil's horns as we speak.'

Hoffman's eyebrows rose. 'You didn't like him?'

'I'm not saying that, but he was an overbearing lech. What sort of idiot tries to have an affair with the boss's wife?'

'I take it you declined in no uncertain terms.'

'I punched him on the nose, made it bleed.'

Hoffman chuckled. 'Why have him in the group if he was such a scumbag?'

'He was Kasia's partner, so he came with her. If he wasn't being randy, he could be funny. I'd even admit to him being bright and interesting. Like and dislike often walk a fine line. He'd been around a bit, the world, that is, as well as every girl in town.'

'Was Kasia aware?'

'Aren't we women the last to know? I'd put money on him having tried it on with Mary and Avani. Not to mention all the barmaids whenever we went out. Kasia thought his chatty behaviour was just who he was, but I always sensed a darkness to him.'

Zelensky wanted to know more about that. 'Dark in what way?'

'Some people want something until the moment they have it. He was one of them. I never got a handle on his relationship with Kasia, but they were partners for a long time. I reckon Charlie had been up to no good for years. The reason I suspect that is because of how confidently she moved on after he died.'

Morwen had regained her cool after the golden share bombshell. A smile here, a smile there. A tilt of her head. A tongue popping out. In fact, she was now staring at Hoffman in a way he appeared to be struggling to pull away from, as though she'd caught him in the spider's web of her beauty.

Even Zelensky was drawn to her, but she was too life-hardened to be influenced. She seized the initiative.

'Do you think the others weakened where you didn't?'

'Some did, sure.'

'Which ones?'

'Who knows?'

Zelensky suspected Morwen did.

'Do most of you in the club get on?'

'Yes, although, as far as I was concerned, Avani was the best of us. Nothing was the same after she died. I got the chance to say goodbye, but only because I was going on holiday.'

Hoffman frowned. 'Can you explain what you mean?'

'Avani wished to bid farewell to those closest to her before she reached the dosed-to-the-hilt stage on morphine. I had two weeks in Rhodes coming up, so she asked to see us all on the day before I flew out. Mary had been before I arrived. Beryl was the final person to visit her. She died not long after she left. Perhaps she'd done everything she wanted and slipped away.'

'That must have been a tough time.'

'It was,' replied Morwen without emotion.

'Tell me about your dealings with the Thwaites, please,' said Zelensky.

'Mary is lovely but having a son like that took a toll on her mental health. I had little in common with Eric due to the age difference, but he seems a pleasant guy.'

With the answers flowing now, Zelensky could tell Morwen was beginning to relax. She had one last biting question to rattle her.

'I suppose there could still be a fairy-tale ending.'

'What do you mean?'

'You and Vijay each own half the business, and you're both single.'

The look that swept across Morwen's face was there and gone so swiftly, Zelensky couldn't be certain if it was anger or revulsion, but it was definitely one or the other.

Morwen rested both hands on the table.

'I find Vijay oily. Over-friendly. He treated my friend, Avani, like shit. She was his pretty little dolly, but he liked her on a shelf, not in his life. He'll make out she was his princess, but that's rubbish. He was bored with her.'

'Was it you he wanted?'

Morwen steepled her fingers and took a few seconds to answer. 'I don't know. He never stepped over the line like Charlie did. Never bumped into me by mistake. No kisses on cheeks that went too close to the mouth. You're aware of how some men can be. Perhaps he didn't dare try it on, with my husband being his business partner. Makes sense now, with Rhys having the golden share.'

'Which is now his.'

Morwen tipped her head in agreement.

Hoffman had been waiting for his strike.

'I was told Avani died quickly. Might Vijay have finished her off?'

Morwen's expression didn't change. 'I don't think he'd have been paying her enough attention to notice or care. As I said, she adored him. I doubt it was the disease that made her fade so fast, it was her broken heart.'

Zelensky had to admire Morwen's strength of character. 'Thanks for coming in. The last question we have is, can we have permission to check your bank and phone records? They help rule people out.'

Morwen got out of her seat. She walked to the door and tapped her foot on the floor. 'Look at whatever the hell you like. You won't discover anything that incriminates me, because there's nothing to find.'

45

DCI BARTON

The team gathered at five o'clock. First, they discussed the day's interviews. Barton rubbed his temples afterwards as he tried to draw some conclusions from all the conflicting statements. Who was telling the truth, and who was lying? But perhaps more importantly, why were there such wide discrepancies between the stories?

Some of the details given seemed deliberately vague, meaning they would be hard to confirm or deny, even if the people involved were still alive, or not dying soon. Barton stared at the whiteboard, covered in circled names, arrows and hastily scribbled notes, searching for a pattern, a clue, anything that could give them clarity.

He dropped into his seat with a good-natured groan.

'Who'd like to start?'

That at least got a laugh from everyone. Barton had been on a CID team early on in his career where complicated investigations caused disillusionment, uninterest, or indifference.

Malik, however, was almost licking his lips.

'Now, this is juicy. Crimes committed years ago might be the key to this. Not the boy, Walter, but he's still worth looking into. Pub flirtations combined with alcohol can initiate affairs, and people remember events differently depending on how they felt they were treated. Both Vijay and Morwen slag

Charlie off, but Kasia is less critical. It's possible she did that deliberately to not draw attention to herself.'

'Is there a needle in that haystack?' asked Barton.

'Perhaps. It's possible Kasia reacted impulsively when she discovered another affair and put the sleeping pills in Charlie's food or drink, thereby causing the crash.'

Leicester frowned. 'I'm not so sure, but there are definitely undertones filtering throughout the group. It was mentioned that Bernie and Avani were close, and Beryl made an angry appearance at the office. Did that stem from a suspicion of something going on between them?'

'Yet Morwen downplayed Beryl's behaviour,' said Zander, scratching his head.

'No,' replied Hoffman. 'Beryl's fury was to do with Bernie being at work when he was ill. Avani had been dead for years by then. The issue is, we don't possess any robust evidence against any of them. Even if Kasia had spiked Charlie's food, there were no guarantees he would crash his car and kill himself. He might just have nodded off in the car park.'

'Succinctly put,' said Barton. 'But neither would anyone have been confident Rhys would die from the heroin.' He waited a few seconds for added impact. 'Luckily, we have the weekend to focus on all of this.'

The grumbles were few.

'I'm doing end-of-year stuff, so I'll be in the office both days,' said Zander.

'Well, I'll be at home,' said Barton to some friendly grousing. 'I'll come to why in a minute. Right. Tell me what needs doing.'

Parveen wasn't present, which surprised Barton. Caroline explained.

'Parveen called the hospital to confirm we were still okay to head in. The victim's blood pressure spiked today, and they didn't know why, so they said to wait until tomorrow afternoon. She's gone back to Huntingdon to liaise with her team.'

Hoffman raised a hand. 'We should check what the drug unit is doing, so there's no crossover, then divvy up the jobs between us.'

'What are those tasks, Leicester?' asked Barton.

'Seems too many to list.' He waited for the chuckles to die down. 'We need to study the death certs and coroner's reports for Avani, Charlie and Walter.'

'If someone had called me Walter,' stated Hoffman, 'then I'd—'

'Don't say it,' interrupted Barton. 'Carry on from what Leicester was saying.'

'Okay. We've still got CCTV and ANPR to search, in the city where the homeless hang around, and on the main roads to and from Stilton, especially now we have a description of Mark Kilby. That includes council cameras, private residences and businesses. How about looking at people's laptops and their actual phones instead of only their records?'

Zander shook his head.

'We don't have sufficient intel to warrant that as yet. We've all learnt people are happier with us analysing their bank accounts than checking out their browser history. Hopefully, we'll gather enough evidence to get warrants for those items or to search the houses we haven't been to. CSI found nothing suspicious at Morwen's property. There wasn't even a trace of heroin in the house, but there were cake crumbs found in the car, which makes me suspect that that's where he ate it.'

Barton nodded as Zander confirmed what he'd suspected.

'Were drugs found in the crumbs?' asked Barton.

'No, but it is the same cake. Pieces from the edge perhaps.'

'Have the tech guys been able to access Rhys's phone or computer?'

'No, and I doubt we will now. He had a passcode, and fingerprint and face scan set up.'

All the detectives understood the technology nowadays used capacitance to detect a living fingerprint. No electrical charge meant a phone wouldn't open, so they couldn't use a finger from his corpse. A person's dead features appeared quite different from their living one, so face or eye recognition, which had a liveness detection anyway, wouldn't work either.

Minton was next to speak.

'We've got to find this Mark Kilby, assuming he was dealing the drugs. I asked the Met to attend the probation address, a minuscule bedsit in East Ham, but there was no answer. The officers said those they spoke to responded cautiously when Kilby's name was mentioned. One neighbour confirmed Kilby had been living there but hadn't seen him for a couple of weeks.'

Barton slowly looked around the room.

'Have this case running through your head all weekend. Perhaps a theory will slip into place. If something's not obvious, what territory are we in?'

'Left field,' said Hoffman. 'Maybe this book stuff is a front, and it's secretly a swingers club.'

'It already sounds a bit fruity,' said Leicester. 'To think I've been wasting my time at the gym.'

'Libraries are the place to be, my friend,' replied Hoffman. 'I thought everyone knew that.'

Barton shared a swift smile with Zander. The banter was back.

'What about Vijay and Morwen?' asked Zander. 'Tell them not to leave the country?'

'Yeah, that'll have to do,' said Barton. 'Send them home. We'll know if they've tampered with anything, and I can't see another obvious victim or suspect, although perhaps that's a concern.'

Zander nodded in agreement. If they didn't have any clue as to why Rhys was dead, then they couldn't say if anyone else was in danger.

'Surely everyone will be on their guard after what happened to Rhys,' said Hoffman.

Barton wasn't so sure. 'None of them know about the heroin side of it yet, or, if they do, they're impressive actors. Even if they were aware of the substance, apart from Kilby, they'd probably be ignorant of the dangerous chemical it's been mixed with. They may think he overdosed on something else or ate a household poison. Their guards might be down, guessing Morwen was responsible, and that Rhys's demise was the end of it.'

'I'll make certain everyone is warned to be cautious,' said Zander.

Barton only had his outside theory remaining to suggest.

'As I said, I'll still be available for calls all weekend. You'll survive without my input. I only want to hear about progress. Locating the dealer would be a particularly welcome development. Watch your drinking over the weekend, it might be all hands to the pump with little notice. Now, who remembers the name of the book the club chose?'

No one replied. Barton smiled.

'*The Slay Before Christmas.* Anyone done any research on that?'

Nobody had.

'I found the book on Amazon. Police procedural. Grim detective seeking a slasher by the sounds of it. Obviously, our case is a little different, with a handsome, heroic, dashing acting chief inspector pursuing a dastardly poisoner. I've bought it on Kindle and will read it this weekend.'

'Good idea, sir,' said Zelensky. 'Who knows? Perhaps the solution is inside the pages.'

'Maybe. I'll leave you with this. The picture presented to us doesn't seem to make sense with what we've heard. There's contradictory evidence. All that means is there are hidden factors we aren't aware of but should become clear. Stay positive. We'll get there.'

Barton didn't say it, but he hoped that was before someone else died.

46

THE BOOK CLUB KILLER

So, the police are closing in. Little by little, as the pieces slot into place. I wonder if anyone from their team has bothered to read the book. I couldn't stop turning the pages the first time I devoured it. Clever, how the author made the killer so human. Cold, sometimes, but life had moulded them so. Crazy at others, but aren't we all?

So many of us running on empty, insisting we're fine. Rushing around, flashing grins like laser beams, then collapsing like falling stars when we drop through our front doors.

It makes me consider whether my actions have given me a new burden. What are my thoughts on what I've done? Okay, I guess. There has been an extra load all these years. An added weight that I've been forced to bear myself. I sense it lifting, not all the way, but I anticipate freedom coming my way.

Rhys wasn't expected to die, but, if I'm honest, I haven't been feeling much of anything lately. It's probably too soon for guilt. In fact, I'd say it came easier than what else I've done.

I was more emotional when I was younger, but poor old Avani really cried out for the end. Overwhelming anxiety about the eventual conclusion ate away at her dwindling hours. She wanted someone to step up, and I did, hard as it was. I helped her. I'm sure she was grateful.

Funnily enough, I used to be scared of dying, too, but not now. The closer

I am, the more alive I feel. I bet for many at the end, a simple touch could ignite their hearts. A cherished scent would recall bygone days, and a few chords of familiar music prove balm to their restless souls. My passing is unlikely to be so tranquil, but I will have found peace.

Go with a smile, the Joker said. Wise advice, but not easily followed. Perhaps my cool will desert me. I've seen it happen to others. Even Avani desperately struggled to remove the pillow in those final seconds, but I understood what I had to do.

47

DCI BARTON

Saturday

Barton spent the first few hours of the morning reading the newspaper and then wishing he hadn't. He felt as though politicians were gaslighting him by claiming one thing, when clearly the opposite was happening.

The second half of the morning was occupied by wanting to break his Kindle, which seemed to have more bugs than a *Gremlins* movie. First, it wouldn't turn on, then it wouldn't connect to Wi-Fi. Next it failed to update, before finally it refused to switch off. He imagined the tiny critters inside the device, each one laughing maniacally and giving him the finger.

An unfamiliar, uncontrollable rage surged through Barton. He stamped into the kitchen away from the carpet, then placed the Kindle face down on the hard floor. Pent-up frustration, the accumulated irritation of countless technical failures, the sheer unfairness of a device designed for leisure morphing into torture, focussed into that one solitary moment.

He pushed down, all of his weight, every pound of his twenty-plus-stone frame, driven through the heel of his shoe. There was a fracture, a sharp, clean sound that resonated, not just through the Kindle's plastic casing, but through his very being. It wasn't joy, exactly, but a pure, visceral release. Pressure, which had been coiling tighter around his heart for months, faded away.

Was it the job, his future, the case, or just the knackered reader? It was hard to say, but a sense of peace enveloped him. Adrenaline, which had been sharp and potent, drained from his system. For a fleeting moment, everything was clear, simple, easy. Then, as swiftly as it had arrived, the sensation scattered, like leaves in a gentle wind.

He peered down at his broken Kindle, the smashed screen glinting in the overhead lights. The anger, rage even, had vanished, to be replaced by a quiet, unnerving calm. Damn, it felt good.

'What the hell?'

Barton's attention jolted to the doorway, where his wife stood, hand to mouth, eyes wide.

Holly stepped inside, incredulous. 'That's my Kindle.'

'What?'

'I think I saw yours in a drawer somewhere.'

'Ah! Sorry.'

Holly tipped her head back and roared with laughter. 'Only kidding. That is your one. It's been knackered for ages.'

Barton prodded a huge finger at her. 'Evil woman.'

'Jeez, your face. Get in the game, mister. A word of warning, though. The remote in the lounge needs new batteries. I'd hate to go out and return to discover your forehead buried in the TV screen.' She paused for a moment. 'What's got into you?'

'I'm not sure. I really do need some time to find my equilibrium.'

'Well, you'll have it after Christmas. Why don't you read whatever it is you want to read on the tablet, like the last occasion we realised that particular Kindle was broken? It's in the dining room.'

Barton marched away and found the device. He spent the next ten minutes turning it on, loading the app, then couldn't open the book. Gizmo, sensing his master's mood, got up from the floor where he'd been lying and crept away.

Holly wandered in.

'The silence was worrying me.'

She relieved him of the tablet and swiftly uploaded *The Slay Before Christmas* without commenting further and left the room. Barton puffed out his cheeks, dropped into a seat and opened the first chapter.

Barton read for the next three hours, after which he pottered around the kitchen, tidying and cleaning. At five, he drove to Longueville chippy, where he bought four portions of fish and chips. The children descended like bats from their roosts when he returned, quietly plated up slightly more than their fair share of chips, selected the biggest pieces of fish, doused the offerings in ketchup while chuntering about 'how come we never have Heinz any more?', and glided back up the stairs.

Barton and Holly chuckled at each other as they ate theirs, with no words needing to be said. They took an unenthusiastic Gizmo for a quick walk afterwards, then the kids left their crypts briefly to watch a re-run of *Gladiators*, in preparation for the new series starting in January. It was one of the few shows they watched together on TV and always led to some banter.

Barton loved these family moments. It reminded him of when the children were young, when all of them could fit on the sofa. Holly even got a new tub of Quality Street out when *Gladiators* started. It was the second one she'd bought, with the other ravaged by marauders the previous weekend, despite both being purchased for Christmas.

Luke peeled the tape off the side, filled with happiness about getting in first. His small fingers searched through the chocolates, scrabbling harder and faster.

He looked up, his face contorted with shock.

'Hey! Where are the Toffee Fingers?'

His accusatory gaze locked onto Barton.

'Hey, don't glare at me. My teeth haven't been able to cope with them for at least a decade.'

Holly took the tub off her youngest son, stared into it with hope, then at Barton with disgust. 'And there are no Purple Ones.'

'I don't like them either. Besides, it's a new box. I saw you remove the Sellotape. Just unlucky, I guess. I had a packet of Fruit Pastilles last week, and there were no red ones. None! I was tempted to write to Nestlé, but I suppose there's not someone monitoring the production line, ensuring an even distribution of each type or colour.'

Layla grabbed the tub.

'Ooh, there are lots of green chocolates.'

'Lob one over, please,' said Barton.

Holly peered over Layla's arm.

'I've never seen so many strawberry and orange creams.' She slapped a hand to her forehead. 'Oh, you twat.'

Barton knew she didn't want to glance over at him, but she was forced to take in his grinning chops.

'You opened them,' said Holly, a smile creeping onto her face. 'Took out our favourites and put in last week's remnants. You're a sick man.'

'Who's still got it, baby?'

'Please don't tell me you ate the ones you removed.'

'Not the Toffee Fingers.'

Barton dodged two missiles, but an Orange Crunch hit him in the chest. That was cool. He liked them.

Barton left the room, returning with the other box where he'd hidden their favourites, and calm was restored. They enjoyed the action on the screen together. He checked his phone at 8 p.m. and found a text from DC Caroline Minton about her visit to the hospital.

> Spoke to the victim on the ward. Dealer confirmed to have large gaps between teeth, and coat with furry hood. It's our guy, all right, but no further leads to his whereabouts.

He replied.

> Nice work.

Zander had sent a briefer message.

> Nothing urgent in the office.

Barton responded.

> Cheers, Zander. We've been watching Gladiators. I still reckon I could win it.

Barton chuckled to himself after sending it. They'd been joking about the programme for years.

'What are you laughing about?' asked Holly.

He gestured to the screen. 'I've texted Zander to tell him I could be the champ.'

Holly smiled. 'I don't fancy your chances of getting up that travelator.'

Barton tapped his thighs. 'Explosive power. No problem at all.'

Layla cracked up. 'Oh, wow! I just had a vision. Imagine Dad in one of those cages in Rocketball. He'd be rolling around aimlessly like an enormous red-faced hamster.'

Luke choked with laughter. 'And while wearing a leotard.'

Barton didn't want to get into why he would be wearing a ballet outfit. He picked up the tablet and rose from his armchair with as much dignity as he could muster. It was time for an early night.

48

DCI BARTON

Sunday

Barton woke late, having read into the night. Holly brought him a cup of coffee as he was stirring, with Layla waiting in the doorway. The pair, tightly wrapped in Lycra, were heading to a Pilates class. Barton's offer to join them was politely declined by his wife and met with a gagging sound from his daughter.

Holly pointed to the tablet on the bedside stand.

'That book must have been gripping for you to still be awake at midnight.'

'Yeah, it was, in a dirty-secret type of way.'

'Ooh, is it trashy?'

'Not in a style you'd appreciate. In some ways, it's utter bollocks. There are cops planting evidence, side hustles, the inspector drunkenly shagging one of his PCs in the cleaning cupboard, cocaine snorted off the boardroom table, guns waved in people's faces, witnesses bribed, even bogeys wiped on officers' computer screens. It's not been like that in my department for at least six years.'

'Well, I'll take your word for it on the bogey thing.'

He chuckled.

'But it is strangely compelling. There are scenes from the murderer's point of view, and you can kind of get where they're coming from. As though they didn't particularly want to do what they felt forced to. Most of the victims have been vermin, so I've enjoyed reading about them being electrocuted and riddled with bullets.'

'Did you finish it?'

'No, I must have dropped off. I've got about 20 per cent left. I'm planning to crash on the sofa and read the last bit with breakfast. Is there anything nice?'

'I bought a pack of Ayrshire oak-smoked middle-back bacon.'

Barton licked his lips. 'My favourite. I thought you said it had got too expensive.'

'It was on offer. I picked up some Lurpak too.'

'Also on sale?'

'Half price. It will be muesli and porridge in the new year, so enjoy it while you can.'

It was Barton's turn to make a retching sound, then he grinned. 'Just kidding. Yum!'

Holly shook her head.

'Lily's coming over at twelve, so get up and have a shower. No walking around in your underpants. She's been through enough.'

Barton laughed. 'Bringing the baby?'

'Of course. I'm taking them both into Queensgate with Layla, see the lights, then Christmas shopping. We'll have a late lunch, so you and Luke can fend for yourselves today. He's gone out on his bike, anyway. Jacob's mum, Danielle, will probably feed him. Luke said he wanted to put the tree up with you tonight.'

Holly left the room, and a few minutes later, Barton heard the front door slam. His daughter didn't appear able to shut one quietly even when she was happy.

Barton read a bit more of *The Slay Before Christmas*, drank his coffee, then took a shower. The bacon had just gone in the warming oven when Holly and Layla returned. It was the lazy way to cook it. The girls had done their make-up at the gym, so they were ready to go twenty minutes later when Lily arrived.

It was Barton who opened the door when she knocked.

'Hand him over!'

'Sorry, John. Tommy's asleep in the pram. I brought you some company, though.'

Lily dragged Vince into view, reached down and unclipped the lead. The dog poked his head around the door. His tail spun theatrically, and he slipped past Barton into the house.

'I didn't want to leave him on his own for too long. He likes you.'

Barton smiled and it wasn't just at the sight of the hound. Lily had also applied make-up and styled her hair, but it was her eyes that were different. They were clear, and she seemed chilled.

'Okay, okay, he can stay. You don't need to butter me up. I have to say, you look well.'

Lily couldn't help a bashful smile. 'I'm getting there. Holly's been such a help. It's a shame my ex won't return my calls.'

'Perhaps someone should have a word with him.'

'I doubt it would be of any use. Some men do as they please and don't care who gets hurt, as long as they get what *they* want.'

'Well, it's not only blokes, but I understand your point.'

Barton waved the women off, then went back to the kitchen and made his bacon sandwich with four brown eyes watching his every move. Even though he knew he was alone, Barton peered around theatrically before giving each dog a small rasher. One slice wouldn't kill them, and it would stop him from eating it all.

Gizmo headed straight to his usual fireside spot, while Vince stopped at the doorway, where his woeful gaze fixed upon the other dog. If greyhounds could roll their eyes, Gizmo would have, but as the retriever padded in and settled close by, Barton suspected both the animals were secretly beaming.

Barton relaxed as he ate his sandwich, gentle snoring in front of him. He could get used to this.

He cracked on with the book, laughing out loud numerous times at the antics of the killer and the lack of procedures and common sense for the police, who always seemed to be one step behind.

After a nap of his own, Barton finished the last page mid-afternoon, then rested the tablet on his lap. Bloody hell. He hadn't been expecting that. He jumped when his phone rang.

'Decent timing, Zander. I've just read the book the club members selected.'

'Okay, great. I'm going to call it a day here. The guys are ploughing on, but it's draining work. There's so much CCTV to trawl through, and that's with us sharing the tasks with the drug unit.'

'Fair enough. Get some rest for next week. See your family.'

'I need to nip to the shops and choose Kelly something special for Christmas Day.'

'Putting yourself under pressure, aren't you, leaving it this late?'

'Well, when I say choose, last week I found a page ripped out of the Samuel's catalogue on the kitchen table. A necklace had a big black circle drawn around it.'

'Ah, subtle. I picked up a cracking bargain during Black Friday.'

'What was it?'

'A robovac. Should have been £300, I got it for £169.'

'And that's Holly's main present?'

Barton's eyes narrowed. 'I also got her a dog-walking hat. Waterproof from Sealskinz. Very nice.'

'Oh dear.'

'Do I need to get her something else?'

'You do if you don't want to see Boxing Day through black eyes.'

'Right. You'd better pick me up.'

Zander chuckled.

'No problem. So?'

'So what?'

'What was *The Slay Before Christmas* like?'

'Funny and sad. Tragic, crazy, unrealistic at times, piercing perception in other moments into what people are capable of. The coppers were bent as nine-bob notes. Perjury, harassment, intimidation, hiding evidence, theft, corruption and the beating of suspects all part of their working week.'

'Someone else recently mentioned the good old days. How did it end?'

'Our hero, the detective, who is far from perfect himself, solves the puzzle and heads to confront the murderer with his partner as backup. The villain admits to his yuletide massacre and laughs in their faces. Before the main man can draw his gun, his partner, who turned out to be working with the killer, shoots him in the spine. The book finishes with the two chuckling murderers spreading out the head and limbs of the more honest officer under the Christmas tree. Like bloodied presents.'

49

DCI BARTON

Monday

Barton arrived at the office at six in the morning. He felt a little guilty about having the weekend off, but he'd had a relaxing and enjoyable time, which led to him imagining what he'd missed out on in the past while working extra hours.

It was lucky he hadn't been at work, though, because while Zander was buying Kelly a necklace, Barton had suddenly recalled numerous comments from Holly about needing a waterproof smartwatch to help when she was busy in the café. She had mentioned the name of a good brand, Garmin, and said they did an ivory and gold one that would match a necklace she already owned.

Zander had shaken his head with horror at how close Barton had been to becoming another Christmas statistic.

The first thing Barton did after sitting at his desk was read through the case file to refresh the information in his head. Then he browsed a variety of reports from the computer system, HOLMES. It was used for major crime investigations to manage and prioritise inquiries about potential suspects.

Barton observed his team appearing in dribs and drabs. He smiled when Parveen arrived and immediately got into a deep conversation with Minton. A fruitless weekend could drain the enthusiasm from detectives, but there was laughter and mickey-taking occurring amidst focused discussions. He gave them until ten to get their brains in gear and the paperwork up to date.

He made a cup of coffee, then strode to DCI Cox's office.

'Morning, John. I was wondering when you were coming to see me. Thanks for all the updates and cc'ing me on various communications. I can spot a messy investigation from a mile off.'

'Yeah, but I think we have the suspect in our sights. Either one of the book club, possibly a staff member at the pub, the drug dealer, or an angry former customer.'

'Making much progress?'

'Yeah, we are. We've had a lot of people to talk to, hours and hours of CCTV to trawl, and we were beginning totally from scratch. The guy who we assume to be the dealer has a probation appointment this morning at nine. He's not missed one since his release.'

'I take it the Met will be ready to pounce.'

'Yes. Over the weekend, my guys traced a couple who had been unhappy clients of Jones and Singh. They ran a modelling agency and might have been enraged enough for vengeance. We found out the husband was returning to the UK late last night. His secretary said to ring him at his business this morning.'

'And the book club crew?'

'It could be any or all of them. There's some suspect behaviour going on, but it's possible none of them are responsible. This dealer is the key. A type just out of prison after a long stretch. We get him, and we'll be dancing on the desks in our underwear and letting off party poppers.'

Cox's face showed no emotion. 'I should hope not.'

Barton wasn't sure if she was pulling his leg. 'Sorry,' he replied. 'It was in this book I read yesterday.'

'Okay, keep up the great work.'

Barton smiled at her. Even though they were in effect the same rank, it had never really felt like that. He could tell she had something to tell him.

'What is it?'

'I've had confirmation. Your old team, Zander's current team, is being dispersed. If they have any requests, whether that's moving to a different department, or a wish for a specific team, tell them to email me. Have a good day.'

Barton trudged to the main office and sat at a desk. While he was there, the incident with his Kindle kept demanding to be focussed on. At the back of his mind, he'd known the object was broken, or at least he wanted to convince himself of that, but it had given him an insight into some offenders' impulsive behaviour.

Many criminals were repeat offenders. They either loved it, or it was part of their being. An inner drive. Yet other culprits were of good character. They were pillars of their communities who snapped, like celebrities who finally lashed out at a hostile press. As he had with the screen of his device.

Barton had experienced a calm afterwards, but, he realised now, also a sense of shame at the loss of control. Was one of the book club members feeling that emotion?

Honest people's guilt had probably solved as many cases for MIT and CID as the detectives had. Having a conscience was a sure-fire way to get caught. He hadn't sensed any tremendous remorse from Kasia or Morwen, but Vijay seemed unsettled. The Goodmans and the Thwaites also ticked that box, but perhaps for different reasons.

Barton recalled that the members would meet again on Christmas Eve. He considered the characters who might be responsible and realised with a sinking feeling that, if there was going to be another incident, time was not on his side.

50

DCI BARTON

When everyone had gathered in the meeting room, Barton asked for an update, starting with the most important detail. The missing drug dealer.

'Not brilliant news,' said Hoffman. 'Kilby no-showed for his probation appointment this morning. He called the main number, as opposed to his handler, to say he was ill. The person who took the call passed him through, but Kilby hung up. It might seem like an annoyance, but it firms up our suspicions on his involvement.'

'Have there been any more overdoses?'

Leicester nodded. 'I just got an email a few minutes ago. Another twelve.'

Everyone present froze as though they'd been running on mains power and the plug had been yanked out.

Barton recovered first.

'Sorry, that sounded like you said twelve.'

'Yes, but not all were in Cambridgeshire. I was trying to think outside the box yesterday and realised we'd assumed, because all of our victims were local, we only had to check Peterborough City Hospital. But remember, PCH is struggling.'

Barton nodded. Peterborough had been one of the country's fastest-growing cities for the last decade, and the hospital was fifteen years old. A & E and Resus were flat out. They could cope, no problem with staffing levels, but bed space was the issue.

'Corridor treatment most nights,' said Barton.

'Yes, but they also redirect some patients to the A & E at Hinchingbrooke.'

'Ah, you win a star. That's where they were?'

'Only one was. He recovered quickly and discharged himself.'

Barton scratched his head. 'I assume he was homeless and not easily traceable.'

'Afraid so.'

Barton was about to ask where the other eleven were when he worked it out for himself. 'Make that five stars, Leicester. The other overdoses were in London.'

'Yes, at Newham University Hospital. It's located in Plaistow.'

'Which is next door to East Ham, where Kilby was staying. Fatalities?'

'One woman.'

'Okay. Link the post-mortem there to Mortis here, but it's going to be Kilby. He's the link. Put out a BOLO for him. East London and here. Let's have every officer in both areas hunting him down.'

'Will do.'

'Contact the other London hospitals. Warn the Met about a rogue batch of heroin.'

Parveen raised a hand with a confused expression. 'I'd already checked London hospitals and warned both the Metropolitan Police Service and the City of London Police last week. There was nothing.'

'These all occurred on Friday,' said Leicester.

Barton paced up and down at the front of the room. 'Which means Kilby returned to London and sold the rest of his drugs. He's got to be insane to do that if he had guessed the heroin had been mixed with a nitazene.'

Zander cut in. 'It's more likely he didn't know. He'll have gone back for his supervision appointment today. After seven months, all it would have been was an "I'm fine" conversation, so his plan would have been to sell his wares, check in with his probation officer, then...'

Barton began to grin at Zander, then it faded away. 'But he rang up instead of attending.'

'He must have got spooked. Maybe he flogged it cheap to people who lived near him and saw the ambulances arrive.'

Barton thought of the sort of person Kilby was. He could guess what he would do.

'He'll come back here. To his old stomping ground, perhaps in a panic.' Barton waited for the hubbub to die down. 'Kilby is our primary focus. Think about where he might be. Scour his past case files. Look for former addresses. Is his dad still alive? I presume CCTV hasn't provided anything yet.'

Zander shook his head. 'Nothing.'

Barton ran a hand over his jawline as he thought. 'Right. What about coroners' reports on the untimely deaths of Charlie and Walter, and GP notes on Avani?'

Zander had a writing pad with him, which he consulted. 'Coroners' reports remain pending, but we only put the requests in late on Friday. I emailed Mortis this morning. He'll jump on them when they land, which will hopefully be today. They'll be big files, but he should fly through them, knowing all the terminology and how they're laid out.'

'And the GP records on Avani?'

'Still waiting.'

Barton clicked his fingers. 'I bet it's the same GP who came out to confirm life extinct for Rhys. I reckon the receptionist at Jones and Singh can tell us who that is. She'll probably have the healthcare cover, too.'

Zander smiled.

'Nice thinking. Chances are he was Walter's doctor, too. Rhys seems the type to have provided a family plan.'

A persistent unease gnawed at Barton regarding Rhys's murder, considering the generous benefits he'd offered, but he suppressed it.

'Excellent. We're cooking on gas. I was hoping for a break over the weekend, but even though you probably didn't realise it, you've made plenty of progress. What else can we check this morning?'

Minton and Parveen both said the same words at the same time.

'Social media.'

'Well volunteered. I've had the TIE reports from HOLMES. It's not telling us anything we aren't doing, but make sure you carry on sticking to its formula, which I know you will, or we'll get in a tangle.'

TIE reports were generated by the system to track the progress of eliminating individuals from an inquiry. Barton took his seat again and told them about the contents of *The Slay Before Christmas*. Gruesome was the general verdict. And worrying.

'I think Bernie recommended that novel,' said Barton. 'I'm going to head off with Hoffman and visit him, then go to the Thwaites'. If the four of them don't start being less evasive, they'll be coming back here in a van with Uniform.'

Hoffman's face fell. 'Hey, I don't want my body parts ending up as gifts under a Christmas tree.'

'I'm afraid you'll have to be brave. We need to go now, too, because there's no time like the present.'

Genial groans rang out from everyone.

The meeting room door opened. It was an officer from one of the other teams.

'Sir. A call has come through for you with a personal request.'

Barton frowned. 'What kind of request?'

'It was from a Bernard Goodman. He said you have his address. He'd like you to attend his house as soon as you can. It's nothing dramatic. A declaration of sorts. But arrive alone or he won't talk to you.'

'Okay, thanks.'

Hoffman held out his hands. 'Does that mean I don't have to come with you?'

'What are you on about?' replied Barton with a grin. 'You're going in first.'

As the team left the room to get on with their tasks, a last thought struck him. All a dying man had left to lose was his reputation, and Barton wasn't sure Bernie valued his enough.

51

VIJAY SINGH

Vijay clattered down his stairs and stopped in front of the large antique mirror, which Avani had so loved. Every time he stared at the damn thing, which was a lot, he felt a pang of remorse. Or was it regret? He wasn't sure of the difference. Perhaps one was about feeling sorry for his wife, and the other was about hoping events had turned out differently for him.

Vijay smoothed his hair. Yes. Buoyant. He had his father to thank for that. The funeral director, a family friend, had said, before his ninety-year-old dad's burial, he'd never seen such thick locks on a man his age.

Vijay spied a rogue long grey hair in his eyebrow. He huffed and went to get the tweezers. Ageing sucked. That definitely hadn't been there a few days ago.

Five minutes later, after removing some fresh ear hairs, and making sure his Gucci suit hung just right, Vijay stepped outside. He was tempted to drive, even though Morwen lived only a few minutes' walk away, but decided a bracing stroll would liven him up.

A present, wrapped in snowy Christmas paper, had been left at his front door. He picked it up, feeling its weight. Got to be a bottle of wine. The tag simply had a large black X on it. Their club's code for a Secret Santa parcel, so nobody recognised anyone's writing. Damn. With everything that had gone on, he'd not given the tradition a second thought. The idea was to deliver your gift secretly to whoever you had selected. At the next club meeting, people guessed who sent whose.

There was no prize, but it was always good for a few laughs. Eric had once caught Charlie sneaking out of his back garden at 3 a.m. having been woken up by their dog growling. That was a long time ago, but even last year Bernie had been spotted dressed up as a postal worker. The village postie had lent him his coat, but Morwen had just happened to be opening the curtains.

Vijay decided to bring the bottle and marched away from his house. He could guess who was most likely to have bought it for him. Bernie. They often chatted about wine while they worked. In fact, everyone knew of their shared passion for fine wines. As Vijay set off, he realised he was going to miss the old boy. Nearly thirty years together in the same office, and he couldn't remember Bernie and him arguing. Disagreeing about the superiority of a New Zealand Shiraz over a Californian Zinfandel, maybe, but no hint of malice or anger had ever arisen between them.

Bernie's wife was a much feistier creature. Beryl had once bumped his trolley in Marks & Spencer, and never even said hello. Her expression had been furious. Vijay suspected she was losing it, blaming him as well as Rhys for her husband's illness. She'd once walked into the office because Bernie had forgotten the salad she'd made for him, and had met Vijay arriving as she'd left.

'Stress kills,' she'd hissed at him.

Vijay had pondered if their home life was tormented somehow, but suspected the truth of the matter was Bernie enjoyed his job and loved his wife. Beryl simply didn't appreciate having to share her husband, and she was furious about losing him to such a terrible disease.

Vijay's attention switched to Morwen, his cool and calm vanishing, as it always did at the prospect of being in the company of Rhys's wife, and now widow. It had been that way from the first moment he'd set eyes on her. Fortunately, the bottle was in wrapping paper, or it would have slipped from his grasp when his brain reminded him she was a single woman. He knocked and waited, mouth resembling the Gobi Desert, armpits like crocodile swamps.

Morwen answered the door in a pair of cut-off jeans and a faded T-shirt. Sweat had gathered on her top lip and brow as though she'd been through a long exercise workout.

As with most times she deigned to speak to him, her tone carried a hint of sarcasm.

'Vijay. To what do I owe the pleasure?'

His voice had an almost imperceptible stammer. 'I thought it would be a smart idea for me and you to talk.'

'What about?'

'Rhys. The business. Being arrested.'

'I wasn't arrested.'

'Neither was I, but that's how it felt.'

Morwen gestured to what he was holding. 'You're supposed to sneak the Secret Santa around, not ring my doorbell.'

'No, it's for me. I found it outside my house when I left.'

'Any idea who deposited it there?'

'My money's on Bernie.'

Morwen dragged a hand through what he imagined was damp hair, leaving Vijay at risk of collapsing.

'I'd ask you in, but, seeing as you might have killed Rhys, maybe I shouldn't risk it.'

'It's me who's taking the gamble, considering I'm not responsible.'

'Nor am I.'

'Would you tell me if you were?'

Morwen stood back from the entrance, smiling broadly. 'I suppose not.'

Vijay edged past her, his breathing shallow. He picked up the scent of her, some floral perfume combined with a faint whiff of body odour. Pure catnip to the already entrapped. His blood pressure spiralled upwards.

'You'll have to excuse my clothes. I'm doing the housework. Better than any Pilates class for keeping your butt cheeks where they ought to be.'

Vijay beamed, but didn't trust himself to reply. When they reached the kitchen, he distracted himself by pulling the wrapping from the bottle of wine.

'Definitely Bernie,' he stated.

'Why do you say that?'

Vijay held the bottle up to the light so he could read the small writing on the label, but he'd recognised the brand.

'This vintage comes from the Blackman Vale Estate. It's a wonderfully perfumed and elegant Cabernet Sauvignon, showcasing the best of the cool

Margaret River region. If I recall right, aged for eighteen months with a splash of juicy Malbec.'

'Sounds expensive.'

'That particular winery is one of the founder estates of Western Australia's industry. There's a long, sunny growing season producing fine wines they can sell at a premium.'

Morwen didn't bother to hide her yawn.

'More than the £20 maximum we're supposed to spend on Secret Santa gifts?'

'Not loads more, but that's why I guessed it's from Bernie. Beryl wouldn't have a clue. Eric and Mary like a nice glass of wine, but would they pay £30 for one as a joke? You weren't responsible and Katarzyna probably wouldn't have remembered my story at last year's Christmas meet.'

'The tale where you bought a fancy bottle during a vineyard tour at the start of your Australian holiday, carried it in your luggage for three weeks, survived the flight home, then left it to mature for three years. Finally, the day arrived for savouring the wine, you sneezed and the bottle smashed on the floor.'

Vijay grinned. 'So, you remember?'

'Of course. The telling of that story was hilarious.' She rested a hand ever so lightly on his arm. 'Perhaps your finest hour.'

Vijay felt heat rising all over his face. 'Shall we have a glass? It'll keep for five years, but a Cabernet Sauvignon can be enjoyed now.'

Morwen glanced around her as though searching for an excuse, then let out a sigh. 'Okay.'

She went over to a cupboard and took out two glasses, waving them at him.

'Only the one. Or I'll be undoing all my hard work, but we should talk about what's next for the firm. If I'm honest, I just want to sell it.'

Vijay's hand shook at that comment, and he nearly spilled the wine over the work surface as he poured two glasses.

Morwen was watching and couldn't help laughing. She put her fingers over her mouth as a poor attempt at concealment.

'Vijay. I can never decide whether you're petrified of me or in love with me.'

Vijay would normally swill his wine around the glass, smell it, take a sip, breathe in air as it swished around his mouth and then swallow. Instead, he took a huge gulp of wine and swallowed as Morwen caused his synapses to detonate like a misfiring firework display, thoughts scattering in every direction.

'I've always considered you to be a wonderful lady.'

He gently slid her glass towards her across the work surface. Weak rays from the low sun shone through the window and caught the curve of her mouth as she took a sip of the drink. The wine clung to her lips, glistening like blood. A shiver of desire swept down his spine. No, it was more than desire. A yearning. Hunger that grew ever stronger. A starvation that was almost out of control.

Morwen ran a tongue across her top teeth.

'That's extremely sweet of you. I have to say if it was affection you felt, then you've been quite the gentleman. Not a move in thirty-odd years of knowing me.'

Vijay's voice came out husky. 'I am a gentleman.'

'Perhaps I'm losing my touch if you men have stopped trying.'

Vijay smiled back at her. He wanted to leap across the metre distance between them. Tear her T-shirt off with his teeth. Nibble her everywhere, then gaze into her eyes and declare his undying obsession, but he knew he would not. His upbringing had been steeped in religious tradition, where marriage was forever, and commitment was total. He had to admit, Rhys being his boss with the golden share might have been a factor, too.

The problem had been that ever since he'd met Morwen, she was always on his mind. It was as if he'd spent three decades in a daydream. Avani had been a lovely person, but so quiet and gentle. She had paled next to this raging, vibrant, unpredictable Welshwoman. His wife had tried to be sexy for him, to turn him on, but it had been as if he couldn't see her any more.

Life's unjustness and cruelty had become starkly apparent when it had been she who fell ill, not him.

Still, to have these moments with Morwen, just the two of them, was complete bliss.

Vijay experienced a scintillating time, chatting with the beautiful, clever lady about his plans and hopes of expansion for the business. Morwen laughed often and seemed genuinely interested. She appreciated another half-glass, and he finished the bottle, feeling decidedly merry when she ushered him out of her house.

As she went to close the door with him on the other side of it, her expression took on a calm focus.

'I'll see you at the funeral, I expect.'

'Naturally.'

'As I said earlier, I plan to sell my share in the company. I'll appoint solicitors to provide a fair value for the firm. Liaise with them if you wish to buy me out, or it will be sold externally.'

Vijay had been so mesmerised by her energy and poise, he'd forgotten the golden share passed to him.

'Morwen, when the partnership was drawn up, it clearly stated in the event of Rhys's death, his half of the business passed to you, but the golden share became mine.'

'Yes, that's correct. I read that first draft, and I made Rhys change that line. I thought it prudent you weren't told about the alteration and suspected, when you came to the house to sign the document, you wouldn't check, merely assuming it was identical to the one you'd read.'

Vijay's face formed a rictus grin. He remembered Morwen's dinner party for just the three partners and her. She had played the perfect host, in a short red dress, which made his mouth go dry even all this time later. Vijay had only had eyes for one thing that evening, and it hadn't been the contract.

For the first time, he saw the Welshwoman for who she was. Clever, calm, controlling and utterly ruthless. Vijay had been a fool.

'You bitch.'

Morwen's eyes met his and coolly held them.

'Women, eh? I've found it helpful to keep my cards close to my chest, letting other people assume I'm weak or clueless. That includes the police, and it certainly includes you.'

The door was closed in his face.

52

DCI BARTON

The biting chill of a December breeze nipped at their faces as Barton and Hoffman exited the police station. With a shared glance at the leaden, motionless sky, they climbed into a pool car and set off for the Goodman property with an air of trepidation hanging heavy in the vehicle. Hoffman's manoeuvring around a roundabout was nowhere near as smooth as normal.

Barton rested a hand on the dashboard.

'We'll be beating Bernie to the afterlife at this rate.'

'Sorry, sir. I can cope with virtually anything, but I'm not comfortable with dying people.'

Barton gave the driver a brief glance.

'Didn't I hear you once went into a field after a motorbike accident to search for the head?'

'Yeah, that was me. It took ages to find it. The impact had thrown the helmet into a bush.'

'Surely that's more traumatising than talking to a relatively old man who probably still has some time left.'

'The decapitation thing was weird. I know I shouldn't say this, but there was a hint of a farce about it. I mean, walking out holding the head. Release of pressure and all that.'

'Please don't mention those words to anyone else ever again.'

Hoffman remained quiet until they reached the next junction.

'My grandad died of cancer, and he desperately didn't want to go. We visited him near the end. I was just a teenager and felt so awkward. He so wanted to see the grandkids grow up. I always feel sorry for people like that and struggle with what to say.'

'It's fine to feel sorry,' replied Barton, who then softened his voice, 'but you still have a job to do.'

'I guess it's business.'

'Right, and what's the most probable reason he asked to speak to us?'

'You! He specifically requested you.'

Barton laughed. 'Okay, what does he want to tell me?'

'I reckon he's made a trapdoor at the front of his house, planted some spears tipped with the secretions from a golden poison frog underneath, then when we press the buzzer, it's game over.'

'Nasty for you if you end up going down first, and I land on top of you.'

'At least it would be quick.'

'Well, I hope that's down the list of possibilities. He obviously wants to talk, probably to come clean, but the question is, will it be a full confession?'

'I reckon a partial admission of something criminal. Obviously, I was only joking about the frog.'

'Take it from a man with experience. It's usually best to provide the correct answer first, then opt for comedy. That reminds me. I had a quick chat with Zelensky.'

'She said you trapped her in the car.'

Barton smiled. 'That's not the term I'd have used. Are you two planning to make a go of it?'

'I think so.'

'You sound about as convincing as me saying I'm going to get serious about the gym in January.'

Hoffman frowned.

'We argue a lot.'

'Do you know why that is?'

'No.'

'It's because you're both a bit irritating. She can be frosty and dismissive. You can be rude and flaky.'

'Cheers.'

Barton chuckled. 'No problem. Apparently, retiring is similar to dying. It means you're allowed to say what you like. A wise but grumpy Scotsman and a going-on-a-world-cruise GP taught me that. Look, no relationship is perfect. You're in your thirties now. It's a pivotal moment in your life. There'll be changes in the new year. Both of you will have to focus on new challenges. You in particular need to buck up your ideas. Think before you speak. Take your job more seriously. It's acceptable to be the comedian in your twenties, but jesters don't get promoted.'

Hoffman groaned. 'Sometimes stuff slips out. You know, comments.'

Barton gave him a stern look. 'Try harder, and that applies to how you are with Maria, too. Women like her don't grow on trees. Be more disciplined, or you'll cock up your career and relationship so badly that, whatever you do, you won't be able to save either of them.'

Hoffman nodded beside him. Barton suspected he already knew most of what he'd just said.

'Okay, let's get our heads in the game. What are your thoughts about all of this?'

'For the first case in my career, I'm genuinely stumped. We went through all the phone and bank records we received back so far. There's nothing obvious. CCTV and ANPR are ongoing, but it's time-consuming and we've checked the most likely spots.'

'I'll admit it's frustrating.' Barton stared hard at the Goodmans' property when they arrived, as though it might give up the answers to their puzzle. 'Let's hope Bernie's in a conversational mood.'

Hoffman parked and they got out. Professional pair that they were, neither could stop themselves from tapping the paving slabs in front of the door with their shoes to check if any were loose.

Barton raised his eyebrows and pressed the buzzer.

'Seems okay!'

Bernie arrived swiftly and gave them an unusual smile. Kind of dreamy.

'Come in, come in.'

They followed him inside, but he staggered when he opened the lounge door. Barton had to grab his shoulders, his hands easily going all the way around seemingly thin bones. When Bernie reached his hospital bed, it was obvious he didn't have the strength to clamber up. The room smelled of death.

Hoffman had stayed back in the doorway. Barton analysed his face, which implied he'd prefer to be chin deep in a septic tank.

Barton lifted the frail man up onto the bed as though he were laying a child in a cot. Bernie's eyes had closed. When he hauled them open, his pupils were dilated, and the sclera was a light yellow.

'Thanks for coming so quickly,' he whispered.

'I'm never late for the truth. Beryl not in?'

'No, she went out early this morning. I'm not sure what she's doing. Didn't take the car. She'll be getting me a few treats. I can still enjoy a bar of Dairy Milk. Chemo first time round ruined my teeth, but I let it melt on my tongue.'

'My favourite, too.'

Bernie patted Barton's arm. 'Beryl's been a brilliant wife. Loyal and kind, and a little feisty. Everything you need for a long marriage.'

The big officer's mouth set with quiet affirmation. 'You're spot on.'

'She left a note saying not back until the middle of the afternoon. That's why I've put things in play.'

Barton's eyes narrowed. 'Like getting us here?'

Bernie had been holding his head up off the pillow, but it suddenly dropped back. Barton moved closer.

'Are your meds making you drowsy?'

'Yes, very. I'd better get on or I'll be snoring. I did this for you.'

Bernie took a small piece of paper out of his pocket and handed it over. Barton scanned the words, then read them aloud.

> 'A book club blooms,
> Ten gather in rooms,
> Wealth and friendship bind,
> Their secrets entwine,
> But fate's cruel hand,
> Claims lives on demand,
> It's a deadly game,
> But who is to blame?'

53

DCI BARTON

Barton's hackles rose, but he managed to stay relatively calm.

'What's this?'

Bernie smiled. 'A poem.'

'I don't think now's the time for witty rhymes. Lives have been lost.'

Bernie smirked or grimaced. It was hard to say which. 'I reckon you're not wrong. Beryl often moans about me making jokes at unsuitable times. Words just appear to slip out.'

'Easily done,' said Hoffman, who'd ventured forward. 'You're saying Rhys's death is connected to the book club.'

'Yes, that's right.'

Hoffman took the poem off Barton and read it again. 'There was another murder, perhaps years ago.'

'Maybe more than one.'

Hoffman asked the obvious question. 'How do you know that?'

'I've got eyes and ears, and a brain for these types of things. I love an intriguing mystery.'

Hoffman fixed him with a critical look. 'You should have told the police. Withholding information about a murder is often considered to be assisting an offender, which is a crime. Not to mention the strong moral and ethical factor.'

Bernie's eyes had closed again. Barton put his hand on Hoffman's shoulder to make him aware he was taking over. Any chance of further intel was dwindling fast. Their confessor was about to be unconscious. Wasting time by chastising a dying man wasn't the right call.

Barton spoke loudly. 'We all love a conundrum, Bernie. Who did your suspicions rest on?'

Bernie replied but kept his eyes shut. 'Oh, quite a few. It didn't make sense back then, but when I was at the book club last Friday, one person acted differently.'

'Did you see them tamper with the cupcakes?'

A smile crept onto the poorly man's face. 'So that was how it was done. No. Their general demeanour had changed. With knowing the rest, I could speculate about the entire truth.'

Barton's thoughts were going like the clappers. 'Are you referring to the other murders?'

'Yes.'

'Who was it?'

Bernie's eyes opened as slivers.

'I'm afraid I can't say. I'm not completely sure. Not 100 per cent, anyway.'

'I don't mind hearing a guess.'

'Sorry, I can't.'

Barton unclenched his jaw. 'Why not? You shouldn't be protecting a murderer.'

Bernie shifted his head so his distant gaze could refocus on Barton's face. 'A long while ago, that person did something glorious for me, and I've never forgotten it.'

'What was it?'

'They saved my life.'

Barton took a measured breath, the last grains of time slipping through his fingers. He had seconds to formulate the right question.

'Saving one life doesn't permit you to take another. I need to hear that name.'

Bernie laughed, or choked. It was hard to tell.

'I've never felt robbed by cancer. I had a terrific run. A few mistakes here and there. More years than many. More love than most, but I'm a bit annoyed about checking out now. I'd have loved to see how all this pans out. That's the problem with death. The end of the lives of the people you know, the denouement of their stories, I suppose, will forever remain a mystery.'

Barton couldn't help growling his response. 'That's a cold attitude.'

The older man licked his parched lips. 'I know, but there's a chill to death. Sometimes you forget you're dying. You make plans, then you realise you won't be about. That's tough.'

Barton saw Bernie was struggling to concentrate.

'You should tell me everything. Other innocent people might be at risk.'

'Yes. Pro certo habeo.'

'What does that mean?'

'I hold it as certain.' He swallowed deeply, which appeared to be an effort, then peered at the man next to his bed. 'Will you ask the boy to leave?'

It was then that Barton understood. Bernie wasn't falling asleep. He'd taken something. Barton took out his phone and turned it on.

Bernie's eyes blazed, but the lids were still hooded. 'Put that away. Don't you dare have them resuscitate me, only for me to die in agony a few weeks later. You'd be too late, anyway. I'm well beyond help.'

Hoffman looked more than happy to leave, so Barton gave him a nod. After his officer had vanished, he stared down at the fading man. As if sensing the end, the shadows in the room seemed to crawl closer, as though preparing to take their next guest. Even the light outside appeared to have dimmed.

Barton shifted tack. 'Had the pain become too much?'

'It hadn't been too severe, but the last few days, unbearable.'

'Painkillers not able to be upped?'

Bernie coughed weakly. 'There's not enough morphine in the whole world for where I was.'

Barton took a deep breath. 'What have you taken?'

His voice dwindled to a quiet murmur. 'Everything. Chemo tablets, paracetamol, statins, various opioids, a few of Beryl's. All washed down with a glass of Alka Seltzer, so I didn't barf it up.' Bernie's face relaxed and his eyes closed. 'I'm sorry, they won't stay open. Do you mind revealing how Rhys died?'

Bernie might have been lying about what he'd taken, but Barton decided to risk telling him.

'Heroin.'

Bernie smiled. 'That makes sense.' He took a few deep breaths, as though uncertain of something. 'I have a favour to ask. Will you sit with me?'

Barton gasped. 'You bring me here and give me a cryptic rhyme, then fail to tell me who the killer is. Forgive me for not wanting to watch you die.'

'You don't have to hold my hand.' Bernie sniffed. A weak effort. 'You can leave if you want, although I don't fancy being alone. Nor did I wish to put Beryl through it. Her last memory would never have been of me screaming in pain and begging to go. I couldn't bear that. She deserves better after giving me a wonderful life, but she'd have rung for an ambulance in these circumstances. I know she would.'

Bernie's voice was getting even quieter and his speaking slower. Barton had to lean over him to hear. His nose twitched at Bernie's breath.

'If people are at risk from a killer, I have to know their identity. My job is to protect the public. You're a decent guy. Think of them. Their wives or husbands. Their family.'

Bernie slowly shook his head. 'The person deserves a chance to get away with it, like I did. So let me tell you this.'

The room went quiet, then Bernie inhaled deeply. 'I had a brief affair with another at the club. That should set the ball rolling for you, but Beryl isn't aware. I'd prefer it to stay that way. I made a silly mistake, for a few weeks, that's all.'

Bernie's hands, which had been resting on his stomach, dropped to the sides. His breathing rattled in his chest. His ribcage barely rising at all.

'Bernie?'

There was no reply. Barton glanced around for a chair to sit next to the bed but couldn't see one. Striding from the room, he grabbed a high stool from the kitchen and went back to the lounge. He inhaled deeply, then reached down beside the hospital bed and lifted Bernie's hand up. He held it. The dying man's eyelids flickered briefly but remained closed. Barton felt the faintest pressure being returned.

A minute later, the wheezing gasps came less often, each one a shallow, trembling rattle. The lines of sixty-four largely happy years on Bernie's face seemed to fade, the worry for his wife that had clung to his brow smoothing away. The slightest of smiles shone for a few seconds.

Barton wasn't aware when the rise and fall of the man's chest had stilled, nor which faint sigh had been his last, but Bernie, who was mostly a good man, had gone.

54

DCI BARTON

Barton returned to the pool car and clambered inside.

Hoffman stared at him, face pained. 'Is he?'

'I'm afraid so.'

'While you were with him?'

'I wasn't checking the contents of his fridge when it happened.'

'Brutal.'

Barton's shoulders slumped. 'You wait. You'll be forty before you know it. That's when tragedy and illness become more familiar acquaintances. You learn how your health is a lottery. Death can swiftly and unexpectedly arrive.' He gave the younger man a knowing look. 'Seize your opportunities.'

'Doesn't sound like ageing is something to look forward to, but I get what you're saying.'

'It's not all negative. One of the best parts of getting older is appreciating life more as you come to understand how fragile it can be. Right, you'd better contact Beryl and tell her what's happened. Call the office. They'll find her number.'

Hoffman opened his mouth but then took out his phone and dialled.

'I've got the details,' he said afterwards. 'Shall I ring Control first and arrange for a PC to be here?'

'No. We'll be staying until Beryl arrives. It's the right thing to do with me being the last person with him. She'll have questions. I can help put her mind at rest.'

Over the next few minutes, Barton tried to let the investigation roll around in his head, like a stone looking for moss, but it wasn't easy with a crying Beryl on the other end of Hoffman's line.

Hoffman finished the call.

'She's at Tesco Extra. She'll be about twenty minutes.'

Hoffman appeared to be in a retrospective mood, but he was a detective through and through.

'What was she doing over there without her car?'

'It's the closest big supermarket. Perhaps she went with a friend.'

'Interesting. Means she could have moved around undetected by us. We should enter her friend's number plate into ANPR.'

'Making a fair few leaps there. I reckon we can rule out any involvement from Beryl.'

'Why is that?'

'The person who tampered with that cupcake was careful. If they were involved in some of the deaths twenty-odd years ago, they've stayed in control since then. Beryl is a heart-on-your-sleeve type of woman. Steaming into the office and shouting. Beryl and Bernie's relationship was pretty special. It was real.'

'Doesn't stop her from being a clever psycho. Or him, for that matter.'

'Well, I suppose, but they loved each other very much. They still argued, like normal balanced people, ones who occasionally make mistakes, but their marriage became stronger because of surmounting their problems. Bernie wouldn't have written the poem if Beryl was involved. He'd have died without commenting, in order to protect her. They were clearly the most important person in each other's lives.'

Hoffman shrugged. 'Unless it was an extremely clever ploy by him to lead our attention elsewhere and save his wife from thirty years in the slammer.'

'I've found dying makes people honest, but you're right. Death and taxes are the only certainties. People will shock or surprise you in your career again and again.'

Hoffman grinned. 'Aren't they the same thing?'

'Which would you prefer, a shock or a surprise?'

Hoffman gave his boss a wry smile but didn't reply.

'Stay focussed when Beryl's here,' said Barton. 'With Bernie's demise, I suspect the next conversation we have with her will be the last that's of any use.'

'What are you saying – that with a love so strong, she'll fall to pieces?'

'Yes, and we can't pester a grieving widow without strong suspicions.'

Hoffman barked out a laugh. 'Is that the real reason why we're staying to talk to Beryl? My, you're ruthless.'

Barton's expression was one of outrage. 'How dare you?' He winked at Hoffman. 'Although, sometimes doing what's right comes with benefits. I do have a specific question that will give me clarity if she answers honestly.'

A few minutes later, a grey Honda pulled up outside the house. They watched Beryl lean over and hug the driver, then get out and stand precariously on the pavement.

Barton left his vehicle and went over.

'Do you want to hold my arm?'

'No. I'm going to be tough.' She lifted her chin. 'At least for today.'

The Honda accelerated away.

'Is your friend not staying?'

'She's coming back in an hour. Your partner explained over the phone you were there with him when he died.'

'Yes, I was.'

She took a deep breath.

'Come on, then. Take me in. Only you, please. Too many people will upset me.'

Beryl did end up taking hold of the inspector's hand. He briefly wondered what his younger self would think, seeing him now.

She peered up at him as they neared the property. 'I seem to be hanging on to you a lot lately.'

'All part of the service.'

They made it into the lounge unscathed. Beryl released a small cry when she saw Bernie lying on the bed. She sat on the same stool Barton had, which he'd left knowing she would want to be next to her husband.

He stood at her side. 'Is there anything we can do for you?'

'What happens now?'

'I assume you've already organised a funeral parlour.'

'Yes. We chose one together.'

'I'm sorry to say there'll be a post-mortem.'

Beryl's head jerked around, the beginnings of a glare on her face, but she was no fool. Her grimace quickly dissolved into a sob.

'Oh, Bernie. He killed himself, didn't he?'

'It seems so.'

'But why investigate his remains? He was dying anyway.'

'Put simply, he poisoned himself. It's procedural. We need to find out exactly what he took.'

Beryl sniffed, then wiped her nose with a tissue from her pocket.

'I suppose Bernie wouldn't mind. He loved his crime novels. In fact, I think he'd have enjoyed knowing he would still be playing a part after he…'

Barton briefly rested his hand on her shoulder.

'Please accept my deepest sympathy.'

Beryl stood and slipped off her coat, revealing another twinset, green this time, and gently rested her fingers on Bernie's chest as though she might wake him.

'He promised to save me from the gruesome end.' Tears trickled down her cheeks. 'I thought he meant by going into a Sue Ryder hospice.'

Barton couldn't help chuckling, and she did, too.

'I feel a bit relieved, actually. I was so terribly worried about the final few days. At least this way, he wasn't in pain.'

'It's obvious you were devoted to each other. He didn't suffer at all. Quietly slipped away.'

'And you were with him?'

'I was. I held his hand.'

Beryl glanced up into Barton's face. 'Like you did mine.'

'Just like that.'

She let out a deep sigh. 'Thank you so much. That gives me some peace. I'm sure you didn't imagine you'd be doing that today.'

'No, but, in a way, it was a privilege.'

'I don't know what to say. Do you have anything to ask me? I'll go to my sister's in Darlington until the funeral. Maybe go to my son's in Cornwall for a bit, although he's very busy. I couldn't stand it here on my own.'

'That's not a bad idea. Look, I'll let you have some time alone with him, but there is one detail that's stuck in my head.'

'Yes?'

'Bernie mentioned someone had saved his life many years ago.'

'Oh, he was being theatrical. He often told me I'd saved him, from a lonely existence on his own.'

Barton wasn't sure how to reply to that. His mind was whirring. Beryl being the murderer didn't fit with what he'd seen. Neither spouse would have jeopardised their union.

'Would you consider your marriage perfect?'

Beryl scoffed.

'There is no such thing. There's commitment and time. That's all. Ups and downs. Highs and lows. He cheated on me once, you know.'

Barton nearly recoiled with surprise. Not with the affair, but with her being aware of it. 'Who with?'

'I never knew for sure, but I could tell. He seemed different. Not my easy-going Bernie. Invigorated, perhaps, but also carrying a burden. I don't think I'd been behaving nicely at that point. Giving him grief for spending so much time at work. He did love his job. I started putting more effort in again, being more attentive, but my suspicions grew. One night, I was planning to confront him, but he appeared so sad when he came home late that evening. He looked relieved, too, so I didn't accuse him.'

'Did you know where he'd gone?'

'Oh, I wasn't sure. Maybe The Bell after work. I asked him if he'd been to the pub, but he answered in a strange way. Said he'd been lost, but he was back now, and he would never leave again.' Beryl smiled. 'I never regretted not asking more. It would have ruined our past and our future.'

He gave her a small, reassuring nod.

'I'll be in touch.'

'Thank you again, Inspector.'

Barton stepped from the house with purpose, Bernie's words echoing in his mind. When Bernie had said the killer had saved his life, Barton now understood what he meant. The net was closing in fast now, and many would feel the effects.

55

VIJAY SINGH

Vijay woke on the sofa. He could barely remember the walk home from Morwen's. God, he was getting old. Two and a half glasses of wine, a whisky, and he'd passed out for a couple of hours. He supposed they had finished their drinks quickly. He raised his head, but a flash of pain bolted through it. His eyes clamped shut, and his head dropped back down.

He had to force his eyes to reopen. The lounge swam into focus with a sickening lurch. Vijay blinked against the harsh light filtering through his pristine window, yet he recalled a dull day. Disorientated, he tried to sit up again, but the room spun.

He vaguely remembered Morwen shutting the door on him... then nothing. He hauled himself to his feet, a loud drum beating against his skull, nausea washing over him, and stumbled into the kitchen, his legs shaky and uncoordinated.

Cold water from the tap, splashed on his face, helped somewhat, but even raising his arms was an effort. Returning to his wife's mirror, he frowned at his reflection. Bloodshot eyes, skin pale, a strange tingling in his fingertips. His usually razor-sharp mind felt as if it had been hammered into mediocrity.

Something wasn't right, but he couldn't pin down exactly what. A shadow near the tall window next to the front door showed a shape leaning against the glass. He struggled with the key, lacking the necessary dexterity, but just managed it, then nearly fell over the sill as he stepped outside.

A parcel lay there. He got on his hands and knees to pick it up, not trusting his balance. It was another wrapped Christmas present with an X on the label. Vijay strained to lift it, even though it wasn't that heavy. Through the paper, he felt something large and rubbery, but droopy and soft. Odd.

Back inside, he flopped into an armchair and peeled the wrapping away. It was an oversized fluffy blue hot-water bottle. A memory tugged at the edges of Vijay's awareness, like a small but stubborn fish, refusing to be fully reeled in.

It was the night of the book club meet. His spine had twinged when he selected his Secret Santa envelope. He'd moaned afterwards about a nagging throb in his lower back if he sat in an office chair too long. Vijay's addled thoughts caught up with the obvious. Two Secret Santa presents. His teeth bared with horror. Unless this hot-water bottle was filled with dynamite, the first gift had been the dangerous one.

His hangover was well beyond the bounds of normal. He dragged his mind back to late that morning, nervously swigging big mouthfuls of wine with the love of his life. Two whiskies when he'd got home, not one, but even though he'd slugged them down like J. R. Ewing in Dallas, they weren't huge pours.

An image of Rhys popped into his head. A serious face of warning. It wavered and dimmed, then abruptly vanished. His old partner had died swiftly and suddenly.

Vijay's phone lay on the armchair. It felt strangely thick as he grasped it. In a few moments, he suspected, he'd be unconscious, and the ability to beg for help would slip from his clumsy hands.

His vision blurred, he stabbed at the screen with a wooden finger, finally managing to enter his passcode. More awkward prods followed. A final, agonising effort peering in at his blurry recent numbers, a poke, then his call connected. He gasped with relief as the dialling tone echoed out.

The voice that answered, gravelly and quiet, seemed to come from a million miles away.

'Yes?'

A single word, wispy and insubstantial, hissed from Vijay's lips.

'Poisoned.'

56

DCI BARTON

Barton and Hoffman arrived in Paston at Mary and Eric Thwaite's property. Neither got out of the vehicle.

Hoffman twisted in his seat.

'So, Bernie was a nice guy, but he erred from the righteous path and was unfaithful.'

'Yep, and we can have a decent guess who with.'

'Avani.'

'Right.'

Hoffman tilted his head from side to side. 'Surely Beryl would have suspected who the woman was.'

'You'd have thought so. How would she have felt about them working together still? Temptation smiling in the room next door.'

'Perhaps she trusted him. If she'd had it out with Avani, the cat would have been out of the bag.'

'It sounds like Avani became ill not long after, anyway.'

'So, Beryl settled for a vengeful choking as Avani lay on her deathbed.'

Barton held out his hands. 'Maybe. It's a tangled web all right. Vijay probably stopped paying his wife any attention. He clearly has a thing for Morwen, which probably started when he first set eyes on her. The strange thing is, I saw a driving licence photo of Avani. She had large, expressive eyes and wonderful long hair.'

'Life's mad, isn't it? Vijay should have felt fortunate with what he had.'

'Yeah, but people can't help how they feel. We were told Bernie and Avani got on together. Even kind, decent people make impulsive decisions at times, especially if they're feeling unhappy or unloved.'

'Helped by Avani being pretty and there being a cosy pub over the road from the office.'

Barton chuckled. 'A nearby watering hole always helps to oil the wheels of illicit romance, but Beryl knew Bernie so well, she guessed at the short-lived dalliance.'

Hoffman took the key out of the ignition, reached for his door, then paused. 'So, nobody saved his life in the conventional way. No one dragged him from a burning wreck. Nobody donated a kidney.'

'Nope. Bernie swiftly realised what a terrible mistake he'd made in having an affair. He ended it before Beryl confronted him, thereby going to his grave believing she never suspected. For all the years since, he worried if Beryl ever found out, she'd divorce him, and he would have ruined everything. Lost his soulmate.'

Hoffman nodded furiously, having finally caught up. 'Gotcha. So, whoever he had the affair with never spoke of it either, which he considered as them protecting him. That would make our killer a woman. Wait a minute. We suspect it's Avani he hooked up with. She can't have killed Rhys, unless this is a haunting.'

Barton couldn't help laughing as Hoffman held his head in frustration.

'I'd suggest we put that line of thought on the back burner for the moment,' said Barton. 'Don't you think it's more probable that someone else rumbled their secret romance?'

'Ah, and they kept quiet, which saved Bernie's marriage, and earned his loyalty.'

'Now you've got it. They might have seen them kissing or leaving a hotel together.'

Hoffman sucked his teeth as he appeared to try and picture that sequence of events in his mind. 'It's still messed up. Bernie wouldn't tell us who it was. If he's such a decent bloke, why would he protect a killer?'

'Bernie was at the end of his days and in a lot of pain. It's easy to suspect he wasn't thinking rationally. He had taken a life-ending overdose of a wide range of drugs.'

'Seemed pretty compos mentis to me. Straight enough to write his ditty, too.'

'Yeah, I'd agree. Perhaps he was simply a massive crime book fan. He loved mysteries and, having enjoyed the distraction before his demise, decided to let it run.'

'Hoping he's looking down as it plays out?'

'Well, I suspect he'd be peering up, with St Peter frowning on those who aid criminals.'

Hoffman smiled, but his face soon became serious.

'He could still have been unforgiving and unhinged, and partly or fully involved.'

Barton bit his lip as he pondered Bernie's involvement. 'Possibly, but he gave me that poem. He talked more than he needed to. Maybe he hoped we would solve the puzzle, but for whatever reason wanted us to do so methodically.'

'Like Sherlock Holmes.'

'Or Columbo.'

'Unless he in part approved of what happened back then.' Hoffman clicked his fingers. 'Perhaps this is related to the previous deaths. For example, maybe Bernie agreed with what happened to Charlie.'

A flicker of excitement sparked in Barton's eyes. 'See, you're a bright guy when you put your mind to it. We're certainly on the verge of cracking this case. A few more carefully placed questions, or if we locate Mark Kilby, and the truth will unravel like rolling out a carpet.'

They left the vehicle, trudged up the path, and knocked on the door. Barton noted there was no Kia parked on the drive.

Eric answered after a brief wait. He showed no shock at their presence.

'Come in. Great timing. Kettle's boiled, and I was about to open my new biscuits.'

Eric was wearing a white shirt, a red tie and a tartan waistcoat. His shoes shone and his trousers were pressed.

'Heading somewhere special?' asked Barton.

'I fancied getting dressed up. At my age, you don't get too many chances to go out looking smart. Quick cuppa. Then I was off for a few beers. Check out the ladies.'

A smiling Barton let Hoffman enter first, then followed, taking a slow look around the clean kitchen. Through the window lay a small but pristine garden.

The officers chose coffee when asked. Barton recalled his and Zelensky's chat about the closed pub nearby.

'Did you ever go to The Postillion?'

'Yeah, I loved it in there. Always stuff going on. Fights, dances, singing, life, you name it.'

'Yes, it's a shame so many pubs have gone.'

Eric triumphantly lifted a box of Marks & Spencer Outrageously Chocolatey biscuits off the worktop and guided the two men through an open doorway into a dining room with a table and four chairs. He settled himself down, peeled the plastic wrapper off and slid the tray out of the cardboard.

'A neighbour bought me these for Christmas. Wanted to make sure I had a few surprises on the big day. If you reach nearly ninety, most of your pals are dead, so it's always a treat to get a gift. Anyway, I open everything immediately nowadays, just in case. Who knows if I'll expire before Father Christmas has been? Especially considering current events.'

A playful smirk touched Eric's lips.

'Where's Mary?' asked Barton, relishing the prospect of a couple of his favourite treats. Although, as Eric had just said, he was glad he'd seen the plastic wrapper removed in light of what had been occurring.

'You've not long missed her. She popped out to deliver her Secret Santa present.'

Barton checked if Hoffman had seen the mischievous expression pass over Eric's face, but the officer was selecting a biscuit wrapped in blue foil.

'We've done an office Secret Santa in the past,' said Barton, feigning ignorance. 'Who are the people she does it with?'

'The book club members. We do it every year. I told her not to bother this year after all that's happened, but she insisted. Apparently, we need fun and mystery to forget about how cruel life can be. I think Mary bought Vijay a jumbo-sized hot-water bottle. I overheard him saying he had a bad back when we last went out, so she probably did, too.'

'Are you playing as well?'

'Yes. I've got Kasia, who's hard to buy for. She seems to have everything anyone could ever want, but there's an underlying sadness in that woman.'

Barton paused mid-chew, unsure where the elderly man was leading the conversation. 'What's the cause?'

'I'm not certain. It's not the loss of her husband, so maybe it's just me who suspects she is. I don't see her often. Perhaps it was an off day. We all suffer from time to time.' He took a bite, biscuit crumbs falling to the table. 'Anyway, we're supposed to guess who sent which Secret Santa at the next meeting.'

'Wait, you already said Mary got a hot-water bottle for Vijay. Where's the mystery if you already know?'

Eric tapped his nose. 'I found it on top of the wardrobe when I was hunting for something else. Hope so at least, otherwise it's for me.'

Hoffman stifled a laugh beside Barton. Eric grinned at them both, then his smile faded away.

'To be honest, Christmas has never been the same since the death of my son, Walter.'

Barton stopped chewing again and spoke with his hand over his mouth. 'It must be tough to lose a child, especially in that way.'

Eric's fingers hovered near his cup, but he didn't pick it up. His gaze fell on Barton.

'It wasn't suicide, if that's what you've heard. He died of an overdose.'

57
DCI BARTON

Barton's biscuit morphed into cement. He took a big sip of coffee to clear it from his mouth.

'Say that again.'

'I forget the terms used at the inquest. Misadventure was mentioned, but I reckon he was merely off his face next to the lake at Ferry Meadows, not suicidal. He adored it down there – nature, peace, water, people, but no judgement. Spent a lot of time at a jetty feeding the swans, admittedly drunk, or later high, but he seemed happy in a way he never was in Stilton or here. It's funny, Mary and I loved the village, me in particular. I felt I belonged there, you know, a part of something, but not every penny fits the same slot, does it?'

Barton was trying to get his head around how that information affected their case, leaving Hoffman to ask what was on his mind.

'How come everyone believes it was a suicide? The coroner wouldn't usually give that as his conclusion if narcotics were present.'

Eric's fingers traced the edge of the tablecloth. 'It was the stigma, you see? Mary seemed to think suicide was somehow more noble. Taking drugs was what pushed Walter's mental health to breaking point. We noticed a change about six months before we left Stilton. He bought them off a guy in Yaxley, the next big village away.' Eric sighed. 'Mary thought his memory would be more tarnished than it already was, if drug addict got added to his lengthy list of identities.'

Hoffman was clearly struggling with what to say.

'I suppose that's understandable.'

'Isn't it? We tried to get him clean. He didn't know anyone to score from in Paston, but I followed him once. He used to catch the bus to Yaxley. I suppose drugs numb you quicker than alcohol. I drove after the bus that day, then kept an eye on where he went. So I knew where the dealer lived and confronted him when Walter had gone. Told him to stop selling smack to my child.'

'What did he say?'

'He laughed at me.'

Barton had been listening intently. 'Why didn't you tell the police about the supplier?'

'Mary stopped me. She was worried Walter might get hurt if he went to score again and we'd caused trouble for the guy with the authorities. Our boy died a week later.'

'Which substances did Walter take?'

'It would be quicker to list the ones he didn't.'

'Heroin?'

Eric frowned. 'I can't precisely remember. Ecstasy, maybe cocaine. Is that the same as heroin, because I'm unsure?' Eric groaned as he pushed himself upright, anger surfacing on his face. 'The post-mortem listed them. The amount and combination from the toxicology reports indicated levels that would have dropped an ox, so, at the least, he'd have been extremely confused. We have a copy, but it's up in the loft. Out of sight and all that.'

'Don't worry,' said Barton. 'We can get another one.'

Eric exhaled wearily as he ran his hand through sparse hair.

'Looking back, we'd have been better off saying it was an overdose. I think people judged us more. You know, that he must have been so unhappy living here, he killed himself.'

Hoffman took a few seconds, obviously thinking hard. 'Didn't anyone find out, perhaps from the local newspaper?'

'No, it's not like nowadays. Months and months passed before the coroner's report was issued. Mary went to the *Evening Telegraph* and persuaded them we'd suffered enough and not to publish the details. The funeral was a terrible affair. Mary didn't want any gossiping, so she kept it to the two of us.

Didn't feel real afterwards. As though I'd just scattered a dog's ashes in the garden of remembrance.'

Barton studied Eric's face. 'Were you furious with the dealer?'

Eric's right cheek twitched. 'Yeah, I was. I returned to his squat, but he'd gone.'

'What did the guy look like?'

The tired old man blew out a long breath.

'Short, lank, weird longish hair at the back. Ratty features. An old aviator jacket. The type with a furry collar.'

Barton made another connection. He parked it for a moment. 'I have some more tough news for you. Bernie died today.'

Eric's face fell. Rheumy eyes met Barton's. 'Nice chap, Bernie. Tried his best in difficult circumstances.'

Now it was Barton's turn to frown. 'What were they?'

'Oh, sorry, poor joke. His wife's a bit of a firebrand. They made it work though, didn't they? Managed to stay sane and together through it all.'

Barton sensed Eric wanting to tell them something. 'Are there skeletons in Bernie's closet, then?'

Eric chuckled, but it soon tailed off. 'Perhaps one or two. He might have had an affair once.'

So at least Eric was another person who was aware of Bernie's and Avani's brief union. Again, Barton pretended it was news to him. 'You don't say. How long ago?'

Eric squinted. 'It's hard to recall.'

'As far back as when Avani and Charlie died?'

'Maybe before then. Dates are difficult at my age. The years blend together when nothing much changes.'

'Do you remember who the woman was?'

'No, I heard a few comments in the office. Suspected something was going on. I was only the accounts administrator at work, so the big cheeses didn't always gossip with me.'

Hoffman had taken out his notebook. 'I was just thinking that, like Bernie and Beryl, you and Mary made your marriage a success, but you have a large age difference. Is it all right if I ask whether that affected your lives, or wasn't it an issue?'

Eric shifted in his seat. 'It was okay for me, but then I had the better bargain. Mary's had to deal with my flagging strength and enthusiasm for the last ten years.'

Hoffman scowled, no doubt struggling with how to frame his next question. 'I hope you won't mind me saying this, but when I first got involved in this case, I had the view Jones and Singh was a great place to work, but I'm not so sure now.'

Eric vigorously shook his head. 'Oh, no, it was fabulous. There was an electric energy in that building at the beginning, and it was so intensely professional that you couldn't help but feel like one of the team. Rhys ran a disciplined yet rewarding operation.'

Barton decided the time had come to shift tack. 'So, letting you go was the right call.'

Eric kept his eyes on the table but slowly nodded. 'Perhaps. I didn't mention an element of that to you before, not with Rhys being recently deceased. Too much water under the bridge, but there was something more to my leaving.'

'More than you not performing?' asked Barton firmly.

'Yes. I found some suspicious paperwork in one of the files. It appeared to me that someone had recorded a strangely large payment for the quantity of work done, so I checked the bank. The amount we received was much less.'

Barton didn't like the sound of that.

'Fraud?'

'I wasn't a qualified accountant, but I've always had a gift with numbers. So, I did some digging and detected a merry-go-round of money. Back then, it was still mostly paper ledgers, not computer systems, so any mischief wasn't easy to notice. Journals were my friends, though, and I found a few more incidents. I took it to Rhys.'

'Sorry,' said Hoffman. 'Can you explain?'

Eric smiled at him. 'The simplest way to describe it is, someone had inflated the accounts to make the firm appear in a stronger financial position than it was.'

Barton had guessed, but Hoffman asked the obvious question. 'Who was responsible?'

'Rhys himself.'

'That's not great, with him being the boss.'

'No, he never admitted to it being him. Said he'd sort the problem out, but it had to be his actions.' Eric scratched his head. 'I suppose I could have been wrong. Rhys explained that the entries had been a temporary shortfall he needed to cover, and it wouldn't happen again. He wasn't lying about that because I didn't find any more proof, but our relationship suffered. He struggled to look at me. Six months later, I received my marching orders.'

'Perhaps he got better at hiding it.'

'Maybe.' It was obvious by Eric's glare that he felt hard done by.

'Must have pissed you off,' said Hoffman.

'A little, but we had problems with our son, and Mary hated everyone in the village knowing our business. Computers were not my forte, anyway, and they were the future.' Eric shrugged. 'I swiftly made peace with it all. Mary was close to Kasia and Beryl, so I bit my tongue. Chose not to stir the hornets' nest. Rhys framed my sacking as cost-cutting, which might not have been far from the truth. He gave me a big severance cheque, covered the family's health cover for the next five years, and told me we could carry on being members of the book club, which Mary and I loved, although that also had its complications.'

Barton wondered if Eric understood he was giving them a motive for wanting to make Rhys suffer.

'What kind of complications?'

'Accountancy isn't exciting, but there's endless pressure, hours of concentration, with rapidly approaching deadlines. Everyone at the firm let off steam in the pub. The Bell is so inviting and cosy, we'd spend hours there. Situations developed. Fate, it seems, is not without a sense of irony.'

Barton's phone rang. It was Control. He held up one finger.

'Inspector Barton.'

'Sir, there's been a 999 call from Caldecote Road in Stilton. The caller was Morwen Jones.'

'What service did she ask for?'

'Ambulance. She hung up after the initial details, but sounded in a panicked way, so she was possibly seriously ill. Response vehicles are en route. Considering what happened to Rhys there, they'll need to assess before the paramedics can attend. Your name is marked against the address to be contacted.'

'Thank for ringing. I'll be at the scene in twenty minutes with DC Hoffman.'

'Understood. Will advise if the situation changes.'

Barton sat quietly. Eric had told them a lot, but he hadn't answered some questions and been vague at times, meaning the picture in Barton's mind of what had occurred still wasn't completely clear. He was close, though. It was as if a wrong jigsaw piece had been pressed in where it didn't exactly fit. Eric hadn't quite given them enough.

Barton pressed for more.

'Who did Bernie have an affair with?'

'I'm not certain.'

'Who might it have been?'

Eric opened out his hands. 'Sorry.'

Barton thanked him for his time, but recognised he'd be back soon. He said goodbye and swiftly ushered Hoffman outside. Barton happened to glance through the lounge window as they drove away.

Eric was already talking on the phone.

58

DCI BARTON

Hoffman drove rapidly but within the limits. If there was anything serious occurring at Morwen's house, such as a crime in progress, Uniform would be at the scene before them to deal with it.

'What did Eric mean about fate having a sense of irony?' asked Hoffman.

'The phrase is a quote from *The Matrix*. Eric knows much more than he's letting on. It was another tip, but I'm not sure if he gave it to us deliberately. Irony is where the outcome is the opposite of what was intended or expected. They set the book club up for entertainment and to bring them together. I think he's implying it will be their downfall. There was something else more important in what he said.'

Hoffman tossed a hand in the air. 'How can you stay on top of all this?'

'You just keep joining the dots. How would you feel if you were sacked for spotting fraudulent behaviour?'

'Furious.'

'If your boy died?'

'Sad, depressed.'

'If a drug dealer who got your son hooked laughed in your face.'

'Murderous.'

'If you had reached the final chapter of your life and felt all of these emotions…'

Hoffman gripped the steering wheel. 'Eric moves up the leaderboard.'

'What was Mark Kilby's description?'

'Fox.' Hoffman slapped his forehead with the palm of his hand. 'Shit. We just heard about a rat. It's going to be Kilby's dad.'

'I was thinking more about the jacket with the fluffy collar. Maybe a young, easily influenced son saw his drug-dealing dad dressed like that and copied the style, perhaps without even realising. I'll phone Zander.'

Barton didn't even hear a ringing tone before his call was answered.

'Are you psychic, John? I had just picked up the phone to call you.'

Barton told him about their visit to Eric and the matching looks and coat.

Zander was quiet for a few seconds. 'That's interesting. What are you thinking?'

'Addicts who live at home get rumbled fast. They imagine they're acting normally, but parents can tell when they're mashed. The stoned also become careless, leaving paraphernalia around, even the drugs themselves. Walter's problems were long-term. Eric and Mary would be familiar with drugs.'

Barton waited while his friend pieced the information together.

Zander hummed down the line.

'Let me get this straight. Eric scored off the son of the man who had supplied their own child, then injected the drugs he bought into a cupcake to kill Rhys, because Rhys sacked Eric twenty-five-years ago?'

'I'm just making connections. Eric has reason to be aggrieved and a familiarity around illicit substances. He was another who mentioned affairs. Charlie was up to mischief at that time. He could be another key to unlocking some of this.'

'Actually, that's one of the reasons why I was calling. The doctor who came out to Morwen when Rhys died was also the GP for Charlie McGrath, Avani Singh and Walter Thwaite. As we suspected, Jones and Singh had family cover for all their employees. The GP has a private practice, which he runs out of his house in Stilton. I heard you're heading there to Morwen's 999 call-out.'

'Send the address. I'll check the situation at Morwen's first.'

'There's more. Mark Kilby has been seen on CCTV leaving Peterborough railway station last night in the direction of the city centre. Parveen's team spotted him. The idiot had worn a trapper hat to conceal most of his face, but he still had that bloody coat on.'

'Brilliant. There are cameras all over there. Where did he go?'

'We're not sure yet. They're checking the council CCTV around the bus station and taxi ranks. Parveen and Minton are going through Kilby's extensive criminal record before he served his long stretch. They've found five separate locations associated with him. They struggled to find his father's specifics at first. Turns out he was only a stepfather to Kilby.'

'Ah, right. Maybe the son copied the mannerisms of his stepdad, as well as his dress sense.'

'Well, he had quite the role model. Dad was a transient criminal in his youth, often moving cross-county, dossing in squats, stealing and dealing, and using variants of his own name when he got nicked.'

'The type of guy who would be in and out of women's lives, popping to the shops and disappearing for months. Not on any council records or tenancy agreements.'

'Exactly, but we've nailed him down.'

'Birth name?'

'Jeremy Lamb. No convictions for fifteen years, though. Parveen's looking into where he might be living.'

Many petty criminals changed their names, often giving the police slightly different spellings of their real one and a subtly different date of birth each time they were arrested. Sometimes it worked, but most times they simply got another alias attached to their record.

Barton considered what needed doing.

'I take it the team is out checking on Kilby's previous addresses?'

'Yeah, all except Zelensky. I've sent her to join you at the scene in case you need another officer. I'll run things here.'

'Good thinking.'

'The coroner's reports for Walter and Charlie also came through over an hour ago. Mortis said to give him a ring after he'd had a couple of hours to scrutinise them.'

'Okay, we're almost at Morwen's house now.'

'Keep me posted. Is the dam going to break?'

Barton took a deep breath. 'I reckon by the end of today, the full picture will emerge, and we'll find a trail of damage decades long.'

Zander made a humming sound. 'That's a reasonable assumption, but what if the ultimate plan is to wipe out all of the book club members?'

Barton recalled the Agatha Christie novel, *And Then There Were None*. A chill swept through him as he realised it was a possibility.

59

DCI BARTON

Barton and Hoffman left the car fifty metres away from Morwen's property, where the police had set up a cordon. A youngster in uniform with a clipboard stared nervously at Barton as he stomped towards him.

'ID, please, sir.'

Barton flashed his warrant card. 'Keep up the sterling work,' he barked. 'Be on your guard about anyone unexpected arriving.'

Up ahead were a line of response vehicles and two ambulances. Barton paced by the officers outside the property. A female officer he recognised stood in the doorway.

'Afternoon, sir.'

'Update, please.'

'Woman in her sixties feeling unwell. Said she was poisoned.'

'How is she?'

'Paramedics are with her now.'

'Has she given any details?'

'There was plenty of mostly incoherent rambling. I was told to wait for your arrival and send you inside.'

Barton brushed past her. He considered the fact he was entering a crime scene, then dismissed it. They wouldn't need CSI to solve this puzzle.

A sergeant directed Barton into the lounge. Morwen, clothed in denim shorts and a baggy T-shirt, lay pale-faced on the sofa. A male paramedic was checking her blood pressure. Another watched on with a syringe in her hand.

Barton beckoned the female and the sergeant into the kitchen. 'What's her condition?'

The paramedic spoke. 'Not great. Given how her husband died, we've injected two milligrams of naloxone.'

'How long ago?'

'Three minutes. No change.'

Two milligrams was what they started with if they suspected an opioid overdose, because naloxone rapidly reversed it. The paramedic was young, but calm. Barton guessed he'd be wasting his time but checked anyway.

'No oxygen?'

'It's not necessary at the moment. Her breathing was erratic, but it's better now we've calmed her down. Some photosensitivity. Nausea. Confusion. It's like she's massively hungover.'

Barton gestured to the syringe in the woman's hand. 'You about to go again?'

'Yes. I'll do two more if necessary, considering we could be dealing with a nitazene. Then we'll blue-light to PCH.'

'Well done.'

Barton cursed under his breath. Naloxone was an opioid antagonist. It would have a stronger affinity for a person's receptors than any opioid they'd taken. It swiftly bound to those receptors when administered, kicking off any opioid present and therefore reversing the effects, including any respiratory depression. If it wasn't working, an opioid would not be the cause of whatever ailed Morwen.

It wouldn't work on cocaine, ketamine or methamphetamines, though. Perhaps the person who'd drugged Rhys anticipated that first responders would suspect the same drug used on Rhys and try naloxone. They might have changed their poison accordingly.

The sergeant cleared his throat. 'When we arrived, sir, the victim wasn't making a lot of sense. We could pick up "poisoned", and "wine", and "Vijay", but little else.'

'As in Vijay poisoned her?'

'Hard to say. There's an empty bottle of wine on the kitchen counter.'

'See if you can clarify that specific fact with her. I'm going to ring a doctor.'

Barton called Mortis. His receptionist answered, so Barton popped back to the lounge while she connected him. The female paramedic had what he assumed was syringe number three ready. She shrugged at Barton.

Mortis came on the line. 'Yes, John.'

Barton rapidly ran through the facts. Mortis tutted down the phone. 'If there's not even been a slight change in Morwen's condition, give her one more jab, then whisk her off to the hospital. I doubt it's our isotonitazene, or at least not on its own. You said something might have been hidden in the wine.'

'Yes.'

'This is my hunch. If the wine had been heavily laced with arsenic or deadly nightshade, the flavour would be affected. It's noticeable. Assuming they or she consumed the whole bottle, my guess would be methanol was added, because the taste wouldn't obviously change.'

'How dangerous is that?'

'Deadly, depending on the dose and time since consumed, but there's a window to counter it with ethanol or preferably fomepizole, which has fewer side effects. A & E will know. I doubt the ambulance crew will have either onboard. Get them on their way. I'll ring you in five minutes to discuss the reports I received.'

Mortis cut the call without saying goodbye. An abrupt method of letting Barton understand time was of the essence.

A groaning Morwen had curled into the foetal position. The other pair of paramedics from outside were bringing in a stretcher. Barton raised his eyebrows at the one he'd previously spoken to.

'Deteriorating,' she said.

'Mortis suspects methanol poisoning.'

The woman paused, then put away the syringe she was holding.

'Understood. We'll be at Resus within ten minutes.'

The sergeant had been crouched next to Morwen. He stood up and spoke loudly so everyone could hear.

'This Vijay she mentioned drank the wine too. But he had much more of it.'

60

DCI BARTON

Barton followed the stretcher out to the driveway and watched as the crew loaded Morwen into the ambulance. He had gathered the sergeant, four uniformed officers, the other paramedics and Hoffman to him, when he noticed Kasia tentatively walking along the pavement towards the house. Zelensky was next to her, a hand supportively around the woman's back.

Brief flecks of rain spotted the air. Kasia wore a thin-looking jumper and a blouse, together with a smart pair of trousers. Only her black shoes were suitable attire for the conditions.

Barton gestured to Zelensky for her and Kasia to stay where they were, then returned his focus to the group in front of him. He gave them Vijay's address.

'There probably won't be anyone else there but be cautious.'

He turned his gaze towards the paramedics. 'It's likely to be a similar situation to here with Vijay.'

Then he focussed on Hoffman. 'Assist the sergeant but report straight back to me.'

'What are you planning to do?'

'I'm heading to the GP's. Now get going. The clock's ticking for Vijay.'

Zelensky had kept Kasia on the other side of the road, away from the departing cars and ambulances. Barton was about to beckon them over when his phone rang.

'Go ahead, Mortis.'

'John, I've had time to scan through what the coroners said about Walter and Charlie's deaths, but there's no sign of any medical records yet.'

'That's okay. I've heard the doctor from back then still lives in the village, so I'm seeing him next. Have you found anything interesting?'

'The reports are as suspected. Walter had a high quantity of heroin in his system, but multiple other substances were also present. Even for a hardened addict, rational thought would have been impossible.'

'So, that puts us in the realms of deliberate or accidental overdose, but not suicide.'

'Right. Misadventure would have been the only conclusion possible for the coroner without other corroborating evidence, which didn't exist. Walter might have walked into the water because he was hot, confused or imagining things, or because he'd simply had enough of life, but nobody could guess exactly what had been going through his mind.'

'And Charlie?'

'Blood alcohol marginally over the drink drive limit, and the presence of diazepam. Combined at those levels, they'd certainly impair judgement when driving fast but certainly wouldn't guarantee he'd have an accident.'

Barton kept his eyes on Zelensky and Kasia as he tried to remember exactly what Kasia had mentioned to him and Malik about Charlie's demise. She'd said her husband's alcohol reading was a touch over, but she'd referred to sleeping tablets. Over the road, Kasia stared blankly into the void, arms crossed tightly, having drifted several feet from Zelensky, who stood poised close by, watching her every move.

He dragged up what he knew about diazepam.

'Better known as Valium. Isn't it a benzo often prescribed in the general population for anxiety? I don't think it's an opioid or a sleeping tablet.'

'Correct on both counts. It does have sedative properties, but temazepam would be used as a short-term aid if sleep issues were the primary concern.'

So, Kasia had probably lied to him. He supposed with it being twenty-five years ago, the cause of death might have become distorted, although he was certain he'd remember precisely what had been in Holly's blood if she'd died.

'No heroin reading for him?'

'None. Appeared healthy, so no long-term addiction issues of any kind.

The verdict was also misadventure, because he hadn't been prescribed the drugs.'

Barton nodded. 'Of course, that information would be in the coroner's comments, even though you haven't seen Charlie's GP notes.'

'Yes. Coroner reports are always incredibly detailed.'

Barton raced through the implications. 'So, how did Valium get in his system if he didn't take it?'

Mortis sniffed at the other end of the line. 'The coroner's officers obviously investigated thoroughly. There was nothing to conclude he may have bought any or had used the drug in the past. They also checked to see if his wife had been prescribed anxiety medication, and she hadn't, either.'

'That's brilliant, thanks. No doubt I'll talk to you soon.'

'Pleasure as always, John.'

Barton stepped across the street to Kasia. He didn't have time for pleasantries.

'What are you doing here?'

Zelensky answered for Kasia, who appeared dazed. 'She was arguing with the scene guard when I arrived.'

Kasia's composure had slipped. She visibly steadied herself. 'Morwen rang me, but she wasn't making sense. I said I'd come, but I was with a client in Alconbury, so it took a while.'

It was a reasonable reply. Barton wanted to head straight to the GP, but there were a few questions he had to ask Kasia first.

'Will you be honest with me?'

It was a strange question to someone who might be a murderer, but Barton often used it as a baseline to check for tells or deceit as they wouldn't be expecting it.

'I'll try.'

'Did Eric ring you a little while ago?'

Kasia frowned, but she didn't break eye contact.

'He did.'

'What did he say?'

'That the police had been.'

'And why would he tell you that as soon as we'd left?'

'We're friends. He was keeping in touch.'

'That's all?'

It could have been the cool breeze, but Kasia's eyes watered. 'He was concerned.'

'Why would he be worried about you?'

'First Rhys, then Morwen. He said to be careful. There's also Vijay now.'

'How did you know about him?'

Kasia's mouth formed a line. 'Morwen told me.'

'I thought she was struggling to speak.'

'I understood that much.'

Barton wasn't convinced. He glanced back at Morwen's house and had a flash of inspiration. Eric had informed them Mary had left to deliver her surprise gift just before they arrived. Barton wondered if that was how the drugs were supplied to Vijay or Morwen. Mary would have been too late to drop off a poisoned bottle, but someone else might have done it.

'Who was your Secret Santa, Kasia?'

Kasia licked her lips, then swallowed deeply. 'Mine was Bernie.'

Barton frowned at another complication. What was going on here?

Kasia, a beautiful woman with soft eyes and a gentle smile, trembled before him. She didn't look like a murderer, but they seldom did.

61
THE BOOK CLUB KILLER

I remember driving to The Bell the night Charlie died. The rain had hammered down earlier that evening, and after I'd parked around the rear and got out, I decided to grab an umbrella from the back seat of the car. In doing so, I dropped my keys, which went slightly behind a tyre. I had to crouch and couldn't quite reach them without having to kneel in a puddle. While I looked for something to put on the floor, I heard hushed, urgent voices.

I'm not sure why I stayed hidden. Perhaps it was not only because I recognised the people who were speaking in strained whispers, but that they seemed an unlikely pair to be doing so. I rose slightly, so I could peer over the car at them. They were grinning fondly at each other, having stopped talking.

Avani made a swift move forward and kissed Bernie softly on the cheek, her grin widening as she moved back. Bernie took her hand and squeezed it gently.

'Go inside,' he murmured with tenderness.

She darted into the dimly lit courtyard, followed only by his smile.

His gaze abruptly swung in my direction, causing me to duck down. I held my breath, waiting for him to walk around the back of my vehicle and confront me.

After a nervous minute of my stooping alone, he hadn't appeared, nor had I heard him move. Then, a steady clump-clump approached, drawing closer.

My lungs felt as if they were bursting, and just as I thought I couldn't hold my breath another second, the footsteps stopped. The silence that followed stretched for what could have been mere seconds, yet felt like hours. Finally, the heavy tread moved away from me.

Despite the cool evening, a layer of sweat had settled on my back like frost. I took a moment to compose myself, then went inside.

The first person I set eyes on was Charlie, animated, mid-flow, holding court to Bernie and Avani, who both had their backs to me. All I received from Charlie was a dismissive glance.

I wandered to my left, decision nearly made, and entered the toilets. I removed the small bottle where I had put the crumbled Valium and returned to the others.

Avani noticed me return.

'There you are. I've got a round in. Shall we chat at the bar while we wait for Morwen and Rhys and the rest, then eat in the restaurant?'

Charlie still hadn't given me the time of day. His back was to the bar where our fresh drinks sat. Avani and Bernie had theirs in their hands. Charlie laughed brashly. Few in the pub wouldn't have heard his braying. I wanted him to understand how it was to be the quiet one.

The fine dust landed on the froth of his new pint. I had a fleeting panic when it didn't sink. The barmaid was serving at the other end of the bar, so I dipped my finger in and whisked the foam. Not a moment too soon. Charlie spun around, grabbed the glass, and took a huge mouthful.

He made a big deal of taking out his flip mobile phone and checking the screen.

'Sorry to say, everyone, something's come up. Work issue. I'll have to skip the meal.'

Charlie might have fooled the others, but by then, he didn't fool me. Sly eyes was the phrase I used for when he was lying. It would be a woman issue he'd planned long in advance, knowing we would all be occupied at The Bell.

Over the next few minutes, he drained his beer to the last drop. Charlie never minded pushing the drink-driving rules, but he would also shortly be bending the drug-driving ones, too.

'Enjoy yourselves,' he said, swivelling on his toes and marching to the door with a brief nod at me as he opened it.

I watched him walk into danger, and guess what? I didn't care. What happened wasn't my plan. Fate was watching, and it took the chance.

I gulped my wine back and plonked the empty glass on the wooden surface behind me. Was that a commiserating look I had from Helen, perhaps an understanding one? It's possible she noticed what I did. She would easily guess why.

As we discussed getting another drink while we waited, I felt someone's gaze on me. Bernie. I found it hard to pull my eyes away from his. What was in their depths?

Did he know I saw him and Avani outside? Or was he watching me inside?

62

DC HOFFMAN

Hoffman sprinted with the uniformed officers that Barton had sent to Vijay's house, while the paramedics ran to their ambulance. When Hoffman reached the property, which was another lovely-looking home, he hung back. The sergeant and his team raced past a gleaming Porsche, which was parked on the left-hand side of the drive. Without ringing the bell, the sergeant tried the door, found it unlocked and edged in. The other two men followed.

Hoffman heard Vijay's name being shouted at varying intervals inside.

A tense minute stretched out, then the sergeant appeared and beckoned the detective over.

'We're searching in the back garden and double-checking upstairs, but there's nobody here.'

The sergeant had opened his mouth to say something else when he abruptly stopped and pointed behind the sports car. A black shoe was visible. The officer cautiously walked over, then crouched so Hoffman could only see his cap.

Hoffman took a deep breath and followed, a knot of dread in his stomach as he prepared to set eyes on the day's second dead body. Vijay lay on his side. Sputum had gathered around his lips. Hoffman stepped closer and helped his colleague turn the lifeless form on his back.

The sergeant lowered his face to Vijay's sagging mouth and held his cheek above it. After ten seconds, he raised his head and grimly shook it.

Hoffman placed two fingers against the neck of the victim as the ambulance pulled up behind them. He stood up and waved the waiting paramedics over, his voice flat.

'He doesn't appear to be breathing, and I can't feel a pulse.'

63

DCI BARTON

Barton considered asking some of the remaining uniformed officers to escort Kasia to the station, but there were only three of them left. He took Zelensky to one side.

'I'll visit the GP, then we'll go from there. Take her inside Morwen's house. She looks freezing. Gently probe. She might be in a talking mood. Then get back to the station.'

'Do you think she's in any way responsible?'

'She knows something. Prise it out of her. Where's your car?'

'Down there. Red Ford Focus.'

Barton took the keys off Zelensky.

'And find out from Hoffman what's going on with Vijay. I'll be in touch after I've spoken to the doc.'

Barton hurried down the road to the outer cordon, spotting Zelensky's vehicle parked on the pavement. He ignored the scene guard as he ran through in his head what he hoped to ask the doctor.

Inside the vehicle, it was a relief to be out of the fresh breeze. He took his phone out and double-checked the doctor's address. It was on North Street, near the edge of the village. Barton had attended a shoot-out there during The Ice Killer case many years ago. They were big houses. He started the car and set off.

When Barton arrived at the imposing property, large, thick wooden gates were swinging wide. A grey-haired fellow in a suit was gingerly opening the door to a black Audi. Barton waited until there was space to enter between the gates, then parked in the middle of the stone posts, blocking the way.

He got out.

'Dr Al-Khafaji?'

Mid-step, the man halted, one leg in the car's footwell. He jerked his head towards Barton, peering over the door's edge. Barton was close enough to recognise a flicker of raw fear in the man's eyes.

'Can I help you?'

Barton took out his warrant card as he approached. 'Detective Chief Inspector John Barton. Cambridgeshire constabulary.'

'Yes?'

'I'd like a word about a couple of your patients.'

The GP shook his head, which made small jowls quiver on his jaw. 'You'll have to speak to my secretary and arrange an appointment. I'm going to play a friendly game of poker at The Talbot.'

Barton strode over to the stooped man, towering over him. 'You *were* going to play poker, Doctor. I need ten minutes of your time now. Either here or down at the station.'

Al-Khafaji closed his door. 'I suppose you'd better come in.'

They approached the house, which, on closer inspection, was covered in Christmas lights. Illuminated when darkness fell, they would make a glorious sight. Barton glanced at the man next to him and wondered if he was at peace or if it was all a distraction.

He accompanied the shuffling figure into a spacious, light-filled, wide hall. The walls were all white, dotted with a variety of large paintings depicting what Barton guessed was the Middle East.

Al-Khafaji saw where he was staring.

'Libya. Where my heart is.'

'Not Stilton, seeing as you've been here so long?'

'This is my house. My life and family are here, but Libya will always be home.'

Barton followed him out of the hall. They turned right and passed through white double doors into a clinical space that resembled a GP's consulting room but was much bigger with more luxurious furniture. Barton's mind made the link. There was something that connected events from twenty-five years ago to the present. It had been staring him in the face the whole time.

Dr Al-Khafaji eased himself into what appeared to be a vintage chair and gestured at the one opposite. Barton lowered himself cautiously, the plush velvet and firm seat a jarring contrast to the armchair he had at home. The high back, more suited to a pampered aristocrat than a world-weary detective, made him feel oddly exposed.

'Walter Thwaite,' said Barton.

Again, the jowls wobbled. 'I haven't seen the forms authorising release of that private information.'

Barton suspected Al-Khafaji's pals enjoyed playing him at poker. Face to face, the man was a terrible liar.

Barton had no time to search for the paperwork or to ring the office. The case was breaking too fast. Instead, he considered why the GP didn't want anyone checking his notes. He decided to be blunt.

'You're a private doctor.'

'Yes. Nearly retired. I have a few individuals I've known for decades. Friends, really, more than patients, but that's it.'

'I'm investigating the murder of one of your friends, but I suspect you already know that.'

'I am aware.'

'Talk to me about Walter Thwaite.'

Beads of sweat had broken out on the man opposite's forehead. 'Doctor-patient privilege,' countered Al-Khafaji.

Barton's voice rumbled from him. 'You know as well as I do that's not enshrined in this country, merely a strong duty of confidentiality. You're going to immediately become more cooperative, or the next few hours of questioning will occur in an interview room while being recorded. It's clear you've done something you aren't proud of. I need the information now. People are in danger.'

'And if I don't talk, either here or at the station?'

'I'll spend the rest of my career searching day and night for your misdemeanours. You may not break, but, mark my words, when folk have died, others will, and the truth will emerge.'

Al-Khafaji's hands trembled as the potential impact of his actions hit home.

Barton pressed his advantage.

'I doubt what you did was for personal gain, apart from helping a friend. I'll try to see that your reputation is protected if you cooperate. Please, tell me what you did.'

A tear from each eye tracked down the old man's lined face.

'I've been expecting a knock for twenty-five years. In a way, you being here is a relief.'

'Concerning Walter?'

The GP flinched.

'A troubled child, experimenting and then being consumed first by alcoholism, then by drug addiction. There's no more to add to that sorry tale.'

'Charlie McGrath.'

'An angry, unpleasant man. Prone to rage and the odd violent outburst, but a charming narcissist for the most part. A classic case of borderline-personality disorder. He wanted to be God but was more like the devil.'

'Did you see him much in your time as his private GP?'

'A few times. Impatient. Couldn't wait five minutes. He would often gripe about being stressed but he didn't have particularly high blood pressure. There were also moans about being tired, but I never gave him anything. If he were a nicer person, then he'd have probably slept better. I told the police that. He must have acquired the pills elsewhere.'

Barton nodded. 'Carry on.'

'He had gout once, which no doubt was God's way of punishing him.'

Barton was about to bark another question when Al-Khafaji raised his hand.

'I can guess why you're here, Inspector. I see the fire in your eyes. Did she tell you?'

'No, I came to my own conclusion.'

'The answer to your query is yes. I prescribed Valium to Katarzyna McGrath.' A choked snort, almost a sob, broke from him. 'Poor Kasia,' he breathed, his voice thick with sorrow.

Barton could guess why the doctor had resisted having his notes checked, but he needed the man to admit it.

'You prescribed them to her off the record. Why?'

Al-Khafaji's silence confirmed it for Barton. Shame was the only logical explanation. Not his, but hers. Kasia wouldn't have wanted anything on her record, least of all for her husband to find out.

The GP surprised him by shifting forward in his seat.

'I'll tell you,' he said, finally with strength in his voice. 'She was living in hell. On the outside, enjoying a privileged life. Rich; wealthy, handsome partner; successful careers; but behind closed doors, he was a monster. In fact, he never even bothered to conceal most of his behaviour. He did it in front of her face. Cheating and lying at every opportunity, but totally dominating her by sheer force of personality, or, on occasion, violence, whenever she tried to get out from underneath his shadow.'

Barton had a good idea about what had happened.

'I suspect you're a conscientious doctor but let me guess. She asked you not to put the prescription or even the diagnosis on her record, but she needed Valium. She was anxious, perhaps terrified, with physical and emotional pain, and the side effects of drowsiness would have been most welcome.'

Al-Khafaji nodded.

'Painkillers, too. Sleeping tablets for a while.'

Barton leaned back. 'But you didn't tell the police or the coroner when Valium was revealed to have been a factor in her husband's accident because you wanted to protect her. Did she deny giving the drug to Charlie? Perhaps slipping it in his drink.'

'I never asked her. She's a special person. A good person.'

Barton crossed his arms. 'She's an attractive, engaging woman. I think you knew and agreed to cover for her.'

'That's not true.'

Barton stood, the weight of the unspoken again hanging heavy in the air. A code of silence, impenetrable and deliberate, had choked this entire case. He hadn't been dealing with a simple puzzle; he was facing a carefully constructed conspiracy. One that was rapidly falling apart.

64

DCI BARTON

Barton had one more place to visit before he finally put the investigation to bed. As he was leaving the consulting room, a querulous voice sounded out.

'What will happen to me?'

Barton turned and glared at the man. 'I'm not sure, but I'll be back.'

Barton returned to the car and called Zelensky.

'Afternoon, boss. That was quick.'

'Yeah, the good doctor confirmed what we suspected. Charlie was a domestic abuser and serial cheat.'

Barton pondered telling his sergeant about the secret prescription, but he made an unusual choice and kept the knowledge to himself for the moment.

'How is Kasia?' he asked.

'Quiet. Wouldn't engage.'

'Have other units arrived?'

'Yes.'

'Go with one of the uniforms and take her to Thorpe Wood.'

'If she refuses to come?'

Barton briefly smiled.

'She won't.'

'Consider it done.'

'How did Hoffman get on?'

'From what he said, Vijay seems to have had the worst of it. He'd fallen beside his Porsche, with a blue hot-water bottle, some wrapping paper and his mobile scattered around him.'

Barton updated her with what Eric had told him earlier. Zelensky was sharp and guessed what had likely occurred.

'So, someone dropped the wine round with the poison inside, disguised as a Secret Santa present. Vijay likes his wine. It's probably a quality bottle. He fancies Morwen. Takes it over. He drinks the majority. Goes home sad, because he's a spurned admirer. Maybe even consumes more at home.'

'Sounds about right.'

'Meanwhile, Mary drops the real Secret Santa gift around, the water bottle. He wakes up in a terrible state, then sees the present. Being a smart guy, he connects the dots. His love for Morwen is pure. Much as Beryl's was for Bernie, so he rings Morwen to warn her instead of calling for an ambulance, then collapsed before he could get help for himself.'

'I assume from your casual tone he isn't dead.'

'I think he was pretty close. He had an extremely weak pulse. Hoffman said the paramedics attached breathing equipment and raced away. What else did the GP say?'

Barton decided on a small white lie.

'He was a little evasive, but he's gathering more information for me. Meanwhile, I'm off to the pub.'

'As sound a plan as any.'

Barton laughed. 'I want to speak to the waitress, Helen. I reckon I have enough now to force her to spill the beans.'

'Do you believe she's involved?'

'Maybe, but I strongly suspect Helen knows more than she's told us. She's kept quiet all these years, but I'm pretty sure I understand why. I'll call you when I leave The Bell and pick you up from the station to visit the Thwaites. Eric's evasiveness will also be coming to an end.'

Barton put his phone down, fired the car up, and turned right towards the pub.

When he arrived, he parked at the front on the main street. He entered the pub and headed for Reception. Alishia was standing at the counter and sensed his urgency.

'How can I help?'

'Is Helen in?'

'You're in luck. She doesn't normally work today, but one of the others called in sick.'

Barton nodded. He would have driven to her house otherwise, but it saved him some time.

'In her usual spot?'

'Yes. Can I help?'

'No.'

'Is everything okay?'

Barton considered her question, then bobbed his head. 'It will be.'

He crossed the courtyard, the satisfying weight of near certainty settling within him. Though every specific detail might remain unseen, he believed enough pieces had aligned to ensure those responsible would face justice.

As always, the bar was snug and inviting, but it was the quietest he'd seen it. A small group of women approximately in their fifties were putting their coats on and a few of the other tables had couples enjoying a drink near to the fire. Helen briefly had an expression similar to the one Dr Al-Khafaji had worn when Barton had visited.

She recovered much faster.

'Afternoon,' she said with a look that was without warmth. 'I thought I'd see you again.'

Barton pulled up a stool at the bar. There was nobody within hearing distance.

'Why is that?'

'Stilton's rumour mill.'

'Is that the only reason?'

'Perhaps.'

'Had any calls today?'

A merest hint of a smile rose and fell on her face. 'Yes, Eric rang.'

'To warn you?'

'To confirm the book club's reservation.'

Barton's mouth dropped open. 'They're still meeting after everything that happened?'

'Yes. Why wouldn't they?'

'There might not be anyone left.'

Helen motioned for him to follow her further along the bar, where she stood behind the pumps. They were out of sight of the other customers.

'Perhaps you don't know everything.'

Barton suspected he never would. 'You need to answer my questions.'

'I can speak off the record.'

'That's not going to cut it.'

She began to wipe down the bar. 'No comment, then.'

For a moment, Barton stared longingly at the selection of enticing real ales. A customer appeared and ordered a brandy and a pint of Birra Moretti. While she served the man, Barton put Helen's attitude up against what he had already surmised. She returned to stand in front of him, her face defiant.

Barton smiled. 'I've spoken to the doctor.'

She folded her arms. A debate flashed behind her eyes, until a sigh crept from her lips. 'Go ahead. Ask your questions.'

'Are you involved?'

'Not as such.'

It was clear he was not only on the right track, but considerably down it.

'Here's what I think happened. The incidents twenty-five years ago don't particularly relate to Walter's demise. That sad event was just a contributing factor, as was Avani's illness and death. Charlie slowly ruined the book club. He tried it on with all the women. Am I right?'

Helen's face was pinched.

'You are.'

'And, I now strongly suspect, some of the bar staff and waitresses, too.'

65
DCI BARTON

Barton placed his hands flat on the wooden surface and leaned towards Helen, whose face was set in stone.

'Obviously, this created bad feeling for years. The five book club couples appeared sound, but each had their own problems. Many of which were aggravated by Charlie's behaviour.'

Helen nodded, so Barton revealed the rest of his theory.

'To put it simply, Charlie was an extremely unpleasant individual. He'd chase and chase, but then when he got what he wanted, he'd move on to his next conquest. It seemed to be a numbers game. Kasia was miserable because it happened in front of her face while he ignored her. Due to his temper and controlling behaviour, she couldn't see a way out. Her mental health deteriorated to the extent she despised Charlie so much, she slipped drugs in his drink, causing him to lose control and crash his car.'

Helen's expression was unreadable.

'Sounds plausible. Nobody missed him afterwards. He was an evil man, better suited to being in the ground rather than ruining people's lives.'

'Life was tough for Kasia back then.'

'Very much so.'

Helen's face softened with compassion for a person who Barton now realised was a much closer friend than he'd suspected, or she had led them to believe. It was clear everyone liked Kasia, but still, why cover up a murder, or, at the least, a manslaughter charge?

Barton studied Helen's body language. He had expected her to be rigid with fear, but she wasn't. It was another clue.

'You weren't involved,' he said. 'Your conscience is clear.'

'Correct, Inspector.'

Barton sniffed as more pieces dropped into place.

'Charlie was drinking here the night he crashed the car. Were you working?'

'Yes. Because of what happened, the details are still clear in my head. I served him two pints of reasonably strong beer that evening. That was normal for him and to still drive afterwards. I remember most of the book club were here that night.'

Barton glanced around him, trying to imagine the scene.

'Where were they drinking?'

Helen pointed next to the hole in the wall. 'They stayed near the bar before taking their table in the restaurant.'

'What did you see?'

'Nothing incriminating. Charlie seemed in high spirits, which means he was acting like a complete knobhead. I was serving but heard him say he had to leave.'

Barton noticed Helen's eyebrow twitch. Was it a representation of trauma, or perhaps deceit, that had fractionally appeared? He swiftly understood Charlie wasn't one to take no for an answer, and that didn't only apply to his behaviour towards his wife.

'I can guess what happened to you. I understand why you said nothing about what you saw.'

Helen hissed at him over the counter. 'I saw nothing! All I noticed was Kasia crying because they were supposed to be having a meal together. Mary had been blanked by Charlie. He laughed as he left. That's when he had the accident, either driving to or from a clandestine meeting.'

Barton frowned.

'Why did people go for dinner with him if he was regularly such an arsehole?'

'Because Kasia wasn't allowed out without him unless he had somewhere better to be. The others were supporting her. It was why he was still invited to the book club. Otherwise, she wouldn't have been able to attend each month. Even so, Kasia often wore long sleeves and unflattering clothes, no doubt hiding the bruises that I would have had if I hadn't slapped his face.'

Helen's eyes blazed into his. She and Kasia had become close, perhaps just as a shoulder to cry on, or more likely as a friend she met.

Barton felt guilty for pushing his advantage, but there were going to be more revelations.

'Did he try it on with Avani as well?'

Helen's laugh was brittle. 'Avani carried a rape alarm when she realised the type of man he was. Mary had become weak, though.'

Barton thought of prim and plain Mary, the librarian. She'd have been cannon fodder under a relentless approach.

'Mary slept with him?'

'Oh, yes. Fell in love. She was in a fragile state anyway, with Walter's ongoing problems. You know how men cope by retreating into their caves? That's what Eric did. I think Mary felt isolated. She tried to attach herself to Charlie, hoping for affection from the wrong person, and he ate her up and spat her out.'

Barton nodded for her to carry on.

Helen grimaced. 'And everyone knew.'

'Including Eric?'

Helen snarled her reply. 'Everyone.'

Barton closed his eyes and massaged his temples as the waves of information filtered through his mind. Mary and Eric struggling through years of tough parenting. Perhaps both on anxiety tablets, but only one of them would have needed to be for them to be used to drug someone else.

Barton remembered Kasia had been driven to Thorpe Wood police station. He would get the chance to question her, but she wouldn't have been likely to put a drug such as Valium in Charlie's drink. Not at those levels. He might have just been spaced out and snoozed till lunchtime, but he might have been suspicious when he woke. His retribution would have been worse than anything she'd experienced so far. Would she have risked it?

Mary, like Kasia, was beaten down by life, rejected by her son, her husband, and then finally her lover. She would have been reduced to nothing.

The soon-to-be-sacked Eric, on the other hand, who had been much younger then, would have been a different beast. One who felt ridiculed. Discarded. Emasculated.

A man enraged.

66

DCI BARTON

A shudder, profound and unexpected, swept through Helen, then she began to sob. The tightly coiled springs of her life, stretched taut for so long, finally unwound. He stood, wanting to comfort her, but that wasn't his job. The door swung open next to him and Alishia entered. She walked around the back of the bar and hugged Helen.

Barton nodded at her. He'd got what he came for, and more.

'Thank you both.'

Alishia must have been watching from the courtyard. For a moment, he considered what she might have seen but dismissed it. Helen had been carrying the weight of her suspicions for a long time, assuming she had been honest with him. Regardless, despite Charlie's appalling behaviour, her knowledge had been a terrible burden but with liking the other book club members, she'd been strong and kept her silence.

Barton returned to the car. After sending a quick message to Zelensky to meet him outside the entrance to Thorpe Wood police station, he fired up the engine, then did a U-turn in the street and sped up the road towards Peterborough.

Barton's scowl hardened as he thought of the victims from this investigation. Many of them were women who had been mistreated by those who should have been supporting them. Lily's face appeared in his mind. What was it she'd said? 'Some men do as they please and don't care who gets hurt, as long as they get what *they* want.'

Even poor Avani had suffered. Her punishment had been to be ignored. Vijay hadn't planned to damage her, but his neglect had been the equivalent of a prison sentence all the same.

Zelensky was waiting on the grass outside the station. As he pulled up and she jumped in, his phone rang. He put on the handbrake and answered it.

'Yes, Zander.'

'No sight of Mark Kilby, but he has been to two of the premises recently. Our guys are taking statements now. One was a former friend's place. He admitted he would have helped Kilby years ago, but he's got three young kids now, so he sent him on his way. Kilby appeared panicked. Reckoned he couldn't stay where he'd been hiding out.'

'And the other?'

'Whoever Kilby knew was long gone. Luckily the bloke who answered the door was a beefy Polish fella because Kilby got aggressive with him. Pulled a small knife out, but when the guy didn't back down, Kilby ran off down the road.'

'Where and when was that?'

'An hour ago, close to the Orton centre.'

'Okay, I'm heading to Eric Thwaite's address. Tell Kasia I'll speak to her when I return, but, between you and me, I'm fairly sure she's not the killer.'

'Have you picked Zelensky up?'

'Just this minute.'

'Okay, cool. We've had another break. Parveen has just discovered two addresses for Kilby's stepfather, Jeremy Lamb. One's out near Wisbech, but the other is a flat at the Herlington shopping centre. A Jason Lamb, another of his aliases, is on the electoral register. It's possible Kilby had been staying with him, but I don't get why he wouldn't be able to continue doing so. Sounds like Kilby's in desperate straits, but I doubt his stepfather would throw him out, even if he was capable.'

Barton focussed on what the priority was. It was the drug dealer. Kilby was on foot. The Herlington centre was half an hour away, less if he ran. The reasons for not being able to live with his stepfather couldn't be positive but if Kilby had nowhere else to go, he'd be back.

Barton knew what he had to do.

'We'll go there now.'

'Great. Minton and Parveen were preparing to head down there, but this Kilby's a nasty piece of work, so I was going to get backup. Prison won't have mellowed him, nor the mess he's got himself in, so you'll need to be careful. They'll meet you in the main car park. ETA ten minutes. Four of you should be sufficient to handle him, but be cautious, for obvious reasons.'

'I'll be in touch.'

Barton cut the call after hearing Lamb's flat number, pulled away and accelerated past The Woodman pub in the direction of Orton Malborne. He updated Zelensky with his findings from Stilton and with what Zander had just told him.

Zelensky gave him a concerned grimace, even though she wasn't the type to avoid any aggravation. 'Shame we haven't got any PPE in the car.'

Barton grimly clenched one of his fists to indicate what he possessed for protection.

'Did you get anything out of Kasia?' he asked.

'No, she seemed really spaced out, so I left it for the moment.'

Two minutes later, they were parked up opposite the Spar shop. The block of flats was above the pub on their left. Barton hadn't drunk in The Dragonfly for years. He'd arrested quite a few of the regulars at one point or another, not to mention a couple of the bar staff. It was that kind of place.

'Let's check the scene out from below while we wait for the others.'

They got out and stared up at the walkway that ran along the first floor. There was a green rail stopping people from falling off. Halfway along, a door was ajar. Barton could make out the number. It was the flat they wanted.

He glanced across at Zelensky. She pointed a finger at him. 'You'd better not be thinking we don't go up there yet because you're with a woman.'

'No, I was wondering if you'd insist on leading the charge.'

'That's okay, then. Although, it's probably best if I cover our rear.'

The door to the stairwell had been propped wide with a brick. Jarring, unidentifiable music blared from an open window. The cool breeze carried the sweet scent of marijuana and spicy cooking as well as the sound of someone's off-key singing. The sharp cries of a baby helped create a fraught atmosphere. Barton led the way. They moved slowly along the walkway, adding their rhythmic footfalls to the cacophony.

Halfway along, about thirty metres from number fourteen, an argument flared up in the flat next to them. The next door along opened, and a youngster with a pram appeared. She shut the door gently, ignoring them. A teary but quiet baby sat in the seat, but the kid started up again as a fluffy elephant slipped from her grip.

Barton sensed something was wrong, although this place had always been the kind where it paid to mind your own business. He edged by the pram, then hurried twenty metres forwards to the still open door and casually walked past it, using his peripheral vision to look for signs of life. He crouched under a smeared window.

Barton looked back to see Zelensky returning the toy to the child, then tiptoeing towards him. He raised himself high enough to peek through the dirty glass and immediately found himself staring into another pair of eyes. They were gone in a flash. Barton edged around the door jamb and was immediately bumped out of the way by the solid shoulder of a fleeing person.

Barton was knocked back, but unhurt. The assailant, wearing a Shearling coat, stopped and turned. He gave Barton a small-toothed smile, then poked the blade of a short kitchen knife in his direction.

'Drop it, Kilby,' snarled Barton. 'The game's up.'

Kilby's hand lowered. He bolted away from Barton, straight towards Zelensky.

Barton set off after him, but the squat, athletic figure was soon in front of his sergeant. Barton roared out a warning.

'Knife, Maria! Let him pass.'

He cringed as Zelensky tried to jockey Kilby against the rail, clearly not having heard his holler amongst the myriad sounds. The drug dealer's arm rose, then swiftly came back down. Zelensky screamed.

Barton was a big man. A heavy man. That had been the case since he'd first become a teenager. Like a train, he took some getting going, but once he did, he could move.

Kilby heard the heavy stomps coming from behind as Zelensky collapsed beside him. He twisted, eyes widening as Barton, huge legs pumping, closed in. Kilby, at little more than five feet tall, raised his weapon again. Barton hoped it wouldn't go through his fat.

Kilby, like every adversary Barton had ever met on the rugby field, recognised too late what was coming. A locomotive that couldn't and wouldn't stop. Kilby dropped the knife as Barton dropped his shoulder.

The young man bounced off Barton and flew through the air, hitting the floor with a thump, as though someone had dropped a dead carcass from height.

A voice shouted up from below. He glanced over to spot Minton and Parveen running towards the stairs. Zelensky scrambled to her feet.

'Stay down,' said Barton.

'It's just my arm.' She pulled back her coat sleeve to reveal a puncture wound that was leaking blood.

Zelensky stared hard at a groaning Kilby.

'Was that straight from the handbook, sir?'

'Yeah, the special edition.'

Minton arrived first, racing along the gantry, cuffs already in her hand.

Barton reached down, grabbed Kilby by the shirt collar, and dragged him to his feet. He shunted the short man against the rails. Kilby groggily stared over the edge. As Minton roughly handcuffed him, Parveen stepped forward to help Zelensky.

Barton told the officers to wait where they were.

He returned to the flat where Kilby had been staying. He discovered a familiar unpleasant odour after crossing the threshold. The same smell that had been in Bernie's lounge. Barton considered caution, but he suspected the danger had been Kilby. He marched inside, nostrils flaring as the stench thickened.

He knew the layout of these flats. The lounge was at the end of the corridor. Barton slowly opened the door. A pall of decomposition hung heavy in the air.

On the sofa, a small man with greasy, mid-length grey hair lay staring up at the ceiling. Barton pinched his nostrils and picked his way through the rubbish on the carpet.

Jeremy Lamb barely resembled his most recent mugshot, but Barton supposed he hadn't offended for fifteen years, and now he'd been dead for at least a few days.

Sticking out of his chest was the handle of a kitchen knife. A knife that was identical in style to the one that Kilby had been wielding outside.

67

DCI BARTON

Barton ran his eyes over the thin, blood-stained T-shirt that Lamb had been wearing when he died. It stretched tightly around the mound of what Barton guessed was a beer belly. The deceased, who just about fitted the description Eric had given them of the guy who'd provided the drugs to Walter before he drowned, had a fleshy neck and flabby arms. It wasn't the body of a hopeless drug addict.

There were at least five distinct puncture marks in his chest, but not much blood. The sofa, filthy as it was, had no crimson stains either. Barton suspected the stab wounds had been inflicted on Lamb after he'd died.

Barton briefly gazed around the room. At initial glance, it had appeared a squalid pigsty, with empty lager cans and fast-food containers on the carpet, but, on closer inspection, some books were in a pile on the fireplace and there was the odd photograph on the walls, even a painting of a beach on another.

He climbed the stairs and opened the first door to reveal a disgusting bathroom, but Barton had seen much worse. The main bedroom wasn't too untidy. A large duvet had been pulled across the double bed. There were a few dishevelled piles of clothing, but a bedside table had various deodorants and even a bottle of cheap aftershave on it.

The other door led to a small box room with a single bed and no other furniture. There was another stack of clothing in the corner, yet this was folded and appeared clean. A pristine pair of white trainers sat atop the pile.

Barton's brain was in prime detecting mode. All the data was absorbed and processed as he clumped downstairs and stepped outside to the three female officers. He doubted Kilby had given them any grief. Few did after the heat of the moment, especially if they'd injured one of the police.

When he left the flat, Barton was therefore surprised to find Kilby standing defiantly between Minton and Parveen, staring straight at him.

'That wasn't me!' he shouted.

Barton stood over him but studied Zelensky, who held tissues over her wound.

'How's the injury?'

'It's not too bad.'

'There are two response units inbound,' said Parveen.

'Okay, get one to secure the scene. The other can provide a lift for Zelensky to A & E.'

Zelensky nodded.

'I take it you're off to Paston.'

Barton smiled. She had realised he would need to immediately visit the Thwaites. He turned his gaze on Kilby.

'Murder to add to your record?'

'I tell ya. It wasn't me. I ain't gonna kill me own father.'

'Stepfather.'

'Whatever. He's all I've got.' The younger man's face fell. 'He weren't around much, but when he was, he looked after me. Took me places. He was the best of 'em.'

Barton didn't have time to delve into those comments.

'You better start talking and quick.'

Any resistance was gone from Kilby.

'I came back here to see him a week ago. I had a bit of business to take care of.'

'Drug dealing. We've seen the trail of destruction.'

Kilby shook his head, face pained. 'I know I've got a shitty past, but I didn't mean for anyone to die. Those shits in London gave me a bad batch. I was just trying to earn some dough.'

'Tell me about your father.'

'I was staying with the old fella. As soon as I heard someone here had snuffed it, I scarpered back down south, but junkies were dying in East

London, too. Probably from the same junk I was given. I couldn't attend my probation meeting, but they had my address down there, so I had no place else to go except back to my dad's. When I arrived at the train station last night, I walked straight here. He was sparko. Stunk the join out. Must have been dead for days.'

Barton already knew the railway cameras would confirm his movements, but to a certain degree, it didn't matter. Kilby would have served only two-thirds of his original sentence. He'd now have to complete the full tariff, plus extra for grievous bodily harm with intent on a police officer, not to mention all the controlled class A drug charges with the aggravating factor of multiple deaths. That would mean decades inside.

Kilby was wilting in front of him.

'Will I be charged with murder for the people dying after taking my drugs?'

Barton felt like saying yes, but he wanted the man talking.

'No. You won't even get manslaughter. The law in this country recognises free will. They made a voluntary choice to take your heroin.'

'Phew,' said Kilby. 'What the fuck was in that stuff, man?'

Barton ignored the question. 'So, if you didn't kill your father, who did?'

For the first time, an expression of guilt rose on the criminal's face. 'In a way, it was me. I've been dabbling down south since I got out. He was the only visitor I had inside, so I bought him a mobile to keep in touch when I was released.'

Kilby's head jerked to the right as sirens sounded in the distance, rapidly becoming louder.

'Carry on,' demanded Barton.

'My old man rang me a few weeks back. Said some old git wanted to score some heroin. Reckoned it was to finish off someone suffering from cancer. They must have had no idea how much it cost cos they offered him two hundred quid. Dad was always brassic, so next time I came up, a week last Tuesday or Wednesday, I gave him a few wraps, so he could make a quick buck. I let him have them for free.'

Kilby had the front to smile at Barton, like a dog waiting for a pat.

The first response vehicle screeched around the corner and slid to a stop outside the pub. Predictably, everyone inside the premises rushed out.

Barton could imagine what fate had fallen to Jeremy Lamb.

'Your dad was a recovering addict. He kept some for himself.'

Kilby nodded, although the armed police sprinting towards the stairs had distracted him.

'I removed the needle myself, but someone had come in and stabbed him up after he died. I swear down that weren't me, either. You need to be tapped for that shit.'

Barton even managed a smile. Now he understood it all. He turned to his two able DCs.

'Okay, Minton and Parveen. When the scene is secure and further units have arrived, have Mr Kilby escorted to the station. I'll call Zander to update him on my way to Paston.'

'Are you heading to the Thwaites on your own?' asked Minton.

'Yeah, I reckon I can handle an eighty-nine-year-old.'

Barton had one last word for Kilby.

'You went back to London, then sold more of a batch you knew to be contaminated. That's going to go poorly for you.'

'I chucked my stuff, truth!'

Barton guessed it wouldn't matter. Kilby had done enough. He even had a tiny touch of understanding for him. Growing up as Kilby had, a lot of the damage to his personality would have occurred while he was a young child.

Yet others suffered similar. The crimes he had committed were his own. Kilby's drug-dealing career, such as it was, had finished.

He would be an old man when he next breathed free air.

68

DCI BARTON

Barton waited at the top of the stairs as the recently arrived officers filtered past. Two more police vehicles were pulling up. He took a moment to centre himself, pushing his feelings to one side. It was almost over. There would be time afterwards to process what had happened and what he'd seen. What he'd done.

A hard-faced woman, who Barton had known since she'd joined the force aged twenty, ran towards him when he'd reached the bottom step.

'Update, please, sir.'

'Situation under control. The officers on the landing will bring you up to speed, then the scene will be yours.'

'Understood.' Concern crossed the woman's face. 'Are you okay?'

'Yeah, it's my last few days. Strange time.'

'I heard, sir. Enjoy your retirement.'

Barton managed a nod, then trailed over the road to Zelensky's vehicle. He got in and set off, having to ask the driver of a police four-by-four to move so he could leave the street. Barton turned left out of the Herlington centre, then pushed the car hard, racing around the parkways to Paston.

Barton stopped outside the bungalow when he arrived, engine idling. The Thwaites' Kia still wasn't back, so he drove a bit further up the street and walked to the property. He opened the gate and knocked firmly on the door.

Eric appeared, looking more dishevelled than he had before, with a smudge of a yellowy substance on his shirt collar. Eric nodded. Barton didn't say anything, just stared him down.

Eric's sharp eyes scanned the detective's face for a few moments before looking away. He bobbed his head once more.

'You'd better come in.'

Barton followed him to the same room where they'd had biscuits and coffee before, noticing a tin of Lidl cream of chicken soup on its side on the kitchen counter as they walked through. Two dirty cups and an opened carton of margarine accompanied it. Even the bread bag had been left open.

Eric dropped into a seat, appearing all of his eighty-nine-years.

'I would have sunk a few whiskies if I'd known you'd be here so soon.'

Barton still didn't comment.

Eric huffed out a breath.

'How did you guess?'

'They call it the Barton belly.'

Eric smiled. 'Good old intuition, eh?' The elderly man's trembling hand, gnarled with age, wearily raked the few sparse white hairs remaining. 'I suppose I'd better tell you why I did it.'

69

DCI BARTON

While Barton got out his notebook, he analysed the doleful man. A range of emotions and feelings ran through him. A touch of forgiveness, some understanding, but also irritation and more than a touch of anger. For time wasted and the lost opportunities to stop what had occurred.

He held out the palm of his hand to indicate Eric should begin.

'I suppose it started with me losing my job. Rhys had fiddled the books and got away with it. The business was back on an even keel, but I had still seen what he'd done. I was a loose end. That's the real reason he got rid of me.'

'Not because you couldn't use Excel?'

'I could use it just fine, but not quickly. There were other parts of the jobs, the old journals, where I excelled. The numbers talked to me on paper, whereas with screen work, I really had to focus. But he wouldn't have fired me for being a bit slow. He wasn't a completely horrible person.'

'Apart from sacking you because you caught him committing fraud?'

'Well, yes, but he'd have seen his actions, both fiddling the accounts and firing me, as saving the company. Protecting the jobs of the other employees. A necessary evil, if you like. Deep down, he was a control freak, though. Vijay was a joint partner in name only. The existence of the golden share took away all of his power. Neutered him, but the pathetic peacock could have at least stood up for me. He knew my worth. All Mary's and my problems began then. We had to move, I had to retire, and finally Walter died.'

'Your son might well have still perished if you'd remained in Stilton.'

'No, he had a few friends in the village. People watched out for my boy. They chatted to him. Ali from Ali's Coffee Box used to give him free drinks, let him stay and chat. He felt part of the community, despite the things he got up to. Believed he had some worth. That was taken from him. Mary was also devastated to leave. You know this area. It's very different from Stilton.'

'So, you bought some heroin and laced Rhys's cupcake in the pub when nobody was looking. How did you make sure he chose that particular cake?'

'I did it after they'd been distributed. Now we're older, one large meal fills us up. We go to the toilet more often. Everyone takes their cupcake home. I dosed my own, then swapped it with his when he was having a wee.'

'Like a cunning magician.'

'Exactly.'

'Did his behaviour justify losing his life?'

Eric didn't raise his eyes from the table.

'He deserved to understand what my son went through. The confusion, the lethargy, the hopeless feeling. I never expected him to die.'

'But he did, so you thought you might as well take out Vijay, too, and, so it seems, Morwen.'

Eric cringed. 'Are they both dead?'

'Touch and go for both. Clever idea, though, telling us the hot-water bottle was Mary's Secret Santa, so we wouldn't suspect her or you.'

Eric flinched as if a jolt of pain had shot through him.

'I didn't foresee him drinking it with Morwen. I like her. She's feisty, but kind-hearted. A lot of her brashness was a cover for how people treated her, judged her.'

Barton tutted. 'Surely Vijay didn't deserve to die just because he didn't try to save your job all that time ago?'

'He was mean to Avani, too.'

Barton shook his head at the weak reason. 'Did you use the same heroin? The substance that could kill in seconds?'

Eric slowly leaned forward. Barton suspected to obstruct the view of his eyes.

'I'm sorry.'

Barton reached over and patted Eric's hand. A gentle gesture, which belied exactly how he was feeling, but he wanted Eric to talk. A part of Barton felt like seizing the man in front of him and shaking him until he thought properly about what he'd done, but he needed to know as much as possible. Most of all, he wanted the truth.

'There's nothing to be sorry for, Eric. I know you weren't responsible.'

70

DCI BARTON

Eric glanced up. A sad acceptance on his face.

'I see. Were you aware before you got here?'

'Do you mean prior to you floundering around trying to lie about something you didn't know anything about to protect your wife? Yes.'

'How?'

'People don't tend to change who they fundamentally are. Take Beryl, for example. She consistently loved Bernie and wasn't afraid to show it. His happiness was as important as hers. She wouldn't have done anything like what's happened to risk upsetting the little time he had left, nor would Bernie have done the same to her.'

Eric shook his head. 'Mary liked Rhys. She had come to see his decision to fire me was for the survival of the business.'

'Maybe that's only what she told you. I wonder if it was also her who drugged Charlie's drink the night he died.'

Eric gasped. 'I always suspected Kasia. She despised him by then.'

'Kasia was a classic case of domestic abuse by an overbearing spouse. You'd be right to consider her. People in that situation can finally come to the end of their tether, but it doesn't tend to happen with cunning and planning. They snap. Those relationships often finish in bloodbaths. I assume Kasia was how you knew about the wine. Did she ring you?'

'A text. Perhaps Helen did it to Charlie. She had to fight him off once.'

'Are you trying to pin it on poor Helen now?'

The tired man closed his eyes. 'Charlie was evil. I hated him.'

'Yet you all drank with him.'

'The full truth only came out afterwards.' Eric's shoulders dropped. He was beyond lies. 'No, you're right. We all turned a blind eye so we could carry on having our fun.'

Barton spoke gently. 'How long has Mary been unstable? It's been a considerable time, hasn't it?'

Eric miserably nodded.

'Back before Charlie and Avani died?'

'No, but that was a hard spell for everyone.'

'It was Walter, wasn't it?'

Eric rubbed his face, then peered at Barton through bloodshot eyes. 'Yes. When Walter went off the rails, he took Mary with him. She wanted to lash out at her son, but it only made him worse, so she took it out on other people.'

'It was you she hurt, Eric. Yet you've tried to protect her for years.'

'I still would have. The prospect of prison isn't so frightening at my age.'

Eric stood and opened a drawer. He pulled out a picture frame, took his seat, and gently slid the photograph across to Barton. It was his and Mary's wedding day. The colours, probably once vivid, had faded away, and the background was an indistinct haze. But despite that, the intensity of their gaze, the tender clasp of their hands, remained crystal clear.

'I always believed she'd come back to me in time. Honestly, I never suspected she was the one who drugged Charlie. In fact, when she may have fallen under his spell, she seemed happier, more balanced. I wondered briefly if it was Helen or Kasia but, in the end, I settled for Charlie having taken the pills himself.'

Barton had met many people in his career who had chosen to believe what they'd preferred to have happened, rather than what was more likely. Sometimes it was the only way to cope.

'Mary was the one.'

Eric still didn't want to believe it.

'Why are you so certain she was responsible?'

'Everyone appeared to think it was sleeping tablets Charlie had taken, but it was Valium. Kasia had been prescribed them, but so, I'm guessing, had Mary.'

Eric had no more deceit left in him. 'Yes, she was on Valium even back when Walter's poison was only alcohol. She more or less has been ever since, but I spotted the pills scattered in the wheelie bin a while back. She refused to talk about why.'

'Did you suspect she was responsible for Rhys being poisoned?'

'She's been acting oddly for a week. Not sleeping or eating properly. Keeping me awake. I suppose my suspicions crept up on me.'

'Did you discuss Rhys's death with her?'

'I tried. She just said it was his fate and nothing to do with her.'

Barton pulled himself out of his chair. He, too, felt exhausted.

'A young girl I spoke to recently said something to me that helped me solve this case. She said some people don't think. They do mean things without caring who gets hurt. It seems Mary laced that cake with heroin, and when Morwen handed them out, it was pot luck.'

Eric licked dry lips as he thought. 'But I might have eaten the one with the drugs inside.'

Barton let him consider why that was. Eric didn't want to accept it, but after a few seconds, he conceded Barton was right.

The colour suddenly drained from Eric's face. 'Actually, there was an incident recently. She came back from shopping a few months ago. Said she'd seen a ghost. Mary had been functioning, admittedly in a haze of anxiety tablets, sleeping pills and anti-depressants, but that was around the time I discovered her thrown-away meds.'

'It sounds as though she bumped into Jeremy Lamb. Perhaps followed him. He's dead now, too.'

'Oh my God. Did she murder him as well?'

'I think she planned to. In fact, I reckon she arrived at his flat to do just that, but he'd already perished. Killed by his own son's drugs.'

Eric's jaw sagged. 'So many lives lost. Such a waste.' Eric glanced down at the photograph again. 'What will happen to her?'

Barton decided not to pull his punches.

'Assuming I'm right, there have been multiple murders. Even with the mental-health angle, which seems to be considerable, she's looking at thirty years.'

'Poor Mary. She'll definitely kill herself in jail. She threatened to do it often enough when she wasn't behind bars.'

The final piece of the puzzle dropped into place as Eric's tears fell. His jumper had ridden up his arms, showing bruises and scratches, many of them old and faded, others fresh, no doubt where he'd fended off a raging Mary.

Barton's eyes narrowed at the sight. 'I'm sorry to hear that. She sounds like a disturbed woman.'

Eric bobbed his head. 'What about me? Am I in trouble?'

'It doesn't sound like you were ever fully aware of what was occurring, so we'll see. You did try to take the blame when I arrived here, but, if I can get to her in time, I'd say Mary will provide a full confession. When was she due home?'

Eric shrugged. 'Hours ago. Are you going to wait for her?'

'No,' replied Barton. 'I have a good idea where she'll be.'

Barton marched from the house, where Eric had begun to weep.

71

DCI BARTON

As Barton walked to the car, he took his mobile phone out and rang Zander.

After an update, his friend whistled. 'Shall I put out an all-stations call for Mary?'

'Not yet. Send a unit to be with Eric but give me ten minutes to find his wife. There's a possible place not far from the station, so I'll do a quick recce, then head in, whether I have her or not. How is Kilby?'

'Singing like a canary. He's desperate to be believed that he didn't kill his dad. Told the duty sergeant he could take another decade in jail, might even enjoy it, but not two.'

Barton knew it was possible Kilby would receive that long even without the issue of his father. He would be assessed on his danger to the public, which, taking into account what he'd done, was considerable. Rehabilitation seemed unlikely.

'I expect you'll be interviewing him shortly, while he's being so talkative.'

'It's already done. It doesn't appear likely he'd have stabbed an already dead body. I assume Mary did it.'

'Yeah. It seems she got the drugs off Jeremy Lamb, who was given them by his son, Kilby. Rhys died, then she returned to kill Jeremy. A fragile mental state had her repeatedly attacking his corpse. What's the hospital saying about Vijay and Morwen?'

'Morwen's talking and lucid. Vijay regained consciousness at the hospital, although he's in a poor state. The doctors are testing for methanol now, but he's got a chance. It's the byproducts when methanol breaks down that cause the problems. Some kind of acid is formed, which leads to blindness and neurological damage, but the pair of them received help relatively quickly, so fingers crossed on that front.'

'That's at least some promising news. I'll talk to you soon.'

Barton had considered taking another officer with him to find Mary, but one other person wouldn't make any difference at this point. The cavalry roaring up unannounced might even exacerbate the situation. Backup would be only a phone call and minutes away if it were needed. He got in his vehicle and drove to the dual carriageway. Fast, but not speeding. He'd either be in time, or too late.

After five minutes, he indicated left for Oundle Road and passed The Gordon Arms pub, then a couple of minutes after that, at Notcutts Garden Centre, he turned right towards Ferry Meadows.

It was on the edge of darkness, and there were only a few other cars parked up. He couldn't see the Thwaites' Kia, but the car park was large and had different sections. A grimace formed on his face as he stepped from his car and felt ice in the wind. Churning grey skies rushed by overhead, giving the occasional glimpse of a bright moon.

Luckily, his coat was a thick one, so he set off towards the café and gift shop. The lights were on in the café and Christmas-tree bulbs blinked half-heartedly at the window, but the staff were the only ones in there, seemingly intent on mopping the floor and tidying up the tables for the following day. The gift shop was closed.

The lake, a dark, menacing expanse, stretched before him. He strained his eyes over the surface, hunting for movement, his trepidation growing. A sudden, jarring thump of footsteps made him flinch; a jogger emerged from the shadows where a lamp light had failed, then vanished in a heartbeat.

Around the next bend in the path, he spotted a place with easy access to the lake. Thick reeds had grown out of the mud, almost camouflaging the person who stood amongst them, knee deep in the water.

72

DCI BARTON

Barton ambled to the shore's edge. He didn't want to spook her, so he spoke loudly, but calmly.

'Hi, Mary. It's Inspector Barton.'

He heard gentle splashing as she adjusted her footing and peered out at him.

'Go away.'

'You know I can't do that.'

'There's no point in saving me. I've nothing to live for.'

He was reminded of Bernie, but, in his case, there had been no hope.

A small hand tentatively came through the reeds and pulled them to one side so he could make her out clearly. She stared at him, her face a blank mask.

'Please leave.'

'You still have something to offer the world.'

Mary made a scoffing sound. 'A life in prison. Don't save me now for me to finish it there. What would be the point? I'd only be marking the days until the grim reaper visited my cell.'

'You could find God.'

Almost the glimmer of a smile, but not quite. 'If I did, I'd have some stern words for him.'

'And him you.'

This time, she did smirk. 'I'm not sure you're a natural at talking people down.'

'Oh, I've done this before.' Barton stepped into the water and carefully walked towards her until there was only a metre between them. He held out his hand to her. 'Come on.'

Mary vehemently shook her head. 'You wouldn't be here if you knew what I'm responsible for.'

'Would you be honest with me if I guessed and got it right?'

The clouds must have parted for longer, because Mary's face stayed lit up, her eyes glittering in the moonlight.

'Yes.'

'You smothered Avani when her time was near, so she didn't suffer.'

Mary blinked once, then a few more times in quick succession. He could imagine the cogs turning in her mind. Nothing mattered to her now. Soon, all the pain would simply cease. A last confession was just a formality.

'Yes.'

'You crumbled Valium into Charlie's drink in The Bell. Not to kill, but to hit back at him, but you never planned for him to die.'

'Yes.'

'When he did crash, you felt he deserved it. You were satisfied.'

Barton wasn't sure if she replied or if it was the whisper of the small lapping waves, so he continued.

'You recently bumped into the man who sold your son the drugs that killed him. That incident tipped you over the edge. You bought heroin off him, put it in one of Morwen's cupcakes, which led to Rhys dying. You didn't think anyone would die, but, again, you felt justice had been done.'

Mary chuckled, but it was low and without warmth.

'I didn't care who got that cupcake. Nobody said anything to my face when Walter was sick, but I knew I had been judged. One of them would experience what happened to my son. As for me, I simply hoped to drag myself out of the never-ending deadness of my existence. I knew the police would investigate. If I could be part of that, perhaps I'd enjoy it, be distracted, and I was.' She took a sloshy step towards him, hooking a thumb back at herself, her mouth in a snarl. 'That's how heartless I am. How horrible! I watched Eric eat his cupcake at home, then I ate mine. I was slightly disappointed when we both woke up.'

Barton nibbled his bottom lip to hide his expression. Heartless wasn't a strong enough word to describe her, but his task was to get her to Thorpe Wood in one piece.

'You've been under a lot of stress, gone through some tough spells, and that's been for a long time. Shall I continue?'

'No, I'll finish. I went to murder Jeremy Lamb, but the scumbag was already dead. I'm surprised the police weren't called then, because it drove me crazy. Screams filled my head as I stabbed him. I certainly felt something then. Robbed!'

Mary's face filled with rage. With fury.

'I lurched home, hit my husband, and not for the first time. I've been cold and harsh to him since Walter became a drunk. When my son drowned, a complete numbness dropped over me. It wouldn't leave.'

'Surely Vijay didn't deserve to die.'

'You were investigating Rhys's death, but not making much progress, so I decided to poison Vijay too. My laptop will no doubt still have the search sites where I selected what to use. I took a taxi early this morning and dropped off some of his favourite wine, then went back later with the hot-water bottle. In my defence, if there indeed is any, I regretted it afterwards.'

'But him dying would have been okay, too?'

'I thought so, but now I've crept fully out from under the fug of the prescription drugs I've hidden under for so long, I feel more engaged with life. A hint of a conscience is surfacing. Not much of one, not enough to stay my hand, but ample to make what I planned to do tonight easy.'

It was clear she wanted to die like her son. Barton had investigated murderers who'd had brain tumours or traumatic brain injuries, which had caused them to act out of character, but many of those who killed had been ground down by life. They'd turned bitter and cold before finally losing whatever it was that made most people human. The voice of reason had died. He briefly considered what ultimately broke some individuals, yet others carried on, bearing the ever-increasing load.

He was close enough now to seize her, but he wanted her to walk out. To give in.

'I've just come from seeing Eric. He'd love to hear you say sorry.'

Mary's mouth dropped open. Her head seemed to wobble.

'That man is everything I'm not. Forgiving, loving. I cursed him for not killing Jeremy Lamb after he finished his last sentence. He insisted that doing so would have made him worse than Lamb. So, what does that make me?'

'Losing a child changes everyone it happens to.'

Mary shivered. 'My son told me life was too complicated for him. He planned to take too much and slip away. Eric and I used to buy his drugs after that. I would inject him. That's why we knew where Lamb lived. It was the only way we could think of protecting him.'

Barton coughed, feeling the chill himself. He would have one last try, then grab her.

'Look at the life experience you possess. There will be youngsters inside. Women like you. Victims as well as villains. Pass on your knowledge. Help others. Find purpose in that. Tomorrow's another day.'

Mary's shoulders slumped, and finally, tentatively, she held out her hand, which Barton took. She squelched out of the muddy water.

'I'll make a mess in your car.'

'That's okay. It's not mine.'

Mary cast him a glance, then a wry smile. 'Perhaps you do know what you're doing.'

As Barton guided Mary back along the dark path, she swayed unsteadily. The frail lady didn't seem like a killer, but she was one. Perhaps a good barrister would get her off a murder conviction in Rhys's case, saying she intended only to let him know how it felt. She wouldn't have known the isotonitazene was present, even though the heroin alone could have killed him.

Luckily, he had her confession, because proving the other deaths were her responsibility after so long would be hard. Although he suspected she would say guilty anyway when the time came to plead.

Even so, a gross negligent manslaughter charge seemed too light for the magnitude of the harm she'd done. Whichever way it was prosecuted, Barton knew her tariff, like Kilby's, would be long. The sentencing judge would swiftly see what a dangerous person this quiet woman was.

Mary abruptly stopped walking. 'Did you read the book?'

'Yes. For a moment, I was worried what was going to be found amongst the Christmas presents under various trees this year.'

'Truth is stranger than fiction, but it was a relevant tale. Fortuitous, because it was Bernie's choice, not mine, but the story shows how people can be driven to extreme actions by wanting justice and revenge. You must be able to understand my actions.'

Barton gave Mary a dark look and suspected at some recent point along life's path, she'd completely lost her mind.

'No, I cannot.'

She began to stride forward with purpose.

'You know, when I found out what happened to Rhys, a part of me wished I'd laced all the cupcakes.'

Barton had no answer to that.

So, as they approached his car, it was a conclusion, heavy and final, for both of them. He would deliver her to the station for a cold, bureaucratic resolution to the cruel decisions that had ruined some lives and ended others. At least lawful justice had finally caught up.

Paperwork awaited, reports to be filed, the inevitable debriefings. But in the quiet of this walk, Barton realised, this was the end.

73

DCI BARTON

It was the Friday before Christmas, and Barton had returned to Thorpe Wood's car park to fetch the cardboard box he'd brought in with him that morning. On the walk there, he shook around twenty hands, then he did about the same number on the way back to his desk. It was a strange feeling to have so many eyes upon him. He guessed some were jealous that, for him, the war was probably over, while others would be pleased that they were still holding the thin blue line.

He had told Zander not to bother with a collection, because he'd had one four years ago when leaving for his desk job. A set of golden handcuffs linked together on a plinth with a small brass plaque inscribed with a single word, Detective, currently sat proudly on the mantelpiece in his lounge.

Yet at five-thirty, the office began to fill. Barton's face heated up as officers, admin staff, support workers, managers and even the duty solicitor filtered through the desks to stand next to Detective Chief Superintendent Troughton and Zander, who had both materialised beside Barton. Troughton appeared harassed but was trying not to show it.

There were more people present than when Barton had left before. He supposed it was different. Then he'd merely been leaving the department. This time, he might be quitting the force.

As Zander stared around through the throng, Barton felt as if the surrounding oxygen were in short supply. Zander rested his hand on Barton's shoulder and waited for silence.

'Thanks for coming through, everyone. I notice a few of you have even stayed beyond the ends of your shifts, so that fact is noted, and will be used against you next time we're busy.'

He received a few playful jeers.

'We are here to say adios, at least for now, to John Barton.'

The room broke into spontaneous applause. Barton caught the recognisable whoop that Zelensky rarely let out. Zander paused for the noise to die down.

'John has been a guiding light to many here. In fact, in Major Crimes, to all of us. If you recall, when he left for his last long holiday, we also did a collection for him.'

The room erupted in laughter. A chuckling Zander shouted over them.

'Our previous boss, Chief Superintendent Brabbins, summed it up perfectly. John is the most reassuring of presences at the most worrying of times.'

Barton's mouth dried as he scanned the sea of nodding heads.

'We wish him the best for the future. We hope he will come back, if not to rejoin us, at least to visit.' Zander paused as people nodded. 'His final case, that of The Book Club Killer, sums up many of John's unique methods, which you won't find in the manual. To solve this investigation, he spent a lot of time at a pub and simply waited for most of the suspects to die or be poisoned.'

The comment was met with smiles and chuckles.

'The John Barton cuffing technique, which starts with a shoulder charge, will no doubt retire with him,' shouted Zelensky.

'I hope so,' replied Troughton. 'In fact, there are a few Bartonisms that need retiring.'

'I once had my end-of-year appraisal at McDonald's,' yelled Malik.

'Me, too,' echoed around the room.

Zander put his hands together.

'I give you Detective Chief Inspector John Barton.'

As those gathered cheered and clapped, Zander handed over a large white envelope and Minton appeared carrying a huge cake with pink icing. On it was a man who loosely resembled Barton, holding a golf club that had snapped in half. The caption above it said, 'Enjoy your break!'

There were shouts of speech, so Barton slid off his chair.

'I'm not going to cry,' he remarked as a tear trickled down his cheek. 'Unless Mary Thwaite's been anywhere near this cake.'

There was another eruption of laughter.

'It's been a privilege to work with you all, and perhaps one day, I will once more. Zander suggested I should do something different this time, like a song or a dance, but you'll be pleased to hear I left my tap-dancing shoes at home. The guys on the floor below should certainly be relieved.'

Chuckles again filled the room.

'You all have a great future here. I'll follow your careers with interest, and I'm always happy to be taken out for beer at any time. I mean, called for advice. To be honest, I don't feel ready to retire, so there *will* be something next. What that is, well, you'll have to wait and see. Thank you all, for everything.'

Minton cut the cake while Barton opened the envelope. The front of his card had a line saying, 'Retirement. When you're officially too old to be told what to do'. There was a picture of a man mowing the lawn while his wife stood next to him with a lengthy list of domestic chores.

Zander came over and shook his hand.

'That was short and sweet.'

'My career?'

'Your speech.'

'Always leave them wanting more.'

The two friends shared a quiet look at the double meaning of Barton's joke. Zander broke the silence.

'The twins are mega excited this year, so Christmas Day should be fun for everyone and something to look forward to.'

'Fun or terrifying?'

'Both, I should think. I'll see you then at twelve.'

Barton gave him a thumbs up. 'Can't wait. Little Tommy should be over too.'

'That's nice of you.'

'I suppose. Lily hasn't got anywhere else to go, but we love having her and Tommy over. Makes Holly and I feel young again.'

'You'll be adopting them at this rate.'

Barton grinned. 'Thanks for today.'

'No worries.'

Barton plopped the rest of his pens and notebooks into his box and slid the laptop inside its case. There was surprisingly little for him to take. He blew out a breath and took what might be a last stare around the room. It contained many memories, but, as usual, in the corner stood a poor example of a fake Christmas tree, which had been decorated by someone whose heart wasn't in it. Although describing it as standing was being generous. It leaned like one of the drunks they often had waiting to be booked in.

Only a few people remained in the office by the time he stood to depart. That would make leaving easier. He spared a thought for Mortis, who had walked out for the last occasion a few days earlier. He'd done a final post-mortem. Bernie Goodman's.

Barton had spoken to Mortis about the lab results, which confirmed the combination of drugs that Bernie admitted to taking, even down to the Alka Seltzer. Mortis also commented that, judging by the tumours he had spotted throughout the body, Bernie had made a reasonable call.

Troughton appeared next to Barton's desk again.

'Quick word in my office, please, John.'

Barton trudged after him, suspecting his boss's parting gift would be to delegate one last task. In theory, he was still employed there until New Year's Eve.

'Take a seat. How are you doing? Confident you've taken the right decision?'

'If I'm honest, exhausted. Similar to when you've planned a big celebration like a christening. They are hard work with elements of chaos, success and failure, but they tend to end well with guests going home happy. When the last person has gone, you're dead on your feet and just want to sit somewhere quiet with a beer. That's how I feel.'

'Sounds understandable.'

'And, yes, it's the correct call for me at this time.'

'You've had a successful final investigation. Not everyone gets that.'

'I suppose so. Talking of which, what was the outcome of the CPS's decision around Helen, Eric, Kasia and Dr Al-Khafaji?'

Troughton folded his arms across his chest.

'I had a long chat with the prosecutors. After reviewing the case file, I strongly suspected there was criminality from all of them, but I took on board what you said.'

'About them suffering as well?'

'Yes. The GP explained he's retiring completely. Most of his clients were employed by Jones and Singh Accountants, and that company has been sold.'

'I hadn't heard that.'

'It's not public knowledge yet. I went to see Morwen, who is much recovered from her bout of poisoning. She was at the office. Vijay's vision is never going to be perfect again, so staring at spreadsheets is out. Kasia has decided to retire as well, so in effect the company had no staff.'

'Just a receptionist.'

'I spoke to her. Feisty lady. She's made up her mind to apply to the police.'

Barton considered the girl and grinned. 'She'll be an asset. The public won't know what's hit them.'

'The conveyor belt continues.'

'Yeah, out with the old, in with the new. Who did they sell the business to?'

'A bigger firm in the city centre. Apparently, Rhys had sounded them out some time ago. As for the others involved, Eric is eighty-nine. There's no public interest in seeing him in court what could well be a year down the line. With a full admission from Mary, there doesn't need to be a trial. She told us in her statement that neither Kasia nor Helen ever knew of anything she did. Obviously, trials are hugely expensive and with various people going no comment, even Morwen and Vijay, the decision has been made to put the saga to bed.'

'A decent result in the end. More lives could have been lost.'

Troughton ran a hand over his chin. 'That's the spirit. We've locked two dangerous criminals behind bars where they belong.'

Barton nodded. Mary Thwaite and Mark Kilby.

'So, congratulations, John.' Troughton waved an envelope at him. 'Now, I was planning to bring this around to your house, but, seeing as I'm forced to be here tonight, when I should have been at a dinner party, I thought you could have it before you left.'

'I was wondering why you were still about.'

Troughton's gaze sharpened, but there was humour present. 'Are you saying that at 6 p.m. on a Friday evening, here is the last place you'd expect me to be?'

'Of course not, sir.'

'A body has been found. A policeman from Huntingdon. Unusual circumstances, perhaps not suspicious. He's being investigated for visiting websites on his PC he shouldn't have. It's going to hit the news shortly, so I've had to prepare a statement.'

'Nothing like a weekend exposé.'

'Yes, but you're free from all this sort of thing, even though when I mentioned the words "a body has been found", your eyes lit up. I reckon you'll come back.'

The sharp look had morphed into one with a touch of mischief. Troughton pushed over the slim envelope.

'A reference?' asked Barton.

'A future.'

Barton studied Troughton's face. What was the wily old dog up to?

'Should I read it now?'

'Of course.'

Barton ripped the envelope open. There was a single sheet containing half a page of writing. He scanned the contents, then rested the paper back on the table.

'Is this even a thing?'

'Not yet, but it could be. When all the superintendents and above get together, this type of idea regularly crops up. We already have the expertise in the country when a serious incident occurs, but it's often involved in other cases, which can mean those investigations suffer when people are pulled from them. I was thinking perhaps a part-time team, who could be called upon as and when. Do you reckon that might be something you'd be interested in?'

Barton glanced at the letter again. He couldn't help grinning.

'Maybe.'

74

LILY'S EX – FRASER

Fraser observed the long vehicle reversing into his cul-de-sac. Two words on the side. Range Rover. He vigorously rubbed his hands together as the lorry's big engine roared in the high gear. Yes, my man, wake the neighbours.

As the drivers unloaded his oh-so-shiny black car, Fraser beamed from ear to ear. He waved at Ernie from number two, who had appeared. He didn't get a response. Old git was probably blind. A slight scowl crossed Fraser's face. Michaela should have been back. Her timekeeping was becoming a problem.

Still, he'd have his new baby parked on the drive, gleaming in the winter sunshine when she returned. Although there were monthly payments, they would be negligible given his firm's rapid growth. He'd closed a fifty-thousand account that week. The future appeared bright as well as shiny.

Despite his best efforts, he thought of his actual baby. Little Tommy. The sides of Fraser's mouth curved upwards. He had been a happy lad. Wasn't much of a crier. Not that he'd spent a lot of time with the boy, not like perhaps he should have. Michaela had become extremely distracting, though. The smile that had been threatening to break erupted as he pictured his girlfriend in the black dress he had recently bought her.

He imagined the Range Rover purring up the impressive driveway of his favourite hotel where drinks were enjoyed on a patio that overlooked the entrance. Him getting out, ever the gentleman, head to toe in Armani, to open Michaela's door.

The air crackling. Conversations faltering. Heads turning. She emerged, a vision in a gown that defied gravity, the fabric a shimmering, liquid coal, slashed high to the hip. Her glossy hair catching the late afternoon light, her lips a vibrant, unapologetic crimson. Long, impossibly high heels, clicking on the porcelain tiles while he nodded at the other movers and shakers.

He pictured Lily in the same outfit. She'd been a cracker when he first met her, but she hadn't coped well with pregnancy. Let herself go afterwards, and then started whingeing at him about, well, loads of stuff. It was no surprise he'd strayed. Bloody lucky he made her sign that pre-nup. Still, he should probably get around to throwing some money her way. It was his kid, after all. Maybe he could take him to the footie when he got a bit older.

A shadow fell over him. He heard them before he saw them. The plodding footsteps of solid men. Fraser was nearly six feet tall, but he didn't have a spare ounce of weight. The heavies in front of him, and he could think of no other way to describe them, were wide and thick. Their suits taut across their chests and bellies.

Fraser's bladder threatened to betray him.

'What do you want?'

The one on the left smiled. A cold leer, which meant that it would be unwelcome news for the man quaking against his garage door, but it was the other fellow who stepped forward. The expression on this guy, the larger of the pair, stated plainly, I might rip your face off. He appeared capable, too.

'We're here to straighten out a few things. Straighten you out, in fact. Are you on your own here?'

'M-m-m...' Fraser cringed at his cowardly utterance. 'My partner will be home soon.'

'We'd better be quick, then. Let's go inside. We wouldn't want to upset the neighbours.'

Fraser considered running, but he was hemmed in. He turned around and walked towards his front door, suspecting the next five minutes would be painful.

75

ERIC

Christmas Eve

After gingerly stepping from the taxi, Eric paused and stared at The Bell's façade. It felt different coming without Mary. He realised her brooding presence had weighed on him for a long time whenever they went out, not knowing what mood she'd be in that night, or when they got home.

Not tonight. He intended to enjoy more than a few beverages. Gammon and chips. Finish with their best cognac after scintillating conversation around that year's book choice. A catch up with old friends on a special evening. What could be better?

A brisk wind rushed down the high street, while the pub windows beckoned him inside. They glowed, spilling honeyed light onto the wet pavement. Real fires would crackle behind the glass. He was unable to resist peering within, spotting contented faces and laughing drinkers raising glasses.

The front door seemed heavier each year, but other merrymakers were arriving, and they opened it for him. At the bar, the first person he saw was Kasia. She signalled him over.

'What are you having?'

'I'll have a Scotch. Anything single malt.'

Kasia ordered their drinks, then ran her gaze over his face.

'How are you?'

'Holding up. I went to visit Mary in jail. They put her back on the medication she had stopped taking, and she seemed, well, normal again. Or at least as normal as she's ever been since Walter died.'

'That's positive.'

'I suppose so. Is Morwen coming?'

Kasia shook her head. 'She's staying home to plan her future. She's going to sell her house and move to London. Hoping to get a job, of all things. Work in a busy café or restaurant. I think she wants to experience a proper life, go to the theatre, visit galleries and museums. Everything Rhys didn't want to do.'

'Good for her.'

'Vijay's still in hospital. His liver is playing up. I visited him and he seems okay. Relieved the business has sold swiftly. He implied he'd see us next year. Beryl said she won't be coming again. Every detail of Stilton reminds her of Bernie and breaks her heart afresh, which was poetic of her. Her sister's single, so they're spending Christmas at hers in the north. I get the feeling she'll move up there to live with her.'

Eric nodded. It would be a small group tonight.

Kasia linked her arm in his.

'Cheer up. Helen has reserved a smaller table, but we're still near the fire. She's waiting for us.'

Eric had invited Helen to join their book club. He couldn't remember when in the past they'd exchanged numbers, but they had spoken regularly over the years. Their conversations had helped when Mary's behaviour had been at its worst. At one point, he'd considered offering to meet for a drink, just the two of them, but he'd never been that type of guy.

Four days ago, he'd rung her to confirm the booking, and they'd chatted for over half an hour. She'd mentioned again how she looked on in envy when the club met. She'd promised to read the novel fast so she could join in with the discussion.

Eric had always appreciated her from afar, but, even with Mary out of the picture, he was beyond romantic entanglements. She would be a great friend to him instead, for however much life remained, as he would to her. Kasia, too. After all, they all had a shared history, like an unbreakable chain, to bind them.

Helen rose from her seat and gave him a quick hug when he and Kasia had taken their glasses over. The three of them settled in their seats and companionably scanned the menus before putting them down.

'Did you finish the book, Helen?' he asked.

She took a sip of her wine, then grinned. 'I raced through the story. Two sittings. The tale kind of lingered with me afterwards. I found it strangely sad, yet poignant, how the characters became the worst of themselves.'

Eric smiled at her. She was right. It was exactly like real life. If you weren't careful, or if you didn't care, it was easy to become your darkest part, and sometimes you couldn't find the way back.

As they settled down into a detailed debate, Eric couldn't help a little smirk. Kasia and Helen wouldn't admit it, and Eric was not daft enough to utter the truth out loud, but he'd rather enjoyed the slay before Christmas.

And the book hadn't been bad, either.

76

DCI BARTON

Christmas Day

Barton just about heard the doorbell over the hubbub in the lounge. He had bought Zander's twins each an electric guitar this year. They were only a bit of fun for young kids, but, even so, they were loud. It was 100 per cent true what people said. Giving was better than receiving. Barton had taken a lot of pleasure from his friend's face when the boys had opened them. Kelly had smiled and mouthed *you're dead meat* to him.

Barton passed his drink to Zander and discovered Lily at the door. He invited her in and took her coat. She lifted Tommy out of the pushchair and handed him to Barton while she folded it down. The child was resplendent in a cute Santa outfit, but he had a bright red face.

Lily rested her fingers on his cheek. 'I'm not sure if the outfit is making him too hot, or he's done something nasty.'

'Smells like a dirty protest. No dog?'

'I'll fetch him after we've eaten. He doesn't have the best table manners.'

Holly appeared from the kitchen and saw Tommy. 'There he is. Come to Auntie Holly.'

Barton swiftly handed him over. 'You might need to check his nappy.'

Holly eyed him suspiciously. 'That's all right. I'm used to mucky boys.'

She reached out and took the changing bag off Lily, who stayed behind as Holly carried Tommy to the dining room to change him where it was quiet.

'John. Can I talk to you about something?'

'Sure, Lily.'

'I had a visit from my ex a few days ago.'

'Okay. Was it positive or negative?'

'Brilliant. He's going to put two grand a month in my bank account. Six thousand has already gone in for the payments he missed.'

'That's quite a change of tune.'

'Yes. He apologised, saying events had got away from him. Whatever that means. I seemed to see through him very clearly. You know, how shallow he is, but I thanked him. He'll always be Tommy's father. It would be nice if they had a relationship.'

'That shows a lot of grace.'

'Yeah, it wasn't easy. I might still slap him. The funny thing is, when he turned to leave, I couldn't stop myself from asking what made him realise we must be struggling. Any idea what he said?'

Barton shrugged. 'Nope.'

'Two thugs came to his house, took him inside, sat him down and politely but menacingly reminded him of his commitments and responsibilities. He asked if I'd sent them, but I didn't know anything about it.'

'Odd.'

'Yeah, that's what I thought.'

'Well, it's nice to know Child Maintenance Services can bare their teeth.'

Lily smiled. 'He mentioned both men were bald.'

'Yeah?'

'And one was black, the other white. Remind you of anyone?'

Barton squinted as he pretended to think. 'Beats me. Sounds like a shady business, although I'm glad it worked out nicely.'

Lily stood on tiptoe and kissed Barton on the cheek. 'Thank you. For everything.'

'Don't know what you're on about. Merry Christmas.'

Lily walked past him, then turned with a grin on her face. 'Tommy's been saying the odd word now. I was watching *EastEnders* last night and Phil Mitchell came on. Tommy pointed at the TV and I'm sure he said John.'

'Brilliant. Not even the handsome brother.'

Lily rested a hand on Barton's arm. 'He likes you so much. I reckon he recognises not only your strength, but your honesty, and your purpose. That probably sounds silly, but I see it, too.'

Barton was blushing by the time he returned to the lounge. Perhaps that was also because he'd bent more rules in his last case than he had during the rest of his career. He briefly pondered that. Sometimes of late, it had felt as though the law had morphed into giving every protection and assistance to the guilty and none to the victims.

Zander handed his beer back to him. 'You look hot.'

'Thanks. I try to look my best for the festivities.'

Barton took a couple of big glugs of his drink as Zander rolled his eyes, but then something caught his attention. He gestured for Zander to watch the action on the far sofa. Mortis was sitting with a woman who hadn't stopped talking since they'd arrived. Quick to laugh and seemingly with few filters, she'd really added to the festive atmosphere. Zander chuckled as the woman reached over to plant a smacker on Mortis, who became tortoise-like as he stretched his neck out to avoid it.

'No Minton this year,' said Barton. 'Some old school friends have hired a lodge up in Scotland.'

'What about Hoffman and Zelensky?'

'Going away, too. Hoffman arranged it on the sly as a surprise. Hotel in Cromer. It's usually nice and quiet there.'

'Zelensky's handed her notice in for Major Crimes. Fancies joining one of the child exploitation teams.'

'I suspected she might leave. Is Minton moving to the drug unit?'

'Yep. Crenwick was impressed with her. Malik and Leicester are coming with me to my new team. If Hoffman stays put, he'll be with us as well.'

'I'm glad you'll have a few of the gang.'

Zander turned to his long-time friend. 'I saw Troughton at your desk on your last day. What did he want?'

'Ah, you noticed him dragging me away. He gave me a letter with a possible opportunity for further down the line.'

'A position in the staff canteen?'

'They wouldn't be so reckless. No, it was to do with murder inquiries that come out of nowhere but need tackling immediately. There aren't always resources available, so the suggestion is to have a team on standby.'

'In the county?'

Barton smiled. 'Anywhere in the country. In fact, the world.'

Zander chuckled. 'Sneaky old Troughton. He can read you like a book.'

'What do you mean?'

'He understands the admin, the politics and all the extra bits that take you away from detecting are what might stop you from returning. He's found a carrot to dangle, and it's a golden one.'

Barton's and Zander's eyes flickered to each other. No words needing to be said. It *was* the end of an era, but perhaps it wasn't *the* end.

Christmas dinner went down a storm. Leicester's place name was next to Lily's. Barton had never watched a couple fall in love in front of him before, but it was as clear to him as it was to them. The lingering smiles, the giggles, the casual touches, despite so many people surrounding them at the two tables that had been pushed together.

He found himself banished to the kitchen after lunch to do the washing up with Leicester. He couldn't resist ribbing the lad.

'You and Lily seemed to be getting on well.'

Leicester had always been one to flush red, and this time was no exception. 'Yeah, she's lovely.'

'How would you feel about taking on another man's child?'

Barton had expected Leicester to laugh it off, but he didn't. He placed his tea towel on the draining board. 'I remember you telling me Holly already had Lawrence when you met her, sir. Did it put you off?'

When Barton had first dated his wife, she'd not been long out of an unpleasant relationship where the father didn't want to know any more. Was history repeating itself?

'I think it's time you called me John.' Barton clapped a meaty hand on the lad's shoulder. 'And you're right. It was the easiest and best decision of my life.'

Everyone wandered to the lounge to take a seat for the King's speech. Barton watched Leicester sit beside Lily, who was bouncing Tommy on her lap. The child had a dreamy, full expression on his face. It wouldn't be long until he was in the land of nod. Lily laughed at something Leicester said. She handed the boy across to him. Leicester sniffed his head, then dropped a kiss on it.

Holly strolled over to Barton and placed an arm around him. 'Why are you throwing withering looks in Leicester's direction?'

'I'm not.'

'You are.'

'Okay, he's stolen my baby.'

Holly laughed for at least half a minute, making him suspect more than a few eggnogs had been consumed. Barton eyed her up. 'Wait a minute. You deliberately put them next to each other.'

His wife winked at him.

'Who knows when Cupid might strike?'

Barton let his gaze wander around the busy room, lingering on Layla and Luke. He thought of Lawrence, who was coming for Boxing Day. He would be sorely missed, but with a family of his own, that was the way of things.

Barton's eyes finally settled back on Leicester and Lily, who were engrossed in each other's company.

Whatever fate awaited this new family – the young couple he knew they'd become and the child who would unite them – Barton wished them all the contentment and joy that life had bestowed upon him.

He hoped their journey would be as happy as his own.

* * *

MORE FROM ROSS GREENWOOD

Another book from Ross Greenwood, *Death on the Norfolk Express*, is available to order now here:

https://mybook.to/NorfolkBackAd

AUTHOR'S NOTE

Well, it was going to be the last Barton, but I had a rebellion from the advance readers. Gnashing of teeth, wailing, floods of tears, you name it, so I gave him a lifeline. If I do another, it might not be for a while because I'm in discussion for a further Norfolk Murders trilogy. Still, by then, Barton will be fit as a fiddle, mostly wearing that leotard I mentioned and boring everyone with his keto diet. We'll be able to enjoy a few laughs again. In fact, I think I have a good idea, so check Amazon and see if there's a pre-order.

Next up is *Death on the Norfolk Express*. If you've not started on that series, time to take a look, because Detective Inspector Ashley Knight and her team are going to have to cope with some devastating news under the vast blue skies in North Norfolk.

I love to read your reviews, so keep 'em coming.

All the best, Ross.

ACKNOWLEDGEMENTS

As always, heaps of gratitude to my talented beta readers, with a few more newbies for this one. Jane Howarth, Richard Burke, Kath Middleton, Diane Saxon and Trish Halstead give me great feedback when the novels are in their early drafts. Paul Lautman's and Alex Williams' skills are always greatly appreciated.

A thank you to my editor for this one, Emma Beswetherick, who got to meet Barton for the first time. Of course, she fell in love with him, and Tommy and Gizmo, too.

The good news is that, if you're following the other series, *Death on the Norfolk Express* will be released in May. The blurb is up for your perusal now.

Final thank you to the readers, particularly those who get in touch. You keep me relatively sane!

BOOK CLUB QUESTIONS

1. How does Barton's personal life, particularly his struggle with work, influence his professional decisions and his interactions with colleagues?
2. Greenwood often explores the grey areas between right and wrong. Are any of the characters in this novel, including Barton, morally ambiguous? Discuss a specific instance.
3. The setting of Stilton is a significant backdrop in this novel. How does the village itself function as a character, and what role does it play in the story's atmosphere and plot?
4. Many of the crimes in this book are deeply rooted in the past. How does the novel's structure, which often hints at historical events, affect your reading experience?
5. Discuss the role of empathy in the story. Does Barton's ability (or inability) to empathise with victims and perpetrators help or hinder his investigation?
6. Greenwood's novels often feature complex and tragic female characters. Discuss the motivations and fates of one of the key female figures in this book.
7. This tale touches upon social issues such as guilt, grief, and abuse. How are these themes handled, and what message do you think Greenwood is trying to convey?

8. How does the novel build suspense? Was there a particular red herring or plot twist that you didn't see coming?
9. Do you find Barton to be a sympathetic protagonist? Why or why not? What are his greatest strengths and weaknesses as a detective and as a person?
10. The ending of the novel is powerful and unsettling. Were you satisfied with the resolution, both for the case and for the characters? Why or why not?

ABOUT THE AUTHOR

Ross Greenwood is the author of crime thrillers. Before becoming a full-time writer he was most recently a prison officer and so worked everyday with murderers, rapists and thieves for four years. He lives in Peterborough.

Download your exclusive bonus content from Ross Greenwood here:

Follow Ross on social media:

instagram.com/rossg555
x.com/greenwoodross
facebook.com/RossGreenwoodAuthor
bookbub.com/authors/ross-greenwood

ALSO BY ROSS GREENWOOD

The DI Barton Series

The Snow Killer

The Soul Killer

The Ice Killer

The Cold Killer

The Fire Killer

The Santa Killer

The Village Killer

The Book Club Killer

DS Knight Series

Death on Cromer Beach

Dear at Paradise Park

Death in Bacton Wood

Death at Horsey Mere

Death at Fakenham Races

Standalones

Prisoner

Jail Break

Survivor

Lifer

Chancer

Hunter

THE Murder LIST

THE MURDER LIST IS A NEWSLETTER DEDICATED TO SPINE-CHILLING FICTION AND GRIPPING PAGE-TURNERS!

SIGN UP TO MAKE SURE YOU'RE ON OUR HIT LIST FOR EXCLUSIVE DEALS, AUTHOR CONTENT, AND COMPETITIONS.

SIGN UP TO OUR NEWSLETTER

BIT.LY/THEMURDERLISTNEWS

Boldwood

Boldwood Books is an award-winning fiction publishing company seeking out the best stories from around the world.

Find out more at www.boldwoodbooks.com

Join our reader community for brilliant books, competitions and offers!

Follow us
@BoldwoodBooks
@TheBoldBookClub

Sign up to our weekly deals newsletter

https://bit.ly/BoldwoodBNewsletter

www.ingramcontent.com/pod-product-compliance
Ingram Content Group UK Ltd.
Pitfield, Milton Keynes, MK11 3LW, UK
UKHW040851281025
8613UKWH00014B/33